Charles Ash Windham, Hugh Wodehouse Pearse

The Crimean diary and letters of Lieut.-General Sir Charles Ash Windham

Charles Ash Windham, Hugh Wodehouse Pearse

The Crimean diary and letters of Lieut.-General Sir Charles Ash Windham

ISBN/EAN: 9783743393585

Manufactured in Europe, USA, Canada, Australia, Japa

Cover: Foto ©Andreas Hilbeck / pixelio.de

Manufactured and distributed by brebook publishing software (www.brebook.com)

Charles Ash Windham, Hugh Wodehouse Pearse

The Crimean diary and letters of Lieut.-General Sir Charles Ash Windham

THE CRIMEAN DIARY

AND LETTERS

OF

LIEUT.-GENERAL

SIR CHARLES ASH WINDHAM, K.C.B.

WITH OBSERVATIONS UPON HIS SERVICES DURING

THE INDIAN MUTINY

AND AN INTRODUCTION BY

SIR WILLIAM HOWARD RUSSELL

THE WHOLE EDITED BY

MAJOR HUGH PEARSE
EAST SURREY REGIMENT

LONDON

KEGAN PAUL, TRENCH, TRÜBNER & CO., LTD.

PATERNOSTER HOUSE, CHARING CROSS ROAD

1897

PREFACE

A N article which appeared a short time ago in one
of the leading weekly journals, also the suggestion
of many friends, first prompted me to publish my
late father's Crimean Correspondence and Extracts
from his Diary.

I thought that, as a sailor, I could not do justice
to the subject, and my friend Major Hugh Pearse
kindly undertook to edit the letters, and to him I
return my warmest thanks.

The veteran, Sir William Russell—and I take it,
no higher Crimean authority exists — most kindly
undertook to write the opening chapter; and I cannot
find words to express how deeply touched I have
been by the interest he has taken in the book.

The letters are those of a man who occupied a very
responsible position, and who had ample opportunities
of forming a correct judgment.

Naturally, I do not wish to enter into any personal
controversy with regard to my father's conduct either
in the Crimea or in India.

I am perfectly satisfied to leave the former in the
hands of Sir William Russell, and the latter to the
dictum of that most accurate and able historian,
Colonel Malleson, who, in reference to the siege of

Cawnpore by the Gwalior Contingent, has placed it upon record as his deliberate opinion, that "Windham saved India."

I may, however, be allowed to borrow one sentence from Lord Wolseley's *Life of Marlborough.* He says, "We must judge of what the public thought of that Great Soldier *at the time.*"

What the public thought of a much humbler soldier *at the time* of the Crimea is well known, for by only a few votes in the Cabinet did he fail to be made Commander - in - Chief (vide *Greville Memoirs* and *Colonel Campbell's Letters from the Crimea*).

If this small book is appreciated by the few friends now living of an old soldier who ever strove to do his duty well and nobly, often under the most trying circumstances, I shall feel more than repaid.

Thinking it might interest old Norfolk neighbours, I have appended a short account of Felbrigg—(the old seat of the Windhams)—taken from the *Norfolk Daily Standard;* also two letters from two of my father's most valued friends.

CHARLES WINDHAM,
Captain Royal Navy.

CONTENTS

PREFACE

BY

SIR WILLIAM HOWARD RUSSELL.

A FEW days after the allies occupied the plateau on the south of Sebastopol—it was, I think, on the 27th or 28th of September—I rode up from Balaclava to take a look at the city, on which we were destined to gaze for so many eventful months ; and, as I was crossing from the French pickets on our left, I came upon a part of the Fourth Division, on their march to take up their camping-ground on one of the ridges over the ravine which runs from the Great Harbour. They were in charge of a staff officer whom I remarked, when the army left the Belbek, warmly expostulating with Lord Raglan's Staff, on account of the orders which had been given for the Fourth Division to remain on the river that night. I had previously seen him over and over again, always energetic, busy, demonstrative, in Varna, and now he was hurrying up the men, who had had a long tramp from the plain below, to their ground in view of the beautiful city—the Queen of the Euxine. I asked the officer, Major Dickson, whom I was with, when he came back from a few minutes' conversation with his Staff acquaintance—

"Who is that?"

B

"A guardsman, named Windham," he replied. "A very good man, I should think; full of ideas. He is very keen, but he's rather inclined to take the bit in his teeth."

It was not, however, till some weeks later that I made Colonel Windham's personal acquaintance. It was on the day after the memorable battle of Bala-clava. The Fourth Division had been ordered down to the plain on the morning of the action to rein-force the troops in the valley. They had arrived late; at least, so it was said. The First Division, under the Duke of Cambridge, had also been sum-moned. The appearance of these two great bodies of infantry, streaming down from the plateau into the Valley of Balaclava, produced, no doubt, a considerable effect upon the Russians; and Sir George Cathcart, a masterful man, who had already worked himself into a frame of mind conducive to violent enterprise, because his counsels, for an instant assault upon Sebastopol, had not been taken, was eager to dash at the Turkish redoubts, and had, indeed, whilst his skirmishers pressed forward and engaged the Russians in a brisk musketry encounter, occupied one of them, when he was once more ridden on the curb, and restrained from the bold offensive which he contemplated.

The next day I rode up to the walled enclosure, which was subsequently named "Cathcart's Hill," because the General's Headquarters were near the elevated ridge, whence there was an extensive view of the city front. There was a group of officers looking down towards the ground on the right, from which Evans' Division had that morning driven the Russians, who had come out to establish themselves in force upon it; and amongst them was Colonel Windham.

Presently, he came to the place where I stood watching the movements of the troops on the extreme right towards Inkerman, and, with an abrupt "Good evening," asked me "if I had seen the cavalry charges down below the day before, and what I thought of the whole affair?" I said I had been all the morning in my tent, continuing the work of the night before, and writing about the battle.

"And what have you written?"

I said "I hoped it would all appear in good time."

"I hope," said he, "that you let people at home understand what a lot of muddling muffs we have out here. What on earth did they mean by hurrying us down there? Two divisions! And then making out that we were late! Late for what? Why, when we did want to do something, we were not allowed. I believe if my General had been allowed to go on, and the whole force had been advanced, we'd have shoved every man-jack of these Russians up into the mountains, and retaken the guns. That's my private opinion, mind you! And I don't want my name in the papers."

Whilst I was living at the Headquarters Camp, I went up nearly every day, early or late, to Cathcart's Hill, and there I found Colonel Windham, his pipe in his mouth and his note-book in hand, very often, but he would not tarry long. He seemed always to have something to do in addition to something that he had done already. His opinions on men and matters were given with refreshing directness, and his views were original, at all events; full of confidence, and always in advocacy of instant action; sometimes to make a dash at the Round Tower or the Redan; sometimes to break up camp and march right away for Simpheropol or Eupatoria. Occasionally he had moments of despondency; he doubted if we should ever take the place at all! Certainly that frame of mind was justified after the battle of Inkerman, and the death of his beloved chief; and it was intensified in the terrible winter, during which Windham became known throughout the army for his indefatigable exertions in providing, as far as he could, for the wants of the Division to which he was attached, and by his liberal criticisms of the officers of his own department on the Headquarters Staff. His military theories, however, were not in favour. He had no experience in war. But he had long service, and in the love of sport and travel, which had led him far afield in the East and in the West, he had all the aptitudes which go to the making of a soldier. Officers of less experience, however, than Windham, considered themselves entitled to express the most decided opinions on the operations. One day, after the first bombardment, Lord Cardigan, accompanied by his friend, Mr. De Burgh, and an *aide-de-camp*, rode up to the front to take a look at the batteries. They were joined by a young officer of Engineers.

"Ah!" said Lord Cardigan. "I see! Those fellows down below are our men, and they are firing at the Russians. Those fellows who are firing towards us are the Russians. Why don't we drive them away?"

The officer explained that there were certain difficulties in the suggested operation. But the gallant General, who was a few days later to distinguish himself in the valley of Balaclava, was by no means satisfied, and insisted on his views with an air of haughty conviction. At last, putting up his glass, and turning to remount his horse, which was down below, he exclaimed :

"I have never in all my life seen a siege conducted on such principles, Squire."

The Squire assented. He had never seen such a siege, either, and they rode back to Balaclava.

Windham was, indeed, a very different sort of man from Lord Cardigan, but if, after a few weeks' acquaintance such as I have described, in constant, if casual, meetings with him, I had been asked what I thought his failing as an officer was, I would have answered, " Reckless gallantry and dash." I say that because I have been induced to write this prefatory chapter by a sense of the injustice done to him by those who expressed the opinion that when he left the Redan on the 8th of September, 1855, and walked back to the nearest parallel to solicit the help to his faltering soldiers, for which he had sent three times in vain, he had acted unworthily.

I was not in the Redan, and I did not see General Windham in the advance or the retreat from it that day; but immediately after the disastrous assault, I heard, from those who were with him, particulars of what came under their personal observation. One fact is beyond question. At the moment Windham left the Redan his presence had ceased to exercise any influence over the shrinking and discomfited men, who were sheltering themselves behind the traverses near the salient. Nothing could save them but immediate support of "troops in formation," the support Windham sought to obtain. His example had had no effect upon these men in any way. They would not follow him. He had endeavoured in vain to induce them to move towards the Russians at the base of the Redan. Our officers felt that without instant help the men would run. There were still old soldiers who disdained to turn their backs and fly, but they knew that if they went forward they could not save the honour of the day, and that they would assuredly lose their lives to no purpose. It was to save those men—perhaps indeed in the hope that he might make good a footing in the Redan—that Windham made his last appeal.

Whatever may be said, or whatever has been said or written, about the part he took, it appears to me impossible to attribute the decision that Windham took, when he crossed the ditch and walked across the open to appeal to Codrington, to any regard for his personal safety. The first thing he did was to stand upon the top of the ditch of the advanced parallel, and ask General Codrington for "the Royals, or for troops in formation," to restore the fortunes of the fight, paying no regard to the General's urgent words—"Get down, or you will be killed!"

The assault was, indeed, a great calamity—a national misfortune, a political disaster. When the story of that day of failure and loss reached England, there was an immense sensation. In the bitterness and humiliation of the defeat, which were not perhaps lessened by the success of the French at the Malakoff, the public rejoiced in the record of the gallantry of the officer, who quickly became known as "the Hero of the Redan." Windham was the only officer in command of a column who entered the Redan. He set a splendid example to his men, but few of them followed it. Reading between the lines of his letters and of the diary referring to the assault, one can see the painful stress which was placed by circumstances on a man like Windham, who felt that he was not responsible for the disaster, at the same time that he could not bring himself to accuse British soldiers of want of courage. It is best to leave the reader to form his own conclusions respecting the conduct and motives of the General, which were very recently condemned by a high military authority, from the letters and from the diary which follow. The opinion that it was dereliction of duty for a commander to leave his men under any circumstances, said to have been expressed by French officers of high rank, was caught up at the time by those to be found in every army, as amongst other bodies of men, who are disposed to accept unfavourable versions of the conduct of others. In letters written from camp on September 8th and 10th, I stated as the results of personal enquiry and investigation the facts connected with the assault ; and anyone who cares to read the evidence of the soldiers who were actually in the Redan, can refer to the volume of my letters published in 1856. I spoke, I think, to every officer who was inside the Redan, and not one of them differed from the general account published in the *Times.* Everyone expressed the highest opinion of Windham's personal bearing, and none, so far as I am aware, questioned the propriety of his seeking, by personal entreaty as a last hope, the reinforcements which one might suppose the General in the trenches would have pushed forward of his own accord. That General was Codrington, as gallant a gentleman and as honourable a man as ever lived. We may form an opinion of the impression left on Codrington's mind by Windham's conduct that day, from the simple fact that soon after he succeeded to the command of the army, he appointed Windham Chief of the Staff !

In recognition of his services, immediately on the fall of the place, Windham was appointed Commandant of Sebastopol, a post which he retained, and a very unpleasant one it was, till the 13th of October, when the notification of his promotion as Major-General—for distinguished conduct on the 8th September—reached the Crimea.

On the 11th of November, Sir William Codrington assumed the command of the army, Sir James Simpson having been permitted to resign on the previous day. From the 17th November, 1855, till the evacuation of the Crimea on the 13th June, 1856, Windham was Chief of the Staff. But the labours of the expedition had nearly come to a close; all the Generals had to do was to obey orders from their respective Governments at home, in case the diplomatic Conferences and negotiations, which occupied so much time even in the midst of war, failed in establishing a basis for treaties of peace. The activity and resources of Windham, as Chief of the Staff, were devoted to the improvement of all that appertained to the efficiency of the troops. Had another winter campaign tried the fortitude of our soldiers, they would not have had to complain of hunger, of want of cover, and insufficient clothing. They were housed in comfortable huts, supplied by a railway with fuel, forage, fresh meat, vegetables, in abundance, there were excellent roads through the camp; and Windham describes, with justifiable pride, the splendid appearance of the forty-six battalions of British infantry, paraded in line upon the heights of Telegraph Hill, on the 25th of February, for the inspection of Marshal Pelissier and La Marmora.

The Brevet-Colonel of June, 1854, returned home in 1856 a General Officer and a Companion of the Bath, a Commander of the Legion of Honour, with a medal and four clasps, a First-class of the Military Order of Savoy, the Medjidieh, and the Turkish War

medal—"a made man"—his name in every mouth.*
But he had not long to rest upon his laurels. At
the end of the year 1857, he was appointed to the
command of a Major-General's district in Bengal;
in December, 1857, he was placed in command of
the Fifth and Sixth Divisions of the Field Force,
under Sir Colin Campbell; and presently, at a
very critical moment in the history of British
India, was left in charge of the important post of
Cawnpore. It may be doubted whether Sir Colin
Campbell would have selected Windham for any
command—for the old soldier, though he became a
Guards General, was not fond of Guards officers, nor
was he particularly partial to the Headquarters in the
Crimea. He had been, moreover, injuriously super-
seded, in command of the Army, by Codrington, his
junior, who had chosen Windham to be his right-
hand man. But Windham was very popular and
very powerful at home, and, indeed, he had been recommended to the Governor-General for the command
of the expeditionary force to Persia in the previous

* The reception which Windham had in England was enthusiastic,
and particularly in his own county, where his family had long occupied
a distinguished position. The public manifestations in his honour
afforded him the liveliest satisfaction. He had not been long in India,
however, before the news of the action at Cawnpore reached England,
and the absence of any complimentary mention of his name in the
General's despatches was taken to imply the dissatisfaction of the
Commander-in-Chief with the General's defence of his post. Ere I
left London, towards the end of 1857, to join Headquarters in India,
I waited on the Duke of Cambridge, at the Horse Guards, to pay
my respects. "Well," said His Royal Highness, laughingly, "we
will see what your Redan General makes of it now." I asked His
Royal Highness whom he alluded to. "Why, I mean Windham, of
course! We all know that it was you made him the 'Hero of the
Redan.'" I intimated my belief that it was Windham, himself, who
had achieved the distinction.

year. He was only passed over because he had never served with native troops, but he was now on the spot; and so Windham was placed in charge of the ill-omened town, which was the base of operations for the force that had just set out for the relief of the Garrison, and of the civilians, women, and children in the Residency and adjacent entrenchments at Lucknow.

The bridge at Cawnpore was the only means of passage from Oudh to the right bank of the Ganges, and the main trunk road, for the great Lucknow column under Sir Colin, with its civilians, women and children, artillery, cavalry, soldiery, stores, guns, baggage, sick and wounded. The instructions Windham received were explicit; but, without plunging into the heated controversy in which Malleson and other writers have given judgment against him, I think that the opinions of an officer like Sir John Adye, who was with Windham in those days of, trial, carry far greater weight than the minute objections of inferior authorities to the details of the operations which had the one all-powerful argument in their favour, that the bridge was saved, and that Cawnpore was held against enormous odds. When I went to Simla, after the actual capture of Lucknow and the campaign of Rohilcund, I met Windham, who was on leave with Sir Robert Garrett. We often had *causeries* about the Cawnpore battles, in which he mentioned matters concerning officers and men— "things not generally known"—which made me feel thankful that he had held the bridge so well and at all! "Had I acted according to orders the bridge would have been lost as sure as you are alive! Why, had I withdrawn my force, after I had displayed them outside the entrenchments and the town, as I was ordered to do, the whole of the 'Budmashes' would have swarmed in on us; but I gave them a blow in the face which staggered the Gwalior gentlemen. Sir Colin felt he had done me wrong, and he made the amends, but the mischief was done. As to the shameful accusations that I was ungenerous in my treatment of Carthew, I can only say, that if I was guilty of anything of the kind, I deserve all the obloquy that has been heaped upon me ten times over. But I feel it is not true." The passages in his letters and memoranda which follow speak for themselves, and the letters from Sir Colin Campbell and General Mansfield, which made tardy acknowledgment of the injustice which had been done to him by his chiefs, are the best answers to those who have assailed Windham for his defence of Cawnpore. That he was judicious and politic I will not say, for I do not think he was either, having regard to his own interests; but that he was as honest and as brave a soldier as ever served the Queen I most fully believe.

W. H. R.

CHARLES ASH WINDHAM, the fourth son of Admiral William Windham, of Felbrigg Hall, Norfolk; and a great nephew of William Windham, who was Secretary of State for War and the Colonial Department in Lord Grenville's Ministry "of all the Talents," was born on October 8th, 1810.

He was educated at the Royal Military College, Sandhurst, and entered the Coldstream Guards at the age of sixteen.

The dates of his Commissions are as follows:

Ensign and Lieutenant	. December 30th, 1826.
Lieutenant and Captain	. May 31st, 1833.
Brevet-Major . .	. November 9th, 1846.
Captain and Lieut.-Colonel	December 29th, 1846.

In 1849, Lieutenant - Colonel Windham married Marianne Catherine Emily, daughter of Admiral Sir John Beresford; and on June 22nd of the same year he exchanged to half-pay.

On the outbreak of the Crimean War, Windham exerted himself to the utmost to obtain employment in the field, and eventually was rewarded by receiving the appointment of Assistant Quartermaster-General to the 4th Division, which was commanded by a distinguished and experienced soldier, Lieutenant-General the Honourable Sir George Cathcart.

Windham had been promoted to the rank of Colonel in the Army, on June 20th, 1854, and thus entered on his first campaign in full maturity of mind and body, and entrusted with duties of much responsibility. He embarked at Southampton on August 9th, 1854, on board the steamer *Harbinger*, and began his diary, which is given, as nearly as possible, in the form in which it was written, on his arrival at Constantinople.

DIARY.

CONSTANTINOPLE, *September 1st*, 1854.—Arrived at Constantinople this morning, and heard that the Army was embarking for Sebastopol, and would probably sail on the 3rd.

The French and English have suffered severely from sickness in Bulgaria. For my part I never felt better, and I sincerely hope I may be preserved to return home; but, above all things, I do earnestly pray that God will grant me strength and courage to behave as becomes a man and a soldier, come what may.

It will be my first battle, and no man can say what effect that may have on him, so I repeat that, above all things, I pray for a stout heart and a clear head when the battle rages fiercest, particularly should we be unsuccessful.

A letter to Anthony Hudson, Esq., Colonel Windham's oldest and best friend, follows:

"CONSTANTINOPLE,
September 1st, 1854.

"MY DEAR ANTHONY,

"This is for you and William, as I have not time to write to both. We have this moment (7 a.m.)

dropped anchor, and we are off again directly, as the Army is embarking for Sebastopol, and we shall be just in time.

"I am happy to say that I never felt better in my life, and lucky for me it is so. The sickness here has been *frightful* (don't let Marianne know this), and I think the attack on Sebastopol is a good deal owing to this. How I pray we may succeed. Our Division is gone on, and I shall have arduous duties to perform without positively one single day's preparation, even for my horses. They have never seen fire, nor have I, so we shall be novices together; but we must do our best.

"Give my best, very best, love to William, Charlotte, and all your family, as I shall not probably have another chance of writing to you for some time. God bless you, my dear Anthony, for all your many kindnesses; and sincerely praying that I may conduct myself well before the enemy, and live to return to old England.

"I remain in good health and spirits,

"Yours affectionately,

"C. A. W."

VARNA, *September 2nd*, 1854.—Anniversary of the death of a great English soldier, Oliver Cromwell. I wonder what he would do if at Varna? I had a long and interesting talk, last evening, after dinner with the General (Sir George Cathcart). He told me all he intended doing, and I am convinced that he is perfectly right in his views. He said almost exactly what I wrote to Bentinck* last February.

* Brig.-Gen. commanding the Brigade of Guards.

VARNA, *September* 3rd.—Went on shore and saw Lord Raglan, Sir George Brown, General Airey, Admirals Dundas and Lyons. Drew some necessaries for servants and the detachment of the 46th Regiment, now on board here. I did what I could to find out what I had to do, but, as to this, got but little information.

I was glad to see Lord Raglan looking so well, and as to General Brown, he looks the freshest man here ; and I do not doubt he will lead the Light Division " like a good 'un."

For my part, what I fear is the condition of the men. They are so dispirited and downcast by sickness that I very much question their fighting in the resolute way I am sure they would have fought had this expedition been undertaken months ago.

I think that, from a strategical point of view, Odessa is the place to attack.

Why we should choose to fight the Russians with a strong fortification to assist them, instead of fighting them with an open town near us that would probably offer no resistance, is more than I can understand.

From what I can learn the French seem to be opposed to the attack (on Sebastopol) ; the English think it too late in the year, and a great many of our superior officers look upon it as hazardous and doubtful. And no one seems in the right spirit to do it.

The French have lost a frightful number of men by sickness, and will only be able to embark twenty thousand ; we shall send twenty-two or twenty-three thousand, and I understand the Turks will send ten thousand.

One thing is certain, we must all do our best.

Codrington has got Airey's Brigade,* which I am delighted at, as I am sure he is a man whose heart is in his profession.

VARNA, *September 4th.*—That the French and English Armies should have been here for months doing nothing, and that now, when they are out of health and spirits, and have lost in effective strength at least one-third of their force, they should undertake to beard in his den the lion that they were afraid of in the open, is certainly wonderful.

Alas! how few men there are who possess common sense. Cathcart does, and I believe he is quite right in most of his views.

Only fancy if we fail in this expedition! To say nothing of the bloodshed, look at the loss of reputation to our arms, to the apparent certainty, or, at least, strong probability, of a split with France; for a defeat would assuredly produce the most bitter disputes; lastly, consider the defencelessness of our island in the event of the Army being destroyed. And what, I ask, are we to gain? Sebastopol! And in what respect will Russia be injured if we have to return it to her at the end of the war?

We shall, if successful, be further off peace than ever,† in my opinion; and, if unsuccessful, it is utter ruin, unless we fall back upon Odessa, and declare the Crimea attack to have been only a feint. God is merciful, and spares many who little expect or deserve it.

We shall assuredly have a rattling fight of it, and I

---

* Brigadier-General Airey had been appointed Quartermaster-General in succession to Lord de Ros, invalided.

† This proved to be erroneous.—W. H. R.

earnestly pray that these lines may stare me in the face hereafter, and prove to me that, though I now think I am writing wisely, I am after all a fool, and that the people in whose hands the nations of England and France have placed themselves are wiser by far than I.

All I can say is that, as I am firmly convinced of the folly of the attack, undertaken to gratify the vainglory of a lot of foolhardy men, I will never expunge a word.

If the Armies were in health and spirits they would unquestionably take Sebastopol, and they may, and, I hope, will do so now.   Indeed, I do not think the odds are two to one against it, but they ought to be five to one in our favour before we undertake so hazardous an operation.

VARNA, *September* 5*th.*—Got up this morning at six as usual, and saw the *Agamemnon* moving about the Bay under steam, and looking beautiful.

A vast portion of the fleet has already gone, and our steam is nearly up.

We soon sailed for Baltchick,* and, on leaving the Bay, ran over the dead body of one of the poor Zouaves who was drowned the other day at the embarkation of his corps.†

" *S.S. Harbinger,*" *September* 6*th.*—Arrived at Baltchick Bay at half-past ten a.m., and anchored.   What a noble armament !   At present everything looks well, the wind fair, and the outside of things all one could wish.

---

* A cape a few miles N. of Varna.
† A boat full, going off to a transport, had been run down by a steamer.

God grant all may go on well, and old England win the day.   So hurrah for success!

BALTCHICK BAY, *September 7th.*—I suppose such a fleet as this was never seen before in any sea.   I cannot help thinking the sight of it will cast a damper on the good folk of Sebastopol.

At about one o'clock p.m. the fleet got into order, the French being on the right, Turks in the centre, and English on the left.

I fancy we shall land nearly fifty thousand men.

" *S.S. Harbinger,*" *September 9th.*—At twelve, noon, we were about thirty-five miles from Cape Tarkhan, and sixty-five miles from Odessa.   Soon afterwards the leading ships cut off their steam and we lay to, I suppose for the rear portion of the fleet.

Their heads are now lying in all directions, so I really do not yet know where we may ultimately go. I still hope it may be Odessa, but fear not.

I find, in an old French work, that all the rivers immediately to the north of Sebastopol, and falling into the sea, namely, the Bulganak, Alma, Katcha, and Belbek are sharp torrents in the spring and winter, but easily fordable at this season.   The weather to-day is cloudy and autumnal, and, I may add, cold.

Had my sword sharpened and loaded my pistol, and then, as soon as my three days' provisions are served out, I shall be ready to land.   At about 4 p.m. the signal was made to anchor, and we accordingly did so in about fifteen fathom water.

Who could fail to admire, by the light of the declining sun, the appearance of this magnificent fleet, or to feel proud of the works of science and civilization?

While I was in the midst of these thoughts the *John Masterman* dropped overboard the corpse of some unfortunate to remind us, I suppose, of our end, as far as this being is concerned.

"*S.S. Harbinger*," *September* 10*th*.—The fleet still at anchor this morning, the sun shining, and everything looking peaceable and happy.

It seems to be the opinion on board that we shall land near Eupatoria, and take possession of the narrow strip of land between the salt lake and the sea.

It may be so, but we shall then be a long way from Sebastopol, and have no easy business to defend our lines of communications against the hordes of Cossacks that I expect will be about us; and there certainly will be an end of carrying out St. Arnaud's assertion (in his proclamation) that we will take Sebastopol in three days, for we shall, unquestionably, not be able, in our present state, to march there in that time, even if the Russians received us as friends, and not as enemies.

The men are ordered to land with their knapsacks, great-coats, and three days' provisions, and to leave their blankets behind them. In my opinion, the knapsack is a perfectly useless thing.

I have walked under weight, and have carried my own provisions for many days, and I am sure that, provided you took a blanket, and put in it a spare shirt, a pair of shoes, and a towel, you might leave your knapsack and great-coat behind you for a fortnight.

A great-coat is a great-coat and nothing more, but a blanket is a blanket and great-coat too, and when men lie down together in twos and threes, they can, with good blankets, make themselves comfortable; at least, I always found this to be the case in my hunting trips in North America, where I have gone through more real hard work than falls to the lot of most men.

The knapsack appears to be a thing to which officers are peculiarly wedded ; which can easily be accounted for by their never having carried them.

If they ever had to do so, they would avoid them as studiously as gipsies, pedlars, and trappers do.

Any weight, in fact, that cannot be shifted is painful for a man to carry ; and as a blanket, rolled lengthways and slung over the shoulder, will carry all that a man can want for a fortnight, I cannot see the use of loading him with more. When going on sentry duty he would leave his trifling effects with his comrade, and use the blanket as a great-coat ; when in his tent, his blanket is his bed.

"*S.S. Harbinger,*" *September* 11*th.*—At about 1 p.m. the fleet got under weigh, and stood for the Crimea.

Before starting, Charles Woodford* came on board, and I asked him whether any information had been obtained as to the original strength and reinforcements of the enemy. As to the first, he said he knew nothing; as to the second, it appears they have positive information that ships have lately sailed from Odessa with troops on board, and have safely landed them at Sebastopol.

This, if true, is a considerable reflection on the vigilance of our fleet.

I suppose to-morrow we shall be off our landing-place, and I hope the appearance of the fleet will have considerable weight with the Russians, and make them overrate our numbers.

* Colonel Charles Woodford, Rifle Brigade, afterwards killed, when under Windham's command at Cawnpore.

"*S.S. Harbinger,*" *September* 12*th*.—There was a sharpish squall in the night, which caused our ships to cast off those they were towing, but they have now resumed their places. We see nothing of the French and Turkish fleets, and don't know if they have gone elsewhere, or dropped astern.

EUPATORIA, *September* 13*th*.—Weighed anchor in the morning, and stood to the southward; land distant about three miles to the eastward; the country looks sunburnt and very open, and has a good deal the look of Newmarket Heath from the lowlands of Cambridgeshire.

The French and Turkish fleets came up during the night, and we made sail, and got fairly off about 9 a.m.

Anchored off Eupatoria. As they have made the signal to land, I suppose we shall do so. The place, though fifty miles distant from Sebastopol, appears in other respects a good and safe place for landing.

DISEMBARKATION OF THE ARMY, *September* 14*th to September* 17*th*.—To our great astonishment, instead of landing at Eupatoria, we were ordered off this morning at two o'clock, but did not start till daylight.

We landed without opposition on the tongue of land between Lake Kamishli and the sea. The prearranged order of landing was soon abandoned, and we got on shore as best we could.

In the 4th Division, Sir George (Cathcart) went first with Elliot, and left me to follow with the remainder of the Staff, excepting Smith, who remained in charge of the horses.

We did not land till just dark, and found the General with the 1st Battalion Rifle Brigade.

It soon began to rain, and we passed a wet, unpleasant night on this spit of land, a good deal in want of water.

We remained in this position till the 19th September, during which time the tents were re-embarked, which was wise; but a vast number of stores had also to be re-embarked, or, what was worse, to be abandoned, which was unwise; and showed, what has subsequently been too clear, that we had hardly any transport, and no method with what we had.

September 18th.—At 8 p.m. I was sent for by the Quartermaster-General, and, in his tent with the remainder of the A.Q.M.G.'s, I wrote down the order of march, and galloped back with it to Sir George Cathcart.

Nothing had been arranged by the Commissariat, but it was still determined that we should march early next morning.

BULGANAK VALLEY, *September 19th.*—Accordingly, off we went, with the exception of the 63rd, and the two complete companies of the 46th, who were left behind, under Brigadier-General Torrens.

We had a hot, dusty, slow, drawling march to the Bulganak, a mere brook, about four inches deep, and, in most places, practicable for a horse to jump.

On arriving there, the advanced guard (consisting of light cavalry, under Cardigan) had a small skirmish with the Cossacks, who soon withdrew, and we encamped upon the stream.

We had suffered a good deal at our first encampment from cholera, and it pursued us here. I brought a man, with assistance, into our camp in a blanket.

He belonged to the 50th. He kept constantly saying, "I want to go home. I am going home, I know I am."

Poor fellow, I did what I could for him, but found him dead in the morning, and so was Seymour's servant. Poor Beckwith, of the Rifles, was also taken ill, and we never saw him again.

BATTLE OF THE ALMA.

September 20th.—We advanced again early in the morning, and after a slow, loitering march, arrived at the Alma about mid-day. When I first saw the village on its banks it was in flames, but the smoke from it was soon equalled, if not eclipsed, by the fire from the Russian artillery.

The Light and Second Divisions crossed first, and were soon followed by the First. The Third and Fourth Divisions acted in support, and were neither of them engaged during the day, though under fire.

It was my first fight, and I was quite astounded at my coolness. I did not feel a bit more nervous than I should have done in Hyde Park.

The General sent me off to the left to look after some Cossacks, and it was the opinion of some that I should be cut off; my friends, on the contrary, did not try it, but bolted.

We crossed the river as soon as possible, and the General, followed by me, galloped after the Highland Brigade as fast as we could, and arrived in time for "the brush."

We had the pleasure of seeing the Highlanders, aided by three or four guns, pitching into the Russians, who were in full retreat. I found a man of the 42nd threatening to break the head of a Russian who lay at his feet, and, on my stopping him, he said the fellow had shot at him after receiving quarter. I heard the same story from many on the field, and from all I have seen, I believe it to be true.

This battle must have shown the Russians that they had to deal with no ordinary infantry, as they could not hold their very strong position above two and a half hours.

Had they thought less of their trophies, or, in other words, of their brass guns,* and more of their position, they would have held it much longer. Their fear of losing their guns lost them their position.

As for our attack, it was a mere stupid taking the bull by the horns and throwing him. Had we not let him get up again, this might have been excused; and we could have done this by sending in pursuit the 3rd and 4th Divisions, the Highland Brigade, and the cavalry. But we simply let him get up and go off with all his artillery (save two guns), and then sat down on the ground we had previously camped on, and looked out for dinner.

I watched everything very closely, and was much pleased at the kindness and good nature of the men to their enemies.

The great slaughter was at the large *battery*, about half-way up the hill, six hundred yards from the river. Here the enemy lay thick, both on the inside and outside of it, but more on the outside.

As to myself, I had nothing to do. I was never exposed to a close musketry fire. The shells and

---

* The Russians were very badly armed, with smooth-bore flint-lock muskets, converted. They possessed very few rifles.

round shot flew about fairly, but nothing much. At the end, when I *was* near enough, the enemy was making off too fast to put one in much danger.

The more I think of the battle, the more convinced I am that it might have ended the campaign. I thought so at the time, and I think so more strongly *now.*[*]

The battery never should have been attacked. Our left should have been thrown forward and to the left, and have turned the right of the Russian position.[†] Had the Russians then waited for our attack, they would have been driven on to the French or into the sea. Had they not waited, they must have abandoned their batteries and their position.

If it be said, "Aye, but they would perhaps have driven back our attack over the river and ruined it," I answer, "If they could do this without their batteries, why could they not drive back our centre with them?" In fact, we flung away the great advantages of the attack, namely, choice of time and place; and, moreover, when the battle was over, did not follow up our success.

The following letter to Mrs. Windham gives some interesting details of the battle :—

"CAMP ON THE HEIGHTS OF ALMA,

"*September* 21*st*, 1854.

" MY DEAREST,

"We are now in the camp occupied by the Russians yesterday. In 2 hours 50 minutes we carried

---

[*] It appears that the above remarks were written a few days later, at Balaclava.

[†] This was St. Arnaud's plan, which Lord Raglan accepted, but did not carry out.—W. H. R.

their position with the loss, I fear, to us of about 1100 killed and wounded.

"The Guards did beautifully, and have suffered much, particularly in wounded. I saw Charles Baring to-day, arm lost; Cust, killed; Heygarth, arm and leg lost; Percy and Ennismore,* both wounded; Charles Hare, I hear, is killed, poor fellow! Listowel and Richard will regret him much. I am glad to say Ennismore was gone on board ship when I went down to see him. Poor Lord Chewton is desperately wounded in several places, and, I fear, will not recover. Colonel Chester killed, Major Rose ditto, and Montague, of the 33rd, and many others. It was a beautiful military sight, and I watched it as quietly as if I had been in Hyde Park, but I must add, for fear you should think me boastful, that I was in no kind of danger; a few cannon shot and bullets wounded some half a dozen men in our Division, which supported the Guards, and that was all. I am, my dear, perfectly well.

"The Russian General we took prisoner, and who is now on board the *Agamemnon*, says of all the soldiers he ever saw he has never seen anything like the British infantry; they fought more like devils than men. Tell Lord Somerville that the centre battery was 600 yards from the river, and consisted of twelve 32-pounders, supported by 35,000 men and 50 pieces of artillery, and that the allies made a clear sweep of them in less than three hours. It was nobly done.

"We advance to-morrow.

"God bless you, my dear,
"Your affectionate husband,
"C. A. W."

* Present Earl of Listowel.

A letter to William Windham, Esq., the eldest brother of the writer, is also included, as it gives a good many additional details of interest :—

"CAMP ON HEIGHTS ABOVE THE ALMA,

"*September* 21st, 1854.

" MY DEAR WILLIAM,

"We yesterday carried the Russian position in the finest style imaginable, with the loss, I am sorry to say, of 1100 men (British). The French did their work excellently, and are well pleased with us. I cannot enter into plans and minutiæ, as I am writing at night in the open air, without tent, and by a little lantern. The glory rests with the Left Division and the Guards. Our Division, though close up, was untouched save a few wounded, and beyond a few bullets and round shot every now and then coming up to me, and a shell or two, I might as well have been in Hyde Park.

"The Russians had an immensely strong position, 30,000 men and 50 guns, besides a battery of twelve 32-pounders, and they were driven to the devil in less than three hours. Tell Anthony it would have done him good to have stood, as I did, by Lord Raglan on the height with the Guards and Highlanders, and to have seen the whole plain below strewed with Russians. The Russian General we took says we fought more like devils than men, and how such a position could have been carried under a loss of eight or nine thousand I can't think.

" We have to-day been burying the dead and carrying in the wounded. You could trace the route of the Russian columns by the dead, dying, broken arms, lost knapsacks, &c., as clearly as you could a road, and, in less than five minutes, the Highlanders, at 600 yards, killed a hundred men whilst they were running.

"Give my best love to Anthony, and I will send more particulars if I am not bagged on the Katcha; but I think they have had a sickener, and won't stand long before us whenever we meet. We lead next time.

"Yours ever affectionately,

"C. A. W."

ON THE ALMA, *September 21st and 22nd.*—Assisted some of our own, and many Russian wounded. Much pleased at the conduct of our men towards the latter, but greatly hurt at the want of exertion and system in getting the wounded away. The whole of the 4th Division ought to have been employed, as well as others, in collecting them; whereas hundreds of men were walking about giving them bread and water, but no fatigue parties were employed to carry them in, and bury the dead, until nearly forty-eight hours after the battle. Cholera on the increase, I am sorry to say.

KATCHA, *September 23rd.*—The allies left the Alma, and marched to the Katcha.

Sent fifty-two of the division to the beach, sick, mostly, with cholera; also my servant.

Had to destroy my brown mare before marching.

This (Katcha) is a beautiful valley, and full of the finest fruit, particularly grapes, and most handsomely were they plundered. This was very natural, as the inhabitants had all deserted their houses, so the men could not buy the fruit.

The 57th Regiment joined us.

What a strong position for the Russians to have abandoned!

BELBEK, *September* 24*th.*—Left the valley of the Katcha late, and advanced to the Belbek, a stream running through another valley, rich in fruit, and about as big as the Katcha. Crossed it, and camped on the bushy heights to the south of the river.

Cholera still in camp.

THE FLANK MARCH, *September* 25*th.*—Under arms at 7 a.m. The rest of the Army marched across country in a S.S.E. direction. We (4th Division) remained as a rear-guard, and to protect the sick and baggage. In the afternoon Smith * was sent by Sir George with despatches to Lord Raglan; lost his way, was fired at (from Sebastopol), and one of the two dragoons who were with him was killed.

Smith got back about midnight.

BELBEK, *September* 26*th.*—At about one o'clock this morning Sir George desired me to go to the Katcha, and inform the senior naval officer on the station that Lord Raglan wished the base to be considered changed to Balaclava, and the fleet to be moved accordingly. I was also to get all commissariat stores, transport, and sick on board the fleet.

I rode down to George Paget's † tent to ask him for a dragoon, when his charger kicked me, with all its force, upon the right shin, and hurt me most severely. However, after having had my leg dressed, I rode on, and gave my orders, first to Admiral Dundas, and then to Sir E. Lyons, who took me in his ship, the *Agamemnon*, to Balaclava, where I witnessed the capture of that place.

---

* Captain Hugh Smith, "The Buffs," D.A.Q.M.G. of the 4th Division.
† Lord George Paget, at this time Lieutenant-Colonel of the 4th Light Dragoons.

In the afternoon I was attacked by either colic or cholera; was given calomel and opium every ten minutes for the first two hours, then every hour. The Admiral and Captain Mends both extremely kind.

BALACLAVA, *September 27th.*—I may think myself very lucky to have had this attack here, as on shore I might not have got over it. Stayed on board the *Agamemnon* by the advice of the Admiral, Captain Mends, and the doctor, and wrote to Sir George Cathcart and to Powlett Somerset,* explaining my absence. The *Agamemnon* entered the harbour of Balaclava this morning; the entrance very narrow.

BALACLAVA, *September 28th.*—Went on shore and saw Powlett Somerset and others of Lord Raglan's Staff. When there, although still ill, I determined to join my Division immediately, hearing that 26,000 Russians were likely to attack it. Accordingly, I borrowed Powlett Somerset's pony, having sent my horse to camp, with the orderly I took with me to the Katcha, and rode up to camp, where I arrived ill and uncomfortable.

The following letter to Mr. Hudson shows how fully it was expected that "the Flank March" would lead to the immediate fall of Sebastopol :—

" H.M.S. ' AGAMEMNON,' BALACLAVA,
" *September 28th,* 1854.
" MY DEAR ANTHONY,
" On the 24th, the French Army encamped upon the right of the road, running from the second bridge

---

* Colonel Powlett Somerset was an officer on the Headquarter Staff, and an old friend and brother-officer to Colonel Windham.

(further from the sea) of the Belbek to Sebastopol, and the English Army on the left of it.

"About mid-day the French moved to their left and front about four miles, but the English marched by compass, carrying no baggage, S.S.E., to near Mackenzie's farm, through the thickest copse and brushwood, struck the old road from Batchi Serai to Balaclava, and halted at night on the Tchernaya (black water), near Tchorgoun, about four miles from Balaclava. This was done because the Russians have dismantled and sunk all their ships, and placed the guns in battery on the north shore to the south where we now are. They are quite unprepared, and we hope soon to have the place.

"I was badly kicked by George Paget's horse just before starting with the despatches, to announce the change of the base of operations from the Katcha to Balaclava to Sir Edmund Lyons, and have accordingly come round with him; and glad I am I did so, as I was attacked with cholera the day before yesterday, and they have crammed me full of calomel and opium. I am now going to get on my horse and rejoin Cathcart, who is within five miles of this. Don't tell Marianne anything about my having had the cholera. St. Arnaud goes home to-day or to-morrow, being nearly dead of the same disorder. Alma was a fine fight as to pluck, and has cast a damper on the Russians; but our loss was over 2000 men.

"Yours ever in haste,

"C. A. W."

September 29*th*.—Leg still bad. After an uneasy night, awoke this morning not much worse. The groans of six or seven poor fellows of the 57th, who died during the night of cholera, did not add to my comfort.

At about 1 p.m. the Russians began firing shot and shell at us, and continued doing so at intervals for the remainder of the day.

At 11 p.m. the outlying picket reported the sounding of bugles and beating of drums in the Russian lines.

At midnight, owing to four or five shots from the outlying picket, we all got under arms, and in the morning we found that they had captured a man from a Russian patrol.

October 2nd, 1854.—It is now a week since we left the Belbek by the "cross-country" march, the best done thing of the campaign ; but instead of turning it to account, we appear determined to allow the enemy to recover from his surprise and despondency, and to let him erect every defence in his power. I am sure Sebastopol ought to have been taken ten days ago. That is my firm opinion. Days and days have been wasted since I first arrived. As for the enemy, they could not have prevented us ; but what with idleness and delay, we have not yet done or begun anything to strengthen our position against an attack from them. They fire at us all day, but, I believe, do no harm.

October 4th.—Not well yet. Russians to-day fired with more success, as they killed one man of the 63rd, and one of the 68th, and severely wounded a sergeant of the 68th.

October 5th.—Worse, and with Sir George's permission went on board the *Agamemnon*, where I slept.

D

October 6th.—Rejoined the camp, I hope for good, as I feel better. Found the General out with four companies of the 57th: three near the Quarry in our front, and one further to the right. I believe the Engineers intend getting one gun into position. Sad, slow work, but I hope it will be proportionately sure.

October 8th.—My birthday. May it please God to let me see some others. Another day and nothing done; the Russians shooting and shelling us, and we looking .on. If Sebastopol is ever taken it will be by the bayonet.

We have now lost many days since we embarked at Varna, and I am perfectly convinced we ought, with energy, to have had the town ere this.

We may still take it, but it will be a long business. The world cannot say we are all talk and no action, for we never hear or say a word. No one seems to know anything as to what is to be done.

October 9th.—A real touch of the coming winter. A strong north-east gale, with searching cold. This, added to a want of wood, bad prospects, starving horses, constant shot and shell from the enemy without any return from us, were certainly cogent reasons for passing an uncomfortable day. A bitter cold night.

October 10th.—Russians more than usually playful with their artillery. I believe we have at last one gun in position, and to-night the 3rd Division and ourselves will turn out in earnest. At sunset a working party of six hundred proceeded to the front, supported by a covering party of one thousand, under Brigadier-General Goldie. The like number were furnished by the 3rd

Division; the covering force, under Brigadier-General Eyre. It is now 11 p.m. The Russians have been firing all night, but over and beyond our working parties. Should they leave them alone till morning it will be everything. The Light Division sent out a small working party and covering force, but somehow or other Captain Gordon lost his trace,* and they came back. Not so, I believe, the covering party. The Rifles, one wing of each battalion, are in advance of all. Lord Raglan and Sir John Burgoyne came to our camp at about 10.30 p.m., and I showed them the way to Sir George Brown's. Sir George Cathcart went afterwards to show them where the trench work was going on.

Powlett Somerset told me the French were getting on famously; they have discovered a fine clay to work in, expect to have everything ready by Thursday, and to take the place in forty-eight hours after opening fire. We shall see.

October 11th.—Rode to Balaclava, and called at Headquarters *en route.* Lord Raglan asked me about the trenches, round which I had gone with Sir George Cathcart at about half-past seven this morning.

A strong fire was kept up upon us, but there was lots of time to bob down if one kept one's eyes open. Got 1500 blankets for the Division.

October 12th.—Was roused at about two o'clock this morning by heavy firing and cheering at the trenches. Was sent by Sir George to find out what was the matter, and was nearly killed by a shell.

* The working party arrived late, and the trace could not be found in the darkness.

Found Torrens* at the trenches, and discovered that all the noise and confusion had been caused by three Sappers getting amongst the Russians, and being fired at.

The works are progressing favourably; and the covering force remained very steady during the alarm. Went to the trenches again at 10 p.m.

October 13*th.*—The General again sent me to Bala-clava. Had the reserve ammunition horses laden with gabions. Was much struck by the extreme carelessness of persons in charge of fatigue parties, and by the waste of that which is most precious, namely, "the means of transport." Without authority, I could, of course, do nothing in the way of reform in one day.

October 14*th.*—At Balaclava, arranging for a house to be used as a store for the Division.

October 15*th.*—Again at Balaclava on the same business. Heard of poor Chewton's† death.

October 16*th.*—At 3.20 this morning, marched 1500 men down to the trenches as a covering force. Stayed there about an hour and a half. Got all the men into position without any killed or wounded.

At a quarter to ten o'clock the Russians began a tremendous fire, from every gun they had, against both us and the French. A grand "tapage" they certainly made, but we returned not a single shot, nor budged an inch.

* Brigadier-General A. Torrens, commanding the 2nd Brigade, 4th Division ; he was mortally wounded at Inkerman.

† Captain Lord Chewton, Scots Fusilier Guards ; mortally wounded at the Alma.

In about half-an-hour this shower of shot and shell passed away, and the sun shone clear again under the smoke.   In our Division we only had five or six killed ; and, amongst others, poor little Rowley,* of the Grenadiers.   I am sorry for it.   He was killed, when perfectly under cover, by a round shot striking a rock, flying up into the air, and alighting on his loins.

Seeing the "weather" well settled after this storm, I rode with Seymour† to Headquarters, and then on to Balaclava, where I brought the Division store business nearly to a close.

THE FIRST BOMBARDMENT.

At 9 p.m. Sir George sent for all his Staff, and read to us Lord Raglan's mems. for the attack upon Sebastopol to-morrow morning, which is to commence upon the firing of three French mortars from their lines: both fleets are to join in it.   Hurrah!   God grant it may be successful.

October 17th.—The batteries opened against the town this morning at ten minutes to seven, and a grand row they made.   At nine o'clock the French magazine of their right attack blew up ; and that battery has been silent since.   (It is now noon.)

FAILURE OF THE BOMBARDMENT.

I am, at this moment, much disappointed at the effect of our fire.   We have certainly damaged the White Tower, and dismounted three guns ; and that

* Captain Rowley, Grenadier Guards.
† Lieut.-Col. Charles Seymour, Scots Fusilier Guards, brother of the late Admiral Lord Alcester.

battery looks sickly. But the "Redan" holds out stoutly, and does not appear to have suffered.

We are now expecting to see the fleets attack. At about 1 p.m. the French fleet attacked, and at 2 p.m. the magazine of their left attack blew up. At 3 p.m. we blew up the magazine of the "Redan," and great was our cheering.

Owing to the smoke, I could not see when the English fleet attacked, but they are firing away now (4.30 p.m.) like mad, and have been for some time. In the afternoon some caissons, in the rear of Gordon's Battery, blew up; and I fear some men were killed. They sent a horse and cart some fifty feet into the air, and, as certainly, have not hurt the battery.

October 18*th.*—Marched the covering party (1000) to the trenches at 3 a.m., and stayed there till 5. At daylight the firing began, and continued vigorously till twelve noon, when it somewhat slackened on the part of the Russians.

I greatly regret to say poor Hood* was killed in Gordon's Battery, about mid-day. We prepared to receive the Russians on our right front, but it is now 3 p.m., and they have not come.

I think the Round Tower looks sickly, and that is all I can say. The French have not fired a shot during the day. The fleet yesterday, I understand, lost nearly one hundred and fifty in killed and wounded.

October 19*th.*—Went to Balaclava with the sick. The pounding match went on as usual, without our

* Colonel the Honble. F. G. Hood, Grenadier Guards, who had distinguished himself at the battle of the Alma.

gaining the slightest advantage, and I am more convinced than ever that we shall lose double the number of men in taking the place (if we do succeed) than we should have done had we attacked it twenty-four days ago.

This long range firing is all nonsense; moreover, the Russians are better at it than we are, and, from all I can see, our present attack is an absurdity.

October 20*th.*—Horsford (Rifle Brigade), Smith, and Maitland went out this morning at half-past one to reconnoitre the Redan; but they could make out nothing except that the hill on which it stands is too steep for infantry to get up in line. Firing commenced at 6.30 a.m., and continued till dark. The Russians I thought rather slack, but this may be fancy.

I believe that the proper method is for us to attack the south-west salient point of the town, in conjunction with the French, storm it and hold it, and leave the Redan and Round Tower to themselves. By so doing we should turn all their batteries, and get possession of that portion of the town, west of the harbour, which we could hold.

Euston,* Newton,† Dunkellin,‡ and D. Carleton,§ came to see me, and I saw also Mark Wood,‖ Percy Feilding,¶ and young Greville.** I do not like the look of things, although (it is now night) they look better in the morning.

---

* Present Duke of Grafton. † Afterwards General Newton.
‡ Lord Dunkellin, afterwards taken prisoner.
§ Present Lord Dorchester. ‖ Afterwards General Mark Wood.
¶ General the Honble. Sir Percy Feilding. ** Killed at Inkerman.
All the above were officers of the Coldstream Guards.

October 21st.—General Goldie was sent last night to Balaclava with 1000 men, but no attack was made there. A small sortie was made upon the French lines, and also upon our 2nd Division. Rode to Balaclava.

This night the General has requested me, upon taking the relief to the trenches to-morrow morning, to advance beyond them, and see what sort of country there is past the house in the left ravine.

Notwithstanding the favourable reports, I don't like the aspect of affairs.

October 22nd.—At 3 a.m. marched the covering party to the trenches. Took Sergeant Rutland and six men of the Rifles, and followed a company of the 21st to the house in the left ravine. When there, found they had been erecting a battery on a hill to the left of it.

About two hundred yards in front of this battery I found a French picket and working party, the latter making a battery within five hundred yards of the salient angle. This is a move in the right direction.

I then went forward, edging off to my right, and got a good view of the town and harbour, but could discover nothing as to the foot of the hill on which stands the Redan, although I got within three hundred yards of the town.

Came up the valley after sunrise under a heavy fire of shot and shell, but was not hit.

After breakfast rode to Balaclava, and put the sick on board ship.

On returning to camp, D. Carleton told me that Dunkellin had been taken prisoner by a Russian picket.

Letter to William Windham :—

> " ABOVE SEBASTOPOL,
>
> " *October* 22nd, 1854.

" MY DEAR WILLIAM,

"I had intended enclosing you and Anthony a bird's-eye view of our proceedings here, but the probability is so great that the *Illustrated News* will have a much better one, that I shall refrain from exhibiting my talent in that line, and stick to the good old British system of grumbling. We have decidedly no Wellington here. Lord Raglan is a well-mannered, brave, and amiable man of business. Sir George Cathcart is the best of the Generals of Division, and he is warped and out of temper ; disappointed, I fancy, at not being more consulted, and, therefore, irritable and angry with most people and most things. After our flank march from the Belbek to the old road from Batchi Serai to Balaclava, we had turned their position, and found the town defenceless on the southern side. To do Cathcart justice, he proposed to Lord Raglan to assault it with his Division immediately, provided he were supported. This was not listened to—people who are constantly sneering at others, and offering suggestions, are apt to get the cold shoulder given them—and I fancy this is the case with him. One thing is, however, clear: the town was not assaulted on the 27th or 28th September. The Russians worked day and night from the 25th to the 17th ult. (the day on which we opened fire), and the greater part of that time we did nothing but wait for the landing of our siege-train ; and on the 9th, broke ground ; and, as I before said, began firing on the 17th, at a range averaging at least 1200 yards. Up to this day we have done nothing beyond killing (according to deserters) the governor and a good many men, and if

the point of attack be not changed, we shall, in my
opinion (which I have expressed for the last fourteen
days), continue the same laborious and useless occupation—it is at present a mere pounding match.   One
good battery thrown up on the ground *between* the
French and English attacks, or, if you will, on the left
of the English and right of the French, would do more
in one day than all the others in one week.   At first the
French thought they could knock down the Russian
works in four hours.   What was the result?   We both
opened fire together at half past six a.m.   Bang! bang!
bang!   Whiz! whiz! whiz!   Every kind of whistle,
hum, and noise, but, singular to say, topsy-turvy goes
over one French gun after another, until nine out of
some thirty-five are upset, when at nine a.m.—exactly
two and a half hours from the commencement—Johnny
Russ pitches a shell straight into the French magazine,
and up goes Johnny Crapaud's battery, with three
officers and a hundred men killed and wounded.   At
half-past two p.m. his other battery is blown up, and
instead of the Russians being silenced, the French are
for two days; and we have to bear the whole brunt of
it.   Our batteries have been well made, and our fire has
been good; we have blown up the Russian batteries,
and killed many of their men; but the arsenal is close
at hand, and at night the damage of the day is repaired,
and we begin afresh in the morning.   I do not say we
shall not succeed—'Patience passes science'—we may
blunder and punch our way in at last; but it is clear we
have not a Wellington, the French a Buonaparte, or the
fleet a Nelson.   I hope I may live through it.   Dunkellin
was taken prisoner to-day by a Russian picket.   It is
now nine p.m, and I have been hard at work since three
this morning; and, as I may be turned out at any minute,

I shall close this letter, though I have not said half what I could say. Menchicoff is at Batchi Serai, and they talk of attacking our right rear, defended by General Bosquet and two divisions of French. I wish they may, as they are pretty sure of getting a licking. He has 13,000 Turks to help him and 2000 British (Marines and 93rd Highlanders).

" Love to Anthony and Henry and Bob.

"Your affectionate brother,

"C. A. W."

October 23rd.—The same as usual—a mere pounding match. The French have, however, advanced a long way, but they have not as yet opened their new batteries.

October 24th.—Our Picquet House Battery, to the left of our left ravine, opened at sunrise this morning. Three 32-prs. and one mortar.

BATTLE OF BALACLAVA.

October 25th.—Horsford had just pointed out to me the confused masses of French upon the hill to our right, and I had just gone to point out the same to the General, when up galloped Captain Ewart, of the 93rd, and ordered us (the 4th Division) off to Balaclava.

We got under arms immediately, and, on arriving at the scene of action, were informed that the Turks had run off to a man without firing a shot,* running straight through our Cavalry Camp. The Russians instantly took possession of the position, but abandoned the greater portion of it on our approach.

---

* This information was quite erroneous. The Turks defended No. 1 Redoubt very gallantly, and lost heavily.—W. H. R.

The cavalry instantly went into action, and the Heavy Brigade did very well. Unfortunately the Light Brigade was ordered to charge, and they did so gallantly; but, being received by three times their numbers and three batteries of artillery, besides riflemen, they got cut up and driven back, losing about half their number.

The 4th Division got there just as this charge was being made, and the Russians abandoned two of the redoubts, retaining only the one furthest to the eastward.

Captain Nolan, who took the orders to Lord Cardigan, was killed, charging at the head of the Light Cavalry. Although a good fellow, from all I can learn, his conduct was inexcusable. His whole object appears to have been to have a charge at the Russians at any cost; but he could not have chosen a worse time.

After the fight was over, and we had been pounded for the better portion of the day, we returned at night to camp, abandoning our original line as too extensive.

My leg wonderfully painful all day, but I held on.

SIR DE LACY EVANS' ACTION, "LITTLE INKERMAN," *October 26th.*—The Russians, rendered daring by their success against the Turks yesterday, made to-day a sortie against the 2nd Division. We (4th Division) turned out, but were not wanted, as the Russians soon beat a retreat, getting a handsome mauling, and losing 500 men in killed and wounded.

They could not stand the fire, and, though they got up their guns, did not fire a shot with them. General Bosquet came down, but too late for the fun. I rode forward and joined the skirmishers of the 2nd Division for a few minutes.   Leg still very bad.

A letter to Mr. Hudson gives an interesting account of the battle of Balaclava :—

> "HEIGHTS ABOVE SEBASTOPOL,
>> "*October* 26*th*, 1854, 10 *p.m.*
>
> "MY DEAR ANTHONY,
>
>> "After two stormy days we have now a lull, and, for a wonder, I do not hear a single cannon or musket-shot, a perfect rarity for one month, I assure you.
>
> "Without entering into particulars of hills and dales I will simply suppose that this is
>
>> SEBASTOPOL.

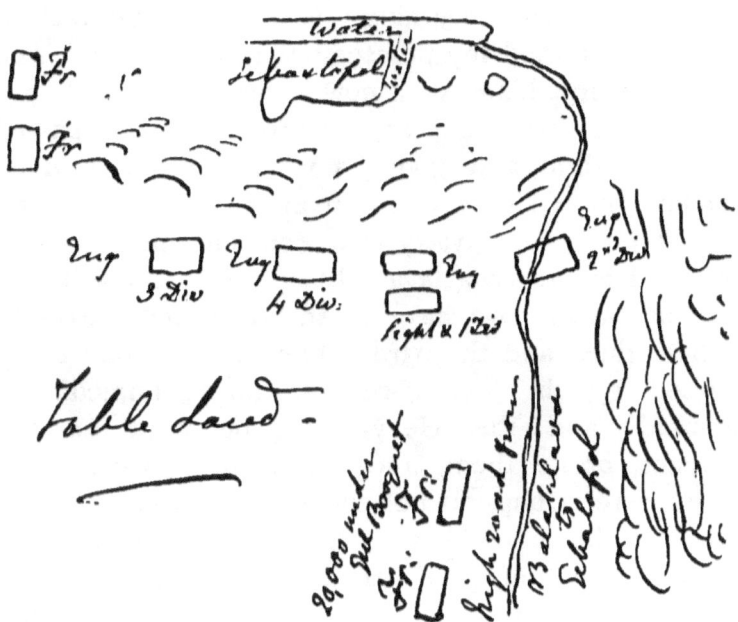

" As before stated this is not a plan of the place, but
a mere outline to let you understand what follows.
Balaclava is distant about seven miles from our camp,
and to get to it you have to descend the heights
occupied by General Bosquet, and then go to your
right. Immediately in front of Balaclava, and to the
right of Bosquet's two Divisions, are a lower range of
heights, on which are four redoubts occupied, up to
yesterday, by as many thousand Turks. (Here I have
been interrupted by a general shout of ' To arms! to
arms! here they come!' &c. I immediately jumped
on to my horse, Sir George Cathcart being absent,
and told the men to stand still and to their front, and
to hold their tongues. I soon discovered that the alarm
came from some sailors, and was all nonsense; so, after
riding to see that everything was quiet, I came back to
the camp, reported my proceedings to the General, who
has just returned, and shall now resume my letter.)

" Yesterday morning at 7.30 the Russians passed
round our right, and, giving a wide berth to Bosquet,
attacked these Turks, who ran away to a man, going
right through our cavalry who were encamped behind
them and before Balaclava. In addition to the Turks
and our cavalry, we have in the town 1000 invalids,
1000 Marines, and the 93rd. The cavalry, upon being
alarmed by the Turks running away, immediately
mounted; and the Heavy Brigade went at the
Russians, broke them, and drove them back. The
enemy were strong, 20 battalions of infantry, 20 guns,
and 3500 horse. They had, however, met with so
rough a reception, particularly from the Scots Greys
(whose horses were fresh from England), that they had
partially withdrawn (the 93rd having pitched into them
heavily), when a Captain Nolan, of the Quartermaster-

General's Department, rode up to Cardigan and told him it was Lord Raglan's order to him to charge the enemy with the Light Brigade.   Cardigan hesitated, seeing the danger of leading 600 men with starved horses against such a mass of cavalry, supported by a battery of heavy guns in their front, another on their right, and a third lot in the captured redoubt.   Captain Nolan got excited, insisted on its being Lord Raglan's order, and Cardigan then submitted, made a most plucky and valorous charge, and left on the field 300 * of his men, and nearly 500 horses.   Captain Nolan was killed, but I have every reason to believe that this melancholy business would never have happened had it not been for his unfortunate conduct.   Major Lowe, of the 4th L. D., killed or knocked off their horses thirteen Russians, and the whole plain was covered with wounded men and horses.   We were sent to cover the town, and arrived in time to see the last onset, and to have the pleasure of passing the day in presence of the enemy—the men lying down and exposed to shot and shell.   I know not who are killed ; Captain Morris,† of the 17th, Captain Goad, 13th Light Dragoons, Lord Fitzgibbon, Captain Charteris, Nolan, and many others are, but I know not all their names.   At dark we marched back to the camp.   This morning, inspired, I suppose, by their success, the Russians thought proper to have a fling at our 2nd Division, under Sir de Lacy Evans, and came up the hill in strong force, but before they could do anything the artillery

* The Light Brigade had 113 killed, 134 wounded, 475 horses killed, and 42 wounded, out of 673 horsemen who went into action.

† Captain Morris was very severely wounded, and reported killed, but survived until July, 1858.

(18 guns) let fly at them, the men went at them with
their Miniés, and Johnny Russ had to bolt with the
loss of 500 men, and go back at double quick speed to
Sebastopol. I do not think he will try it again,
although there is no certainty about it. The siege
is a long, troublesome job, badly managed from the
beginning, more by the French than by us; but I
suppose we shall ultimately take the place, at least,
the French will, as they occupy the only ground by
which it can be taken; and if we had had it, I believe
it would have been over before now, as our artillery
is decidedly better than theirs, and the Russians fear us
the most of the two, at least, so two French sergeants
told me the prisoners they took told them. They
have a great dislike to our musketry. We took some
prisoners to-day, but I know not as yet what information they have given. The town apparently will not
burn; but it is in a good deal of distress from want
of supplies, dirt, disease, and our shot and shell.
They (the prisoners) say they have lost 5000 killed
and wounded, which I should think was much
exaggerated.

"You will, of course, send this letter to William, as I
have not time to write to you both. My leg, where I
was kicked, is still most troublesome to me, and this life
is not the most likely to cure it, as I cannot give it rest,
which, from the inflammation, is what I want to do.
The Russians we defeated to-day were not such fine
men as the Grenadiers we met at Alma; they behaved
steadily and retired with some order, but had not any
earthly chance against us, and never will have, except
in a panic, or with overpowering numbers. My own
belief is that our Army here would, on the level ground,
beat the 40,000 Russians they have in Sebastopol; but

we must not boast; they are well armed, and will give us a good deal of trouble yet; but they are certainly not the good men I expected to see, although I never ran wild about their Army. Tell William and Maria that I hear Ennismore behaved very well at Alma. Give my love to Charlotte and the girls, also to Cecilia and Cecy Suffield and Tad. I generally write my military epistles to you, as I know you like the game more than the rest of my family. If the French cannot take the salient point of the town (and I think they can) we shan't take it at all. Old ——* is really too bad, and it is very unfortunate that he is where he is. I shall not be much surprised if he is tried by a court-martial; he will, however, perhaps be made a G.C.B., which he ought to be ashamed to wear, and the Ministry disgraced who gave it him.

> " Ever, my dear Anthony,
> " Yours affectionately,
> "C. A. W."

October 27th.—Had my leg lanced, which did me much good. Lay quietly in my tent all day, and found my leg much better.

A quiet day; no particular event happened, except that a soldier of the 93rd Highlanders shot a Zouave at Balaclava for not having answered his challenge. I have just heard that in the skirmish yesterday Gortchakoff commanded in chief. Menchikoff told the men (5000, and well supported) that they would meet the same men they met the day before (the Turks); they were then taken to mass, blessed by the priest, and sent on. They were the garrison of Anapa, lately arrived, it being thought wise to try fresh men, and not have any that were at Alma in front. It would

* This name is unfortunately illegible.

E

not do, however, and though they showed firmness, they were soon routed. The Miniés are telling muskets. We only lost 3 officers and 12 men killed and 65 wounded, and this morning we buried in one trench upwards of 100 Russians, besides those in the descent of the hill killed in their retreat. They lost upwards of 700 men. Part of the information comes from the Russian lieutenant who took Dunkellin prisoner three or four days ago, and who was himself taken yesterday. I have just looked out of my tent, and, singular to say, there is not a single light to be seen in the town. I wonder if this forebodes anything extraordinary, perhaps a sortie.

October 28th.—Leg a vast deal better, and I hope by to-morrow to have it all well. Yesterday the General wrote to Lord Raglan concerning Smith and myself carrying the Mackenzie Farm and Katcha despatches.

October 29th (Sunday).—Church parade put off on account of weather: wet and bitterly cold. Said my prayers mentally and imperfectly; who does not do the latter?

This week will bring a change to many, and on this corner of a small peninsula will take place events that will shake States, and make families in countries far away shed many a bitter tear. May mine not be one of them is my most earnest prayer to God.

All quiet; the only news I have heard is that the Russians, in reply to our flag of truce, said that they had only two officers of the Light Cavalry Brigade prisoners.* All the men and other officers were killed.

---

* Lieut. Chadwick, Adjutant of the 17th Lancers, and Cornet Clowes, 8th Hussars, were the officers, both severely wounded. There were also 55 non-commissioned officers and men taken, 39 of them wounded. They were well treated while prisoners.

This looks like foul play to the poor wounded fellows who fell, and corroborates what many of the men said at the time, namely, "They are sticking them on the ground."

October 30*th.*—Hot sun and lots of dust, and a most bitter N.N.E. wind. Reported myself as quite well.

October 31*st.*—Marched the relief down to the new battery at 3.30 a.m. Found the embrasures a good deal knocked about, and the artillerymen employed in shifting a ship's gun, for the purpose of placing another in position to fire hot shot at a ship. Useless labour, as she will haul off if they do not hit her in the first six shots, which they will not do.

At sunrise rode to Bosquet's Division to enquire the cause of firing on our right during the night.

Heard, in the course of the afternoon, that the Russians (whose information is excellent), finding that it was Bosquet's intention to attack them in the low grounds, were so thoroughly on the *qui vive* that they fired into one another.

This night, at about 9 o'clock, the Russians opened a smart fire on the French on our right. It is now half-an-hour later, and I shall turn in the more willingly as I hear Osten Sacken has arrived with 20,000 men, and we may expect daily to be attacked; at least, I should think so; they say nothing at Headquarters.

November 1*st*, 1854.—French getting on well. Rode to Headquarters, and traced out for the General the position of the two Armies, and the attack.

November 3*rd.*—Marched down the covering party without casualty. On my return, there was heavy

firing between the enemy and the French. During
the day rode to Headquarters, and saw Airey about
reserve ammunition.

Rode home with Seymour and General Estcourt.*
Firing heavy against the French, and on their part;
also on our left.

There is no entry in the Diary on November 4th,
but Colonel Windham occupied himself by writing
the following letter to Mr. George Payne, which he
completed after the Battle of Inkerman:—

> "HEIGHTS ABOVE SEBASTOPOL,
> "*November 4th*, 1854.

"MY DEAR PAYNE,

 ". . . . Of Alma you have, no doubt, heard
enough. Our Division was in reserve, and was only
in reach of shell and round shot; but the Staff, being
on ahead, had a good opportunity of seeing all that
was going on. It was certainly a fine sight; *particularly the retreat of the Russians.* I certainly never
saw men take a full pace of 36 inches in quicker time,
or more willingly, in my life. Had the 3rd and 4th
Divisions and Cavalry followed them up, which they
might easily have done, I believe we should have taken
many guns and prisoners; but, I suppose, I shall be
told this would have been a hot-headed method of
proceeding.

 "After waiting two entire days, we moved on at
a snail's pace to the Katcha and the Belbek. From
the latter river, as you know, we made a 'cross-
country' march to the old Balaclava road, and, on
the 27th, were in position before the town. Sir G.
Cathcart was all for an immediate attack, and, had

* Adjutant-General of the Army in the Crimea.

we followed his ideas, I am convinced we should have carried the place; but the suggestion was laughed at, and we were ordered to sit down and smoke for twenty-one days, whilst the siege-train was being landed, during which time the Russians worked day and night, and have made the south side stronger than the north, and all the advantages we gained by the flank march have been thrown away; and, if the town be taken at all, it will, after all, have to be assaulted. The only available part is the salient angle in front of the French, and I hope they may be able to take it. *I think they will.* If they fail, it will be indeed a failure. The 'Scientificals,' as I call them (Engineers and Artillerymen), both French and English, fully expected to bowl over the Russians in about a day, whereas the French batteries were both silenced in three hours. We have been hammering away at them for eighteen days without any result whatever, as we cannot, from the nature of the ground and our position, advance. The French have, however, got very close, and I am in great hopes may succeed.

But artillery is the strong arm of the enemy, and, with a fine arsenal to back them, we have attacked him in the very way, and from the very position, that he would have had us choose. Instead of taking him by applying the *fort au foible*, we have just reversed it; and I believe that our waiting for the siege-train, which was done for the express purpose of saving life, will be the occasion of our losing double, for now every house is fortified, and re-inforcements have arrived.

"The weather to-day is very wet, and we have had some days bitterly cold, and we are all heartily sick of this business, I can assure you; but I know there is no use in grumbling, and an untried man finding fault is dangerous. Since I have been here I have seen lots of pluck, and that is all. The skirmish the other day in front of the 2nd Division, at which I was present at the finish, was well managed by Sir de Lacy Evans, and the Russians got most severely handled.

"The cavalry affair at Balaclava was gallant in the extreme, but destructive to the Light Brigade. These Turks ran a deal better than ——*; and our Division, that was sent to their assistance, had to remain all day for the Russians to pelt at with artillery, on account of their shameful abandonment of the redoubts. We (4th Division) lost 5 men, though we made them lie down, by this stupid day's work. The Russians towards Balaclava are about 35,000, and, I daresay, they will have a try at that place, but we have restricted our line of defence, and got within such a compass that I question, without very bad luck on our part, their being able to succeed.

"The enemy appear to have very good information, which, I fear, is not the case with us; but I am not sure, as Lord Raglan very properly keeps what he hears to himself. As the weather looks a little brighter, I shall walk out, and leave this letter for another day. I hope, old fellow, that I may live to have some sweet and dry with you on my return; but when a man gets shot at pretty often during the week, he must not look too far ahead. I have had but little danger, and very good luck up to this, and I hope it may continue; but there has been a deal of 'craning' at this place, and I fear the leap won't be well taken, but we shall see. 'All's well that ends well,' and who knows what an hour may bring forth?"

* Name illegible: no doubt a playful allusion to one of Mr. Payne's horses.

BATTLE OF INKERMAN.

November 5th.—Marched the relief down to the trenches at 4 a.m., and, on returning, mounted my horse and went into action with my Division: 2225 under arms. Felt quite calm and collected during the fight; nervous and unhappy after it. Loss and carnage fearful.

November 6th.—Buried poor Sir George, Generals Strangways and Goldie, poor Charley Seymour, and fourteen other officers in the Fort. *De facto* in command of the Division.

" The Fort " is better known as Cathcart's Hill.

Colonel Windham commanded the 4th Division during the battle of Inkerman, Sir George Cathcart having been killed, and the two brigadiers mortally wounded.

Colonel Horn, of the 20th Regiment, was senior to Windham, but, having been detached to a particular region of the battlefield, could not assume command of the remains of the Division.

Lord Raglan called on Colonel Windham for an official report of the proceedings of the Division, which follows the letter to Mr. Payne.

Continuation of letter to Mr. Payne — written on November 6th and 7th :—

" I left off about 3 p.m. on the 4th. In half-an-hour afterwards we had conjectures afloat as to what was going on at Headquarters by Sir Geo. Cathcart having been sent for. Yesterday I marched the covering party down to the trenches at 4 a.m., and on my return at daylight the Division was immediately got under arms, the right having been attacked again by the Russians.

And what a day, my dear Payne! What pluck! What confusion! What havoc! And what death! I hope to God I may never go through such another, although I was cheerful and quiet enough, except an occasional 'damn' during the fight, which lasted about eight hours. Poor Sir G. Cathcart was shot through the heart, just by me; Charles Seymour through the shoulder, and afterwards bayoneted; General Goldie through the body. Col. Swyney, of the 63rd, Majors Wynne and Townsend, together with nine other officers, are among the killed of this Division; C. Maitland, Col. Smyth, Gen. Torrens, and twenty-eight other officers of this Division, are wounded. It was a fire with a vengeance. I had the command of what was left of the Division nearly the whole day, and formed them on the left of the Guards, and again advanced to the front, where we had to stand a complete cannonade for about two hours, that killed with shell and round shot the thirteen men to the front, right, and left of me. If we had had ammunition we should have made a more splendid example of them than we did. They attacked us with near 40,000 men, and we had about 6000 to oppose to them,* and I think every man bagged his enemy, for the dead lay by far thicker than at Alma. I am proud of the ways of my countrymen, and see plainly that we have far fewer skulkers than the French; but the Zouaves, both French and 'Indigénes,' fight uncommonly well, and go at it like a quick fencer.

"I shall not bore you about my hair-breadth escapes, &c. When I tell you that now (November 7th) the return of killed and wounded is made out, that we have lost (in the 4th Division) forty-two officers and 705 men

---

* This appears to be an accurate estimate. See Kinglake.

killed and wounded, out of 2225 that we took into action, you may guess that they must have been pretty numerous to a mounted man in the thick of it. Our loss altogether you will see is heavy, and as I rode into the action I met poor little Napier Sturt, Percy Feilding, and many others being taken to the rear. The Guards are cut to ribbons. Poor little Greville* killed in his first fight, and so many of my old friends that I cannot bear to think of it. I am assured that the Russian corpses on the hill in front of the 2nd Division are upwards of 5600, to say nothing of those removed, and those not found. So in England they ought to be proud of the conduct of 6000 of their countrymen ; for I don't believe there were above that number in action. The Russians are now, I understand from officers taken prisoners, about 68,000 strong ; and I have a great notion, if our countrymen and the French don't send us reinforcements, we shall be done.

" So much for this stupid expedition. I always told you the proper place to attack was Odessa ; then we should, with the French, have formed the right with near 100,000 men ; the Turks the centre with ditto ; and the Austrians the left—have taken Bessarabia, and threatened Poland, and have obtained peace. Now God only knows what we shall do ; hold our own, we hope ; but even if we take Sebastopol, I see no chance of doing permanent good in this country.

" My best regards to all old friends.

" Yours very truly,
" C. A. WINDHAM.

"*November 7th.*—P.S. I have not time to write to my dear old friend, A. Hudson, Esq., Norwich, so pray

* Lieutenant C. H. Greville, Coldstream Guards.

forward this to him, and he will afterwards forward it to my family. Don't forget this.

"My dear Anthony,

"This letter was originally intended for Geo. Payne, but as I have not time to write (the whole Division being on my hands) to you or William, I send this first to you, and wish you would direct it afterwards to Payne, at the Turf Club, Arlington Street; send it first to William and Marianne. I got your letter yesterday; sensible in some respects, but not based on correct data. My escapes yesterday were marvellous, and I give you my honour I never once bobbed my head or flinched, although I was mounted on a big horse, and the shot came about somewhat after the fashion of a shower for five or six minutes (800 Russians fired at me alone, at distances varying from 150 to fifty yards; to say nothing of round shot and shell that came six or eight at a time for hours, and a general running fire of musketry whenever I conveyed an order); when I thought it all over, and was moving off the field by Lord Raglan's order, a 10 lb. shell, thrown from a ship, passed just over my cap, and by my horse's ears, fell plump into the body of a dead Russian, burst, and blew all the dirt over me, but did not hurt either me or my horse.

"Yours ever,   C. A. W.

"P.S. The grand total killed and wounded is about 2500, including 43 officers killed and 100 wounded."*

* The losses of our Army at the battle of Inkerman were:

Killed	.	.	. 632
Wounded	.	.	. 1878
Missing	.	.	. 63
		Total .	2573

The official report of the proceedings of the 4th Division follows. It has been decided to include it, as it contains an accurate and interesting account of an obscure passage in the "soldiers' battle."

The very heavy losses of the Division are recorded by Windham, in the Diary, April 16th, 1855.

" *To Brigadier-General Airey, Q.M.G.*

"Camp above Sebastopol,
" *November 6th,* 1854.

" Sir,—In compliance with your request, I make the following report to you, for the information of the Commander-in-Chief.

" Yesterday, soon after daylight, musketry being heard to our right, Lieutenant-General Sir George Cathcart, K.C.B., ordered his Division under arms, with the exception of 1000 men just relieved from the trenches, and the inlying pickets.

" He ordered the different regiments to follow him to the windmill, near the camp of the 2nd Division, but the increasing fire, before he reached the place appointed, caused him to send back his A.D.C., Captain Greville, to order Brigadier-General Torrens and the men left in camp to advance immediately.

" Lieutenant-Colonel Horsford, with the 1st Battalion of Rifles, upon reaching the camp of the 2nd Division, formed line, and advanced into action on the left of the Inkerman Road.

" Brigadier-General Goldie's Brigade, with the exception of the right wing of the 20th Regiment, did the same. This gallant officer, as his lordship knows, fell mortally wounded. His Brigade consisted, on this occasion, of some companies of the 57th Regiment, left wing of the 20th Regiment, under Colonel Horn, and of the 21st Fusiliers, under Lieutenant-Colonel Ainslie, until he was wounded, when one wing, I understand, was commanded by Lieutenant-Colonel Lord West (and taken to the extreme left), and the other by Major Ramsay Stuart.

"Sir George Cathcart, in person, went to the right of the road, and sent Captain Hugh Smith, D.A.Q.M.G., to bring the right wing of the 20th, under Colonel Crofton, to support the Guards ; and he sent me back to Brigadier-General Torrens, to order up his whole Brigade to the right.

"I found General Torrens to the left of the road, and, as Colonel Wood, of the Royal Artillery, rode up and informed me that the enemy had taken two of our guns upon the left, I took upon myself to order General Torrens to send Lieutenant-Colonel Swyney, of the 63rd, to the left (in contradiction of Sir George's order, he having given me authority to do so on emergencies), in support of Colonel Wood, and, I am happy to say, the guns were quickly retaken.   Lieutenant-Colonel Swyney was killed upon advancing further against the enemy, and the regiment remained under the command of Major the Honourable R. Dalzell.

"I took the earliest opportunity of informing Sir George Cathcart of what I had done, which met with his approval ; and I then continued with him in rear of the four companies of the 68th Regiment, who were lower down the hill than the right wing of the 20th Regiment.

"The 68th were led into action by Brigadier-General Torrens, who fell severely wounded when in the act of trying to restrain their ardour, after driving the enemy before them.

" Sir George Cathcart expressed himself to Brigadier-General Torrens, lying wounded on the ground, as highly pleased at his conduct; and then, with his Staff, continued to advance until he saw the enemy in full occupation of the heights above him, which he had previously thought were in our possession.

" He immediately ordered me to get back the wings of the 20th and 68th, and tried to show front with the few skirmishers around him, and with them drove back the enemy twice ; but I regret to say he was shot through the heart. His Assistant Adjutant-General, Lieutenant-Colonel C. Seymour, of the S. F. Guards, was shot through the body, and afterwards bayoneted (he had previously been wounded when with me) when rendering him assistance. Major Maitland, his D.A.A.-General (of the Grenadier Guards), was severely wounded at the same time ; and his A.D.C., Captain the Honourable A. Cathcart, had his horse shot under him.

" I did all I could to get back the men of the 20th and 68th, but it was a work of time, as the ascent was almost perpendicular, and the men were mixed with the Guards and others, who had pursued the enemy even into the meadows.

" I am happy to say that as the hillside was covered with brushwood, and the men protected by a ledge of rock, they moved to the rear without suffering any loss, the only people being exposed being those on horse-back.

"As soon as I could collect the men of the 4th Division in this part of the field, I took them to the rear of the 2nd Division Camp, where I found Captain Hugh Smith had, with his usual zeal and activity, got up the reserve ammunition.

" I beg to mention that at this point I received very

valuable assistance from Captain Street, Brigade Major to Brigadier-General Goldie, who had come to look for Sir George Cathcart.

"After Captain H. Smith had distributed the ammunition, I took the command of the men collected— namely, four companies of the 68th, under Lieutenant-Colonel Henry Smyth; two companies of the 20th; two companies of the 46th, under Captain Dallas; some men of the 1st Battalion of Rifles; and about thirty men of other regiments not belonging to the Division—and formed line upon the left of the Guards; immediately advanced to the front, accompanied by Captains Smith, Greville, and Cathcart, and placed myself under the orders of Major-General Pennefather, in front of the camp of the 2nd Division, and on the left of the road, sending Lieutenant-Colonel Smyth, with the 68th, still further to the front.

"Here I remained until I received, through Lieutenant-Colonel the Honourable A. Gordon, Lord Raglan's order to march the Division to their camp.

"The 4th Division went into action about 2200 men, which you will observe were disseminated by regiments and wings from the extreme right to the extreme left, so urgent were the demands made upon Sir George by officers from different parts of the action, and so necessary was it, in his opinion, to prevent the enemy's reaching the camp.

"The greater part of the Division was on the left of the Inkerman Road, fighting far away from their General, under the independent command of their Commanding Officers.

"Sir George Cathcart had with him but a small portion of the Division when we had the misfortune to lose him on the slope towards Inkerman.

"I reported his loss on the field to the Commander-in-Chief.

"I have already forwarded to you the list of killed and wounded.

"I have the honour to remain, Sir,

"Your most obedient servant,

"C. A. WINDHAM, Col., A.Q.M.G."

In a letter to Mrs. Windham, some particulars are given concerning the death of Sir George Cathcart. After describing the order given by himself to the 63rd Regiment, Windham states that he explained to Sir George why he had thus acted in opposition to his orders, and Sir George, "like a generous and gallant soldier, thanked me, and said I had done quite right."

"Poor Sir George," the letter continues, "I would have given anything to have seen him Commander-in-Chief; he was fitted for great movements and broad views. . . . I cannot help thinking that if he would have fallen back only twenty yards, or I might almost say, if he had stood still, he would have been saved; but he would go on. When Seymour was first wounded, he leant against me, and I said to Sir George: 'Sir, those are Russians on the height.' He replied, 'They are, and we are in a scrape.' His horse then had its fore feet on a small rock.

"I answered him and said, 'Yes, Sir; shall I ride on and try and get the 68th back?' He replied, 'Right again, Windham; do so.' (This 'again' referring to the matter of the 63rd.)

"I rode forward to the right, he to the left, and in one minute—I might almost say in ten seconds—he and Seymour were killed, Charles Maitland wounded, and A. Cathcart's horse shot.

"I soon rallied, or rather got together, a few men of the Guards, 30th, 68th, 46th, 20th, and 47th; and I repeat, had the General, on seeing the scrape, fallen back as many yards as he advanced, I really believe not twenty, he might have been spared to us; but he declared for the bayonet, and with a dozen men tried to repulse twelve hundred, and being on horseback was, like all the mounted officers but myself, killed or wounded.

"He is a loss to the Army, God knows, and time will, I fear, show it.

"I had him buried in the centre of the old fort, round which he used continually to walk, with General Goldie on his right, as belonging to his Division; and General Strangways (an old friend of his) on his left; Charles Seymour at his feet; and sixteen other officers of the 4th Division, who fell on that day, in two lines, a few yards off.

"I bought Sir George's black mare, presented to him by General Murray; should she live to get home, I shall be very happy to let any of the family have her for what I gave, which, in fact, was the reason of my buying her.

"She was a great favourite with him, but he did not ride her on the day of his death. Pray let them know this: I do not like to write upon such a subject.

"C. A. W."

November 7th.—Was turned out twice in expectation of an attack. Thanked God often for my many escapes on the 5th. Rode to the 2nd Division Camp and returned with General Eyre. A long talk with him about poor Sir George. With him fell, at any rate, all the dash of the Army. He was not perfect; who is? but he had more enterprise and spirit than all the rest of them put together. He is a great loss to this Division. I suspect it is thought great blame attaches itself to Sir George's having descended the hill to the right. I admit this was a bad move, and Sir George undeniably had faults as a General of Division; but it is ridiculous to throw the blame on him of most of the slaughter and mischances, because he went too far down with 187 men of the 68th, 154 of the 46th, and a portion of the right wing of the 20th.

I myself rallied or collected those men who had gone down *into the valley.* They consisted of Guardsmen, 30th, 49th, Rifles, and odds and ends from the 1st and 2nd Divisions. The 68th were almost the only men of our Division that did go down. When the enemy rushed into our centre and fired upon our inner flank, killing the General, Seymour, &c., the 20th and 46th were mostly on the hill, and I owe my life to having gone forward and downward to get back the 68th and other loose skirmishers.

The only men I could get to stand by me were some of the Coldstream, who knew me, and asked me by name to stop the men on the hill from firing at them, taking them for our own people till I undeceived them.

I had no idea of the difficulty of stopping men retiring, not running, under a heavy fire.

I made all the men of one company lie down until I brought them fresh ammunition, after which, I led them all to the front.

In fact I worked hard; feel convinced that I did my duty like a good soldier, feeling no funk. I am sure I showed none, and, therefore, whether I am mentioned or not in despatches, is a matter of indifference.

Had Sir George lived, I am sure I should have been, as he thanked me for having, on my own responsibility, ordered the 63rd (contrary to his original orders) to the left to retake the guns of Townsend's Battery.

I suppose, however, that General Pennefather, who deserves much praise, will get all that is given.

They will make out that a most plucky and brave resistance of individual detachments was a well-planned and able defence ; whereas I know there was no plan at all, and not half the officers knew who was commanding them.

Poor Seymour was first wounded in the foot, leant upon me, and said, "Charley, I 've got it." I handed him over to a man of the 20th, and rode to get back the 68th. Before I had gone ten yards, he, the General, Maitland, &c., were all down, and the shot flew about me like hail, so much so as to make me smile at the whistling.

The quantity of Russians killed here was great ; they lay so thick that I could scarcely get through them, and on getting off my horse to slip down a precipice to the men, I took the sword from one big fellow, who, in his struggles, had twisted his belt off his shoulder. At least, the sword lay close to him, and I suppose was his.

Wrote a report of the proceedings of the 4th Division to General Airey, for Lord Raglan's information.

November 8th and 9th.—Hard worked. Remainder of 46th arrived on the 8th. In hourly expectation of an attack from the Russians. We are now strengthening our right, but, like everything else in this Army, far too late. The mischief has been done, and they will next try somewhere else. Besides, I question their holding the Redoubt three days, unless they make better practice than heretofore, or the enemy worse.

(The Diary is very scanty for some days after Inkerman, but the following letters are of interest.)

" *To Mr. Hudson.*

"CAMP BEFORE SEBASTOPOL,
"*November 12th,* 1854.

"MY DEAR ANTHONY,

"I was so pressed by business the last time I took up my pen, that I had no time to pour into your ear my sorrows and grumblings at what is going on here, and at the unceasing blundering that has taken place in the conduct of this expedition; notwithstanding the publication of Wellington's despatches, and the experience that was, or ought to have been, acquired in Bulgaria since the landing of the British Army in the East.

"By my letters to you, from on board the *Harbinger,* you are aware that I always thought the attack on Sebastopol to be a bad move, both from a strategical and political point of view. To my letter to Cathcart, as soon as I heard of his arrival in the Channel (absolutely before he landed), pointing out Odessa as the proper place of landing, I believe I may attribute his taking me out with him, and his talking so much to me as he did. A word or two by way of episode upon his character. He was a man more fitted to be first than second. His views upon great questions were decidedly above par, and, provided he was master and had everything his own way, his temper, naturally irritable (though amiable), did not get *riled;* and his judgments, under such circumstances, were clear and sound. As a General of Division he was out of his element; with neither eye nor speech sufficiently clear or rapid, he saw not the points of attack with sufficient quickness, and from an over-explanatory way of giving out his .orders, he both confused others, and often contradicted himself. He never (or rarely) called regiments by their right numbers, or placed them in their proper brigades; and though I, who knew him, could see what he wished, and took the meaning for the word, others did not, which had the effect of putting him on his high horse, frightening the bringer or carrier of the order, and made confusion worse confounded. Since he arrived in this country his temper has been infinitely worse than it ever was, and from his never having been willingly consulted, he felt himself aggrieved, *I fancy* (for he never said anything to me to that effect), and tried to find occupation in fidgeting about trifling matters he had much better have let alone. Having said this much as to his faults, I ought to say something of his merits. Although hard as a commander, he was kind and good-humoured as a man, extremely vigilant and active, both mentally and physically, most undeniably brave; to private soldiers kind, much averse to martinetism, and a good strategist. Oh! how I wish his advice had been taken after the arrival of this Army on the heights. It was simply to assault the place the next morning. Had we done so we should have succeeded, and instead of losing, as we have done in the trenches and the battle of Inkerman, 3000 men, to say nothing of sickness, we should have been in the town with half the loss, and, I trust, out of the country.

"As it is, I do not see my way. The Russians have as many men as we, a more numerous Artillery and Cavalry, and a decided equality as to science in the former arm. If the French assaulted the town to-morrow they would get in ; but, I fear, not hold it ; yet something must be done! To suppose that men can winter on these heights, sleeping on the cold, damp ground, without being killed by dysentery, is nonsense, and to descend into the valley of Inkerman and attack their Army, although it would, probably, be successful as to the fight, would not advantage us much, as we should have to abandon our siege-train, and could not follow them up, as we have no means of transport, and, therefore, could not leave Balaclava. If I were Lord R. I would reduce the size of the camp, hut the men as soon as possible, remove from our batteries all the guns worth having, fortify our-selves strongly, then wait patiently for reinforcements; form, in the course of the winter, another Army to the north; land it, and, in connection with this one, begin again next spring without leaving out the north side.

"I have a strong belief that a one-sided account will be given of the battle of Inkerman; for as regards the 4th Division, notwithstanding its heavy losses, it will be tried to be proved that it suffered from disobedience of orders on the part of Sir George, and that he handled the troops with little or no judgment. But I was present, and I must say, that no man could have been more pestered and bothered by A.D.C's from the front with orders, pressing and contradictory. I do not approve of Sir George's habit—a fatal one, alas! for him—of thrust-ing himself forward and riding about so continually that it was almost impossible to find him ; I do not approve of his having sent forward General Torrens to make a dash without thinking of a reserve, and without having previously made himself acquainted with the absolute position of the forces, aggressive and defensive; but I maintain it to be absurd to attribute to him the greater portion of the mischief, when the real truth is that the action, begun with a surprise, was continued with great pluck and confusion by individuals, every disposable man, as he came up, being sent to the front, in detail, to remedy a momentary weakness; and ended by the courage and resolution of independent commanders (directing steady and bold men) in repulsing an enormous and overpowering force, three separate times. At the fourth attack, had not the French come up, we should, I think, have been done; but, as they did come, the enemy was finally repulsed, and his loss must have been immense. We buried 4081 bodies of the Russians the next day, and there must certainly be 1000 on the ground on the other side of the hill; and we have brought in 1250 men severely wounded, to say nothing of those who got away. I am sorry to say the Russians (officers as well as men) stabbed and killed our wounded without mercy, and if that sort of game is to continue, I see nothing for it but retaliation, which will make matters worse. Poor Sir George was shot through the heart, but as soon as they got to him—by the weight of overpowering numbers—they bayoneted him and robbed him; the same with poor Charles Seymour, and those poor young fellows of the Guards who were slightly wounded, they treated in the same way. In fact it will not do, as has been proved, both at Alma and here, to leave the wounded to their mercy, even for a minute. Bar their artillery and numbers, however, they are not formidable; and I live in hopes and pray that we may never be driven back again.

" The grand error of this campaign, from a military point of view, has been 'the want of transport,' and the not properly considering what we had to do. As we landed without transport and with only three days' provisions, it was, in fact, nothing but a *coup de main* against Sebastopol, with 50,000 men, that could succeed ; but, alas! we moved along at .a snail's pace (and yet, after all, arrived before the town before they had erected any works), and when we ultimately came before the town we did nothing, not even in field fortification, but remained for twenty-one days, smoking, and awaiting the landing of the siege-train. Now, again, there is a strong report (I know nothing as to its truth) that the Army is to hut itself and pass the winter here, and yet they never sent, until two days ago, for any wood or other materials ; and I, therefore, fully expect to be caught by the approaching winter, and this is all owing to dilatoriness and indecision. As for General Airey, he is more like a Private Secretary than a Quartermaster - General, with a quick inconsiderate manner, and no roundabout common sense, which is really what is wanted for such a situation. As to information the Staff appear to have none, and seem to know nothing of the enemy until they see him, and not much then : beyond the common sort of courage to be found in all men of good digestions, they appear, with the exception of Wetherall, to be a moderate lot. If the farm-house in which the Headquarters are now established were only burnt down, we might get them possibly to move.

" During the heat of the battle of the 5th, Sir George ordered me to bring up the whole of Torrens' Brigade from the rear of the left, to the right. When I had given him this order, Lieutenant-Colonel Wood, R.A.,

came and told me the enemy were in possession of two
of his guns, and that our left was turned. I immediately,
in direct contradiction to Sir G.'s order, desired Torrens
to detach the 63rd Regiment, under Colonel Swyney,
to Wood's support, to restore the battle on the left,
and to recapture the guns ; this was done. I should
like to see if Lord Raglan mentions a word of it in
his despatch: he knows it, for I sent him, through
the Quartermaster - General, a full account of the
proceedings of the 4th Division ; but I will wager
not one word of it will be published, as it probably
won't suit their purpose for it to be seen how the
right were sent piecemeal into the fight. I am
afraid we have hard fighting and bad times before
us, but we must do our best ; and with Providence
on our side, and strong reinforcements from England
and France, we may weather the storm ; but it will
be *no easy matter with the absence of head we have
here.* Lord R. is a bold, gentlemanlike, amiably-
mannered man, and a good 'red - tapist,' but no
General. Dundas is worse. Lyons, a good fellow
and clever man ; and of Canrobert I know nothing,
but that he is a fat, punchy fellow of forty-five ;
they say, with a good head and great courage.
Of our subordinates I know none of any mark,
Brigadier - General Eyre perhaps the best of them ;
plenty of them have courage, but there are very few
with ideas beyond a field-day. Our loss has been
severe, and I expect, during the winter, to see an
immense deal of sickness ; but I suppose the Russians
will have their share of that, as they are without tents,
and supplies will get shorter. Would to God we had
gone to Odessa ; our troubles had now been over, and
the Emperor probably inclined to peace. As it is,

I know not what will happen. I send you a copy of the report I wrote to the Quartermaster-General. This ought, in fairness, to be published, but I am afraid it never will, as it shows too plainly that no one was, in fact, in command on the day."

THE GREAT STORM.

November 14*th.*—At 6 a.m., the breeze freshened; at 8 a.m, our tent went; and by 9, it was blowing a perfect hurricane. Every tent down; and what with snow, rain, and wind, all in camp were thoroughly miserable. I can hardly imagine men living through a worse day; indeed, many did not.

Some further details of the effects of the storm are given in a letter to the Earl of Caledon :—

"I believe the Russians are a good deal pinched, and I, hope they are; but certainly, in the way of shelter, they have the best of it, as no one can fancy anything much more bleak than the top of this hill. The weather, when we first landed on the 14th September (except that individual night), was hot and fine, until the middle of October, when we had two or three days of severe cold, then a sort of fine Indian summer until the 14th inst., when one of the most terrific hurricanes of wind, snow, and rain brought in the winter. Heavy losses occurred amongst the transports and shipping, and every tent in the Army was blown down; the men had to remain for twenty-four hours as uncomfortably situated as any mortals could possibly be. You, I daresay, can fancy what a gale of wind you could not stand against, accompanied by heavy drenching showers of rain, followed towards night by a Canadian poudré, would be. It was, I think, the worst day, consideration being paid to the ground, I ever passed in my life. Still, here I am alive and kicking, never better, and only wish others were as well off as I am."

On November 15th and 16th, Windham occupied himself in exertions for the benefit of the men of his Division, and had no time to make an entry in his diary.

November 17th.—Rode with Wood, of the Artillery, to Monastir, to look after wood for hutting the Division; found none.

November 19th.—Going on with my house—it is decidedly too big. A day of heavy wind almost as bad as the 14th. Had to turn out without shoes or stockings to get up the —th at 4.30 a.m. Men perfectly miserable, and sickness greatly on the increase.

Went and saw Codrington; from what he told me, I hope the French will do something towards Inkerman.

In the letter to the Earl of Caledon, an extract of which has already been given, appears the following account of the gallant attack on "The Ovens," on November 20th, under Lieutenant Tryon, of the Rifle Brigade, who had already highly distinguished himself at Inkerman:—

"*November 25th,* 1854.

"I firmly believe the Russian defences in our front are, at this moment, stronger than when first we began firing at them in October. The nature of the ground admits of our advancing but slowly, and it was only four days ago that we even began to make an attack on their advanced riflemen. This was done, without any direction from Headquarters, by Sir John Campbell (in the temporary command of this Division since Cathcart's death), who sent a party of the Rifles attached to the Division, under Lieutenant Tryon, a fine, gallant fellow as ever lived. He dislodged the enemy by night. It was well done ; Tryon was killed, but the 'green men' held their own, and repulsed the enemy twice, after dislodging him with the bayonet. We hold the ground still. This was, and is, the only fight (and a small one it certainly was) that showed the slightest scheme or forethought since we landed. Tryon was a really good officer."

Further on in this letter occurs the following passage, which shows the disgraceful want of forethought, and mismanagement of land and sea transport, which wrecked our army :—

"Our horses of all ranks are literally starving, while every animal in the French camp is living positively in plenty ; and they sent our Cavalry, the other day, forty pressed trusses of hay to keep our horses alive. In fact, the old Duke's boast of being thoroughly *au fait* as to how to feed an army, cannot be made by anyone here. We have a good deal of dysentery and cholera, and out of 3500 men (4th Division) have 760 at present on the sick list. I really hope they will try and do something."

November 26th.—Heard to-day that the 9th Regiment and 1200 Turks had arrived, also 2100 French ; but the latter is doubtful.*

* The French troops alluded to did not arrive at this time.

We ought surely now to do something—have a shy at Liprandi, for instance.

A very fine day: if dry weather would last, we might yet take the place.

Sir John Campbell, a pleasant, cheerful commander, sprained his ankle three days ago, and has since been laid up.

A gap in the Diary is well filled by the following letter to Mr. Beresford Peirse, Colonel Windham's brother-in-law. Some repetitions will be excused in consideration of the spirit with which the story is told :—

"HEIGHTS ABOVE SEBASTOPOL,
"Camp, 4th Division,
"*December 1st*, 1854.

"MY DEAR HENRY,

"As the weather to-day seems to be inclined to preserve its previous character of 'extremely bad,' I shall, as well as a man can in such wet and dirt, try and amuse myself by writing to you. You will be sure to have heard all about Alma, and probably, long ere this reaches you, all about Balaclava and Inkerman. The last battle was begun by the Russians surprising us, our pickets having allowed at least twenty pieces of heavy ordnance (24-prs.) to get up the heights before they ever fired a shot. These guns were supported by heavy columns of troops, who, in the mist and grey of the morning, commenced the attack : first and last, 40,000 of the enemy were certainly in action; and, at the most, 8000 British, from the commencement to the end, were brought to meet them. The ground was all covered with a low oak brush, and on the right, towards the valley of Inkerman, nearly precipitous. Our Army was never commanded throughout the day; it was split up into detachments, and those small bodies luckily fought (almost universally) with the most determined valour. I firmly believe that history cannot show another battle similar to Inkerman. The loss of the enemy, I am convinced, was enormous; I feel sure it was above 20,000 men, and almost all of them fell by musketry. A great portion of our loss was, on the contrary, occasioned by shell and round shot. I was present from nearly the beginning. Every mounted officer near me was killed, wounded, or unhorsed; and at one time, in half-an-hour, I saw thirteen men killed by round shot, within five yards of me. I merely mention this (most of the men were lying down) to give you an idea of the weight of artillery opposed to us—40 field guns, the before-mentioned heavy guns, and a considerable portion of the shipping—all assisted the Russian efforts to dislodge us, but all this, luckily, did not succeed; and, latish in the afternoon, they gave up all further attempts. The enemy showed great pluck and resolution, and had their attack been as strong on the 25th, after two divisions had marched to Balaclava, I think they would have succeeded; as it was, they didn't. They found the British Infantry, notwithstanding the weight of their artillery and masses, too stubborn for them, and they retired, after capturing two French guns that arrived late in the action, leaving us in possession of our old position.

"The day was an honourable, not a profitable one; spoke volumes for the men, little for the General. Why the position had been left utterly unstrengthened, from the 27th September to the 26th October, no one could tell; still more wonderful was it, that after the attack on the 20th October, in open day, no means whatever should even have been thought of, much less executed. One junior officer, who shall be nameless, certainly suggested, many days previous to the 5th, that the ground in the immediate front of the 2nd Division might, at any rate, be cleared so that the Artillery could be sent to the front, &c., &c., but he was snubbed and told to mind his own business; suffice it to say that, with the exception of a 3-gun battery, erected to the right of the road, nothing was done, and with blood we have had to pay for our idleness and want of forethought. Since the 5th, we have been working hard in that quarter, and I therefore think the next attempt of the Russians will not be there.

"As to the siege, you will see more of that in the papers, and better described, than anything I can write; for my own part, I think it has been as badly conducted as it well could have been. At the commencement, everything on our part was presumptuous, and since then the reverse. The same may be said of the French, except that since the conceit was taken out of them, on the first two days, they have worked hard, and, as the ground aided them, have got nearer to the enemy. Why they have done nothing for the last ten days I cannot say; I suppose they have cogent reasons known at Headquarters, but the Army generally knows nothing of them. For my part, I firmly believe that both the French and English Engineers wanted to have a siege of their own, and, therefore, instead of attacking the western side of the town *only*, they have attacked the western and the southern—we the *latter;* and we occupy ground, man and fight batteries, with about 10,000

men, that would certainly require 40,000 to do it
properly. The result is the men are worked to death,
hundreds of them on the sick list, working parties
can't be furnished to carry out the magnificent ideas
of Sir J. Burgoyne, and it would not surprise me
to see the business end in a complete failure. I have
still some hope of the French and their reinforcements, and do not pretend, as I said before, to be
able to judge properly of the propriety of our present
line of conduct; but of one thing I can judge, and
that is, of the present state of the transport of this
Army. . . .

"This Division, on paper, is between 5800 and 6500
men; 900 are absent, sick, and nearly 800 present
sick; those present are dying fast; they lie in the wet
and muck without medicine or any single kind of
comfort. Private enterprise has brought wine, brandy,
cheese, butter, hams, preserved meats, biscuits of all
kinds, bread and vegetables, to Balaclava; and any
officer choosing to spend his money and send down
a horse there may get all he wants, in reason ; but so
miserable is the transport of this Army that the
soldiers can get nothing of this, and, consequently,
have to go with short rations, on several occasions
no meat at all, or rum; this, coupled with the wet
and constant exposure, night after night in the
trenches, will account for the alarming and still
increasing sickness. The night before last the Royals
(1st Regiment) lost 27 men by cholera, of the young
ones that arrived in the last draft, about a week ago.
Six companies of the 46th, arrived here lately, lost
100 men by cholera and dysentery, and have now
upwards of 260 men in hospital. This expedition
I was always firmly opposed to, conceiving it to be

a decidedly bad move. Odessa was the place to have gone to, but we came here, and we came equipped for a *coup de main.* The march from the Belbek to Balaclava was, we all thought, for that purpose; but all of a sudden we are told to wait quietly for twenty-one days doing nothing, until the siege-train is landed. We then begin by making batteries at a mean distance of 1500 yards, and having attacked the Russians in their strong arm (artillery), with a splendid arsenal to back them, we are surprised that we make no impression. In the meantime, the two other arms, in which we have shown ourselves to be their superiors, are sacrificed; and we see how one old General may conduct, and many presumptuous young ones assist in carrying on, a siege, at a time of year the most unfitted, and with numbers quite inadequate to the purpose. I said a siege, but it has always struck me as being neither a siege, a bombardment, nor an investment, but simply a sort of school in which our young gentlemen might try the effect of long-range fire, and of 10-inch shot and shell.

"We receive constantly accounts from Russian prisoners, who all state the enemy to be suffering immensely from sickness, and want of provisions, also from general depression. I yesterday, however, saw two letters from 'two wounded men taken prisoners by them, and belonging to this Division, in which they say that they receive a pound of bread, some soup with a piece of meat in it, and a pint of tea daily. The Russians appear to know everything that passes here; but I fear we are not quite so enlightened as to what goes on in Sebastopol. The French private soldiers have all got an idea that they will attack the place to-morrow; for my part, I don't believe it; however, I hope they may, and I hope they may succeed, for anything would be better than passing one's winter on these heights. A great many officers of standing are going home, and I believe there are not many left that would be sorry to go also, French or English; for my own part, however, I am very easy on that head; I am in good health and good spirits, and if matters were only a little better managed, I should feel easy as to the result. The Duke of Wellington prided himself on thoroughly understanding how to 'feed an army.' I fear his mantle has not fallen on any shoulders here.

"Your letter reached me three days ago, and I remembered you the same day to C. Woodford. One battalion of Rifles, under Horsford, is attached to this Division, and most rapid promotion they have had, although their being much in action has not been much against them. Beckwith died of cholera, and so did poor little Godfrey, the other day. Rooper, I hear, also is dead, and Cook has resigned from ill-health. That poor fellow Tryon, who was killed some ten days ago, was a first-rate young officer, and is regretted by us all.

"Poor Sir George is a great loss to me. I was of essential service to him the day of his death, and, had he lived, I am sure he would have got me a brigade. . . .

"After getting through what I have since September 14th, without a scratch, I ought not to grumble; and when I think that my health has stood when not only hundreds, but thousands, of younger men have fallen in that respect, many never to rise again, I ought to be thankful—and am. Yet I cannot help thinking that I, who have always been so near landing myself,

G

and yet just missed it, cannot be said, in a worldly point of view, to be a lucky man.

"Lord Raglan, I believe, is aware of my services at Inkerman ; at any rate, the Master-General of the Ordnance is, and so was poor Cathcart, who thanked me for what I had done, although it was contrary to his orders. I should have been eternally abused had the movement been a failure ; now I suppose I shall get no thanks, as it seems to be the object to cast dirt at Cathcart's move to the right. It is true he went too far down the hill, and it is also true that he didn't keep his Division enough in hand ; in fact he was, though a good strategist when he had time to think, not a good tactician, and at the time everything was in confusion, and few people in good humour. I smoked tranquilly (without any nonsense), and felt as easy as I do at the covert side ; but the fire was certainly a hot one, and to this day I wonder how I escaped ; the bullets flew so thick about me that I really laughed outright at the whistling. I was glad enough, however, when the French came up to lend a hand. The first of their battalions that entered the fight were the "Zouaves-Indigénes," and they went in well, and the Zouaves (French) are also very fine fellows, in some respects, I may say in most, the best men I ever saw ; but it will not do to compare a regular French regiment of the line with one of ours ; it is altogether a different thing. In everything but discipline and respect for their officers they are our superiors, but in fighting they decidedly are not. A French general, at the time, acknowledged that they never would have held the position as we did, and said they had not the same *talent de se tenir ferme.* They would have retired, probably have retaken it by beat of drum, again been beaten back, and again advanced, &c., but they never would set their teeth tight, and fight it out to the last, as we did. The road through the 2nd Division camp was one of the most wonderful sights I ever saw, the Russians being so thick that I could with difficulty get my horse through them. When I tell you we buried in forty-eight hours 4081, besides about 7 or 800 flung into a chalk pit, and 3 or 400 that still remain unburied on the right and in the valley, to say nothing of the 1400 desperately wounded that we brought in, you may easily guess that they didn't get off cheaply; in fact, they were most awfully mauled, but still they took off their guns, and though they marched off very fast they didn't need to run.

"Now give my best love to George Melville,* and tell him to be contented with Old England. If I live to get home again, we will all talk these battles over again, but there is much to be done before that happens. The poor old Coldstream, tell him, got an awful mauling; and I helped many of them after the fight, and Percy Feilding during it. Many of the men knew me, and, when the skirmishers were retiring, several rallied when I called to them, although they had no ammunition. I was near them the greater part of the day. . . .

"It is now night; the Russians have been just letting fly a couple of 100-pound shot and shell at the French (a nightly amusement), and, as everything is quiet, I shall roll up in my blanket and take a snooze. Except two nights on board the *Agamemnon*, I have not had my clothes off since the 14th September to sleep—very seldom my boots. The Army is good-tempered, notwithstanding its extreme hardships. Tell Geo. Melville that

---

* Colonel Windham's very intimate friend, George Whyte Melville, in whose best-known book, *The Interpreter*, Windham figures.

the 14th November was the worst day I ever experienced—an awful gale of wind, ending in Canadian 'Powder'; every tent blown to the devil; and all hands left to hulk up their shoulders, on a bare lofty hill, exposed for hours to the blast.   Many of the sick died, and plenty of the horses.   I hope Pem* is with you; if so, she will see this.   I have received her last letters, and also the dear children's.   I shall write to her a short note to-morrow.

"Remember me most kindly to all at Bedale, and don't forget to do so to the Duke of Leeds, with whom I yet hope to drink a bottle of claret at Hornby; and with young Fox, who behaved well at Alma.   Describe to him all the wonders and hardships of this campaign. All this sort of thing, my dear Henry, is better to talk of afterwards than to go through; and, though I have really heard nothing but the report of guns and the whiz of round shot for the last two months (no exaggeration, upon my honour), I constantly wake up when these Russian outbreaks begin.   It is true I soon go to sleep again, but what would you have a poor fellow do?

"Love to Henrietta and all your family, and to Jos and Frances Hudson.

"Yours affectionately,

"C. A. WINDHAM."

December 3rd, 1854.—Since the 26th, there have been a few rays of sunshine; but, on the whole, the weather has been very bad, and the roads nearly impassable.

The men, therefore, have never had a regular supply of rations, and sickness has been greatly on the increase. I do not pretend to know what our Generals are about, particularly the French ones; they seem resolved to

* Mrs. Windham.

wait here quietly until the winter has destroyed the Army. Ours certainly will be ruined by it, as our means of transport are truly disgraceful.

How any man who had served under the Duke of Wellington, or who had even read his despatches, could ever have allowed such a state of affairs to arrive, is, to me, incomprehensible.

Sir De Lacy Evans is gone. He was, after Sir George Cathcart, the best of the Generals of Division : in some respects his superior.

Yesterday morning we had a skirmish in the trenches. The Russians killed and wounded some fourteen men, chiefly of the 50th ; and our Rifles had again to recover the advanced trench so gallantly won by poor Tryon. His, by-the-bye, was the only attack made by us with the slightest scheme or forethought.

This morning the Russians killed, in the same way and manner (bayoneted), two men of the —th, when asleep. The men are so knocked up and tired that you cannot keep them awake.

Things look very gloomy, in my opinion ; I hope they will look better soon.

Our chief hope is that the Russians suffer as we do, or more. It is now reduced to a mere question as to which side can receive and feed the greatest reinforcements.

All the advantages we had at first have been thrown away. They have found out that in artillery they are our superiors, that our fleet cannot injure them, and that, if they can only hold on long enough to get reinforcements, they may yet drive us into the sea.

They cannot, I hope, quite do that yet, but certainly we have given them every chance.

General Pennefather very ill : hear he will have to

go to England. Thus we shall lose a very respectable officer.

December 9th.—Rode over the battlefield of the 5th November: how altered! Some few arms of the men, too shallowly buried, sticking out of the earth. Some broken accoutrements and dead horses—no more left of the many thousand that lay stretched on this plain.

We have, in conjunction with the French, erected two redoubts and a battery in these parts, and have certainly much strengthened the position. We now have, too, a very considerable command of the harbour. The enemy are working hard on the opposite side, and, I suppose, a heavy fight, at any rate with cannon, will take place here again.

From the advance battery one gets the best of all views of the town, and the only wonder is that the Engineers should not have found the place out sooner. If we can hold it, the ships must quit this part of the water; that is clear, and we shell a good deal straighter than the enemy. Still, I question if they will not be found just as good men as we are at this long ball game, though they do report that all their best artillerymen are killed.

Our supply of provisions is getting worse and worse, all owing to the want of transport from Balaclava. Now what can be more inexcusable than this?

Here we have a fleet twice as large as the French, with not half the men to feed; and yet they want for nothing, we for much; our horses are literally starved, and everything for the hospitals has to be brought up by the private goodwill of the already overworked men.

This is too bad ; yet it has been represented a hundred times.

Armies are not to be managed in this way. A man's desk is one thing, but his saddle is another; and, for a real soldier and general, more wanted than the former.*

At Headquarters they have every possible comfort, both for themselves and their horses; good beds, good stables, good fires, and good dinners. If their horses stood out in the open air, and could scarcely be kicked along; if they could with difficulty get wood to cook with ; if, like me, they had not (on shore) taken off their clothes since September 14th, they might possibly form a more accurate idea of the discomforts of the men, and discover some remedy, at any rate, for a portion of them.

The Medical Department is disgracefully neglected. One might almost fancy from what one sees (officially stated) in the paper that every sick man would have a comfortable vehicle for his transport. What would the nation say if they knew that one wretched araba, without springs or covering, was all the transport that the sick of each Division had on their advance to this place ; that hundreds of poor devils died upon the road with no means whatever of assistance ; men rolling on the ground with cholera, and not a drop of laudanum for them, nor any means of conveyance, after the one araba (carrying four men) was filled.

This was bad enough, but was to a certain extent unavoidable, as it was a forced march, with a great

---

* Compare with this passage Kinglake's description of Todleben. "It was not at table or desk, but on that black charger of his, which our people used to watch with their glasses, that he mainly defended Sebastopol."

object in view; but what excuse is there now for having left the men six weeks in the mud and water, without shelter or medicine, or any means of procuring warmth when they are taken ill.

Since the 29th, the Royals have had 85 men absolutely die; and the Army loses 200 a day by deaths and invaliding; and yet there are plenty of stores at Balaclava, plenty of horses at Varna, but, unfortunately, no head here.

I have this minute heard that Lord Raglan has been appointed a field-marshal. I hope that, with his "bâton" he will flog matters on a little faster than he has done hitherto, but I doubt it. It is not in him. He has not sufficient energy, and is far too old for his post. He is, however, an amiable, well-mannered man, and in some respects well adapted for the post he fills. Few would have got on so well with the French.

This expedition was, I know, undertaken in haste, and, unfortunately, it has been carried on at leisure.

I know that many reasons of broad policy may be acting on our commanders, of which I know nothing; and they may have very good and cogent motives for acting as they do as to the attack on Sebastopol, The great reasons of State can, however, have nothing to do with the badness of our transport, and the consequent miserable discomfort of the men; nor can they have anything to do with the great and flagrant neglect of not strengthening our right after the skirmish of October 26th, to say nothing of our not having done so from the 27th September to the 10th October, during which period we had nothing to do but to smoke pipes.

December 10*th (Sunday).*—Went to church-parade. The men looked cold, pinched, and unhappy, the reason being that they had had nothing to eat by 11.30, and, moreover, no prospect of getting anything before night. This was the reason of their appearance, not a bad one either.

At 5.30 p.m. a note came from the Commissary, stating that to-morrow we should have a short allowance of biscuit, *no beef;* coffee, sugar, and rum hoped for, but doubtful.

Yesterday 280 sheep arrived, which had taken two days coming from Balaclava, a distance of six or seven miles. This arose from the escort having been kept there for hours because the sheep were not disembarked, and then the men had to return owing to its getting dark. By heavens! the arrangements of this Army are disgraceful.

I repeat that I do not presume to talk of the great questions. The Commander-in-Chief's information enables him alone to judge on them.

But what have the great questions to do with the health and comfort of the men? What have political intrigues to do with the state of the roads here?

Alas, alas, what a thousand pities it is that Sir George Cathcart was not Commander-in-Chief. He was not good as the commander of a Division, but as Commander-in-Chief he would have been all in all.

He had head, energy, and activity; saw things with his own eyes; rode about and looked at what was going on, and decided for himself.

As for the matter of winter clothing, we have scarcely any of it—and why?

The *Prince* arrived laden with it on the 4th or 5th of November (I forget which). She remained outside

Balaclava Harbour, with one single anchor, until the 14th, when she was wrecked with all her goods and every soul on board. How unfortunate! how truly unlucky! was said. I thought she had very good luck not to be wrecked earlier. Good God, do people expect that, because they are indolent, it will please Providence to prolong summer weather into mid-winter? Did none of our naval commanders know that it sometimes blew in the Black Sea?

Oh dear, yes; but the truth is, private traders had got possession of the harbour, and a few days outside *would not matter!*

December 12th.—Now, as this book* is nearing its close, and I shall send it to England to-morrow, I will just say that Sebastopol will never be taken without immense reinforcements. If disease and starvation fall upon the Russians, and the winter prevents their getting reinforcements; if England and France strain every nerve and send every man, I do not say but folly may ultimately be made triumphant; without this, I doubt it.

How creditable to have to say that all our sick are carried to Balaclava by the French mules, our own ambulance corps being found perfectly useless, the pensioners sick or drunk, the mules used-up or dead.

I hope this war will open the eyes of the home authorities as to our inferiority in all, save fighting. The French are organised for war—we for nothing.

As soon as trouble turns up, all has to be organised afresh, and the moment peace is declared, if some jackass of a clerk can discover how a momentary saving of half-a-crown can be made, made it is,

* Colonel Windham's first MS. book.

immediately; thus many a valuable establishment is knocked on the head because it is not wanted at the moment. Why, for instance, should not a transport for the sick exist in time of peace?

Petty economies of this sort will, before this war is over, have cost England millions.

The same may be said about the commissariat, clothing and arming of the Army.

All of these will have to be remodelled ; no one can stand by the French and not observe their vast superiority to us. Entrenching tools, axes, &c., will not—or ought not, at any rate—be supplied for the future by contract.

The Enfield rifle, or a better one, if anything superior can be found, should be the arm for the infantry ; and they should be a hundred times more practised in shooting than they are, *without the bayonet being fixed.*

I can clearly see that what the French call *le combat à la débandade* is the real thing in attacking, with a reserve held in hand.

This is just what the Russians do not understand ; and, therefore, they have been beaten, notwithstanding numbers, artillery, and position.

The French do understand it, practised it at the Alma, and won easy.

We understand it less, did not practise it at the Alma, and therefore lost many more men than we ought, carrying the heights by mere pluck.

Our men are always educated, at least have been ever since I have been in the Army, to look upon the bayonet as a wonderful weapon. They fix bayonets (except the Rifles), invariably, before going into action. This is simply absurd.

No man should, in my opinion, ever fix his bayonet *as a skirmisher*, or ever be ordered to do so. Leave that to him: you may be sure he will do so soon enough if pressed.

A really good Infantry has no humbug about it, and I can clearly see that, with a change of system and the necessary practice, we could turn out ours as fine as any, perhaps the finest in the world.

We are that now as to mere fighting, but we have much to forget, and much to learn, in other respects.

December 13*th.*—Rode to-day with Poulett Somerset and General Cannon round the battlefield of Inkerman, and pointed out to the latter all I knew. He, like others, appeared to think that Cathcart, with the 4th Division, had gone down on the right into the valley. I was glad to undeceive him on this point.

December 16*th.*—Ground this morning quite white with snow. Last night the weather was miserable, and the day is not much better. For the last week the provisions of the Division have been issued with extreme irregularity and great deficiency.

December 19*th.*—Rode to meet the —th Regiment, who are attached to our Division. Found them in rear of the farm behind the 3rd Division Camp, as appointed. They are under the command of an impetuous old gentleman, aged about sixty-five, who ought to have been rewarded fifteen years ago if he ever did anything. Now he comes and cuts out younger and better men.*

* He became a General at last.—W. H. R.

December 21*st.*—A sharp sortie last night against the French and our Green-hill and Right Attack Battery.

The 50th lost fourteen killed, seventeen wounded, and Captain Frampton and Lieutenant Clarke missing. Major Möller is, I fear, mortally wounded.

The flank-companies of the 38th, under the orders of Colonel Waddy (50th Regiment), and commanded by Captains Gordon and Brooksbank, behaved very well.

The Russian prisoners were drunk, particularly an officer, and said that an entire Division had been told off for the sortie—say 8000 to 10,000 men. They were easily repulsed.

December 23*rd.*—Rode to Headquarters and to Bala-clava. Everything was going on the same as ever ; that is, most unsatisfactorily. According to my opinion, if some energetic exertions are not made, half the Army will be lost before the month of April.

December 24*th.*—Weather last night and to-day shock-ingly bad ; cold rain and sleet. Ten men of the 63rd died in the night, and three of other regiments. To-day the 57th had five men killed and two wounded in the advanced trenches. This arose from the poor fellows having to lie down in the wet until perfectly numb with cold. They were then obliged to rise to warm them-selves, when five of them were instantly shot. The others were hit by round shot.

Seeing that we have had this advanced ground a month, surely this could have been seen to ; it has been mentioned more than once—of that I am sure. Like everything else in this Army, reports are made, replied to, and forgotten. I understand that the French are to have this ground. Should such be the case, I will bet any money that in less than twenty-four hours they will put their men under such cover as to be nearly safe.

When I think of the difference of the two Armies, I am ashamed of ours, more particularly the upper parts of it. As to the men, they deserve, in some respects, the most enormous credit: their submissiveness and cheerfulness under their difficulties are wonderful. If the French underwent what we do, they would be in a state of mutiny. Every day in the French Army the men in the trenches receive a good hot dinner, and double allowance of rum. With us there is *constantly* no dinner at all; never a hot one; and sometimes no rum at all.

The English soldier, I admit, has not the *savoir faire* of the French; and why not?

Because the object, or at any rate the result, of our system is to make a fool of him.

I hope to God a change will be made after this war.

January 3*rd,* 1855.—The weather to-day is shockingly bad, and this Army will be ruined if matters continue as they are. The sick are increasing in numbers every day, the means of transport are decreasing, and no move made at Headquarters to remedy our position.

January 4*th.*—Snow deep. How the men are to get wood for cooking is to me the puzzler; and yet, I believe, no steps have been taken to supply them with any. One week of this weather will bring the Army to a standstill, and then what is to be done, God only knows. Heavy fall of snow.

January 5th.—Rode to Headquarters, and delivered McPherson's and Garrett's letters about pickaxes and fuel, with Sir John Campbell's note on them.

Rode home with Yea.*

At this time Colonel Windham was distressed by the death of his eldest brother, to which he alludes in the following letter to his brother-in-law, Mr. Robert Hook.

In this letter, and in another of the same date to Mr. Hudson, painful details of the disastrous condition of the Army are given:—

"HEIGHTS ABOVE SEBASTOPOL,

"*January 5th*, 1855.

"MY DEAR HOOK,

"Notwithstanding the heavy snow and frost, the consequent misery and discomfort of this Army, and the many gloomy matters that are surrounding me on this cursed hill, I can still spare a tear for poor dear William, whose death, from your letter of the 22nd, I look upon as certain.

"It is some consolation to me to know that I never, at any instant of my life, felt ungrateful to him for many kindnesses.

"I can hardly realize the idea of Felbrigg without him.

"Alas, as time rolls on, everything tends to drive me from the old corner of my birth. Anthony Hudson is now almost the only inducement I have to take the train to Norwich. However, my dear Hook, with alarms, and firing, and shot flying, and

* Colonel Yea, commanding the 7th Fusiliers, one of the best officers in the Army. He was killed on the 18th June, when gallantly leading the assault on the Redan.

diurnal deaths from violence and disease immediately beneath my nose, I need not *worry* myself about Norfolk, but simply pray and wish that I may live to get there.

"Our state here is shocking! Our Army so thoroughly helpless; and, on my honour as a soldier and a gentleman, I believe the fault is in our rulers here, not in the Duke of Newcastle.

"I shall be surprised if I see the Generals in authority (appertaining to the British) now in the Crimea handed down to posterity as men of head, or, indeed, as anything but a comfortable, easy-going, gentlemanlike set of do-nothings, who are only fit to scribble a despatch to the Secretary at War. *If this weather lasts a fortnight this Army is ruined, absolutely.* This Division, which had on the 1st December 3760 men under arms and fit for duty, out of 6800 on the roll, has this day only 2500 under arms, and those absolutely crying with cold and discomfort.

"I marched off last night, at 5 p.m., 1200 men to the trenches, 315 of whom had only come off thence at 8 in the morning; they had most of them had no fuel to work with, the snow was four or five inches deep, the wind strong and cold; their shoes (bad English ammunition articles) so small and contracted from wet as scarcely to allow of one pair of worsted stockings, and their spirit crushed by constant fatigue, wet, cold, and discomfort of all kind. They do not, however, grumble. Now, is not this hard, when one thinks of the thousands of pounds Old England is sending out for us? Is it not hard that even the parcels of goods (and I want them, for I have but two shirts, and no winter clothing) sent me by Marianne and Sophie, which have arrived in the *Arabian*, cannot be got, because she is ordered instantly to convey Turks from Varna to Eupatoria? Thank God I am but one of the few who suffer by this, and I can easily bear it; but when I see the same negligence, bustle, hurry, and want of proper arrangement in all that relates to the men, and that these poor fellows have no means of helping themselves, I am fain to sink down in despondency, and to acknowledge that arrangements and carelessness such as we have in this Army can bring, ultimately, nothing but disaster and defeat.

"I most sincerely pray that it may please God to afflict the Russians (excuse the anti-Christian spirit, my dear fellow) with greater hardships than He does us, or else I see no way of getting out of this mess with honour to Old England; for, believe me, we have no working men at our head, no organisation, no forethought. . . .

"Yours ever, my dear Hook, with many thanks for all your kindness to Pem and the children,

"C. A. WINDHAM."

"*To Anthony Hudson.*

"HEIGHTS ABOVE SEBASTOPOL,

"*January 5th*, 1855.

"Seeing the extreme uncertainty of human life in the most favourable cases, I ought not, perhaps, to bother myself about whom I shall meet on my return, but think myself a lucky fellow if I ever get back; but I certainly did hope that poor William, and I sincerely trusted you also, would have been alive to greet me on my return.

H

"I am in capital health, but am much out of spirits owing to this bad news from home, and the state of affairs here.

"The organisation and arrangements here are of the worst possible; and if Parliament does not, first or last, bring the conduct of matters here to light, I shall be somewhat surprised.

"The snow is now about six inches deep; the cold considerable; the utter want of preparation to meet it, wonderful!

"There is scarcely any fuel to be had, and that little got by immense labour in digging up roots. Yet the men go watch and watch about in the trenches, and are completely beaten.

"Our Division (4th), on paper, consists of the 17th, 20th, 21st, 46th, 57th, 63rd, 68th, 1st Battalion of Rifles, and a battery of Artillery—in all, 6700 men (we were near 8000). Of these, we have 1881 men sick at Scutari, 1084 sick in camp; and, deducting servants, bâtmen, and nurses, we cannot get 2500 men under arms, and we lose about twelve men by death, and fifty by invaliding, every night.

"Dysentery rages. Our poor devils have nothing but bad ammunition boots, too small to allow of more than one pair of socks; and, as they are almost always wet and without fuel, the malady goes on increasing; and I fully expect in ten days or a fortnight, if this weather continues, to see the siege brought to a dead standstill. Should this be the case, you will have to thank no one but the heads here.

* * * * *

"The organisation of the French is beautiful, ours a perfect disgrace; and I do therefore hope that, if we have another campaign, we may get rid of all Peninsular heroes."

January 6th.—Tried to get Sir John Campbell into communication with the other Generals of the Division, and to get him personally to see Lord Raglan about the state of the Army—than which nothing can be more lamentable, and a great deal of it owing to want of forethought and proper management. I fear everything is useless; we have not a man of common sense and energy among us, now that poor Cathcart is gone.

January 7th.—Walked with Earle to Headquarters, and suggested to Wetherall the propriety of having three or four thousand snow-boots made out of blankets.

January 8th.—Walked and looked at "the Caves" with Lord West, and went round the batteries at 11 a.m. Wrote to the Quartermaster-General upon the subject of "the Caves," proposing felt lean-to shelters, which would, I think, be much preferable to placing the men in "the Caves," from which they would be a long time in getting, in the event of an attack.

Walked afterwards to Headquarters with Sir John Campbell, who spoke to Gordon about an interpreter, and spoke out well, but I fear we shall not get one. I believe the Headquarter people are desperately afraid of any of the Divisional Staff getting the least information before themselves. God knows, the information we get from them is little enough; and I should recommend them to see if they could not extract a little more from the prisoners than they do.

It is true that Lord Raglan says, in his despatch to the Duke of Newcastle, after Inkerman, that, from "the information he had received, an attack might be expected"; but surely, if this were so, one might have expected a little more preparation on our part for its reception.

January 9th.—Did not go to Headquarters, being sick of doing so, as I never get what I ask for. Received an order for eighty horses for the Division. I wonder when we shall get them, and, when got, whether we shall get any hay or corn to feed them with. I much doubt it.

At this time the authorities are doing at Balaclava what they ought to have done seven weeks ago. What they should be doing now, supposing things had been heretofore properly arranged, is to be forming some system of transport, so that the Army would be able to do something in the spring.

As it is, their whole time is taken up in planning how to feed us to-morrow, and their thoughts are occupied upon peace, or in dreaming how they can escape from the results of their stupidity. What a set! What a set!

January 10th.—Sir John Campbell wrote to Airey, supporting my suggestion of the felt shed.

Late in the afternoon found Lord Raglan in camp. What a pity it is that so amiable a man should not have the truth strongly put before him. I am convinced that this is not done. Every little good he does is magnified; the great evils, that are not attempted to be corrected, are softened down, and kept in the background.

January 12*th.*—Weather still severe, with frost and snow. Everything in the Issuing Department going on with the same slackness. At last got consent to erect felt sheds for the men in the trenches.

January 13*th.*—Walked over in a bitter snowstorm to Chapman's tent about the erecting of the sheds. Then returned and visited the hospital tents of the 46th. Found General Airey in camp enquiring into last night's attack, in which we lost nine men wounded, and thirteen missing.

Rode to the trenches at dusk to see about the felt ; could scarcely find my way back, so thick was the fog, snow, and " poudré."

Heard from Airey that the 1st and 2nd Divisions were to come and camp in rear of us. They are forced at last into doing something to bring the means into something like fair proportion to the task. Until this moment it is perfectly ludicrous to see the way matters have been managed. For my part, I never thought Lord Raglan would command an Army well. I thought it very probable that he might be caught in a trap ; I was not the least surprised that we were surprised at Inkerman ; but I fairly admit that I am surprised that a man like him, so perfect a clerk, so continually calling for details, should have allowed his Army to waste away from want of method and arrangement.

I am afraid the fault must be with him.* How else can it be ? If one department were wrong, it might be supposed that the individual at its head was to blame ; but with this Army everything goes wrong.

* Notice, however, that Colonel Windham believed that Lord Raglan was kept in the dark as to the state of the Army by his Staff, and see entry in the Diary on June 24th, 1855.

January 14*th.*—Snow considerably deeper than we have yet seen it, so deep that I fear that the men will not be able to get any wood for cooking.

Went early to the Commissariat to see what the issuers were doing. Found them not up; but with nothing to issue.

About mid-day Lord Raglan came, and went over the hospitals of the 57th and 21st. He desired me to report upon the sheepskin coats already issued; to get as many bât animals as I could, and, with them and our private horses, to bring up to-morrow from Headquarters a day's rations in advance; and, finally, to breakfast with him.

Since the article in the *Times* of the 23rd December, we have seen more of the Headquarter people than we ever saw before, although the weather has been very bad. It has made them move about, and has, I think, done good.

January 15*th.*—Went to Headquarters this morning with fifty ponies, and sent a day's provisions to camp. Breakfasted with Lord Raglan. The remarks in the English Press have decidedly had the effect of stirring up these gentlemen, and making them open their eyes and their ears.

Did not succeed in getting the felt down to the trenches by the covering-party; hope I shall to-morrow.

January 16*th.*—A very cold day, with a heavy and keen north wind. Two men of the 20th frozen to death on returning from the trenches this morning. One man of the 21st, whom I got carried into my kitchen, will lose his fingers from frost in spite of all our care.

If this weather lasts, the Army will, in my opinion, be ruined, as we have no transport to get up the clothes that would save us, although it is all at Balaclava. Got some of the felt forwarded to the trenches; but it is too cold to do much.

By this time, thanks to the special correspondents, the public at home had become aware of the terrible condition of the Army.

A storm of indignation burst upon the Government at home, and upon the military authorities in the Crimea.

It is clear, from Colonel Windham's Diary, on whom he considered that the blame should fall.

The following letter to Mr. Hudson throws further light on the gloomy scene :—

"HEIGHTS ABOVE SEBASTOPOL,
"*January 16th*, 1855.

". . . This Army is in great peril. The weather intensely cold, the snow deep, the Commissariat infamous, the transport damnable, and *no fuel.* Not a word that you see in the papers is exaggerated. . . .

"By energy and determination something might yet be done, but when I tell you that we have this day only 11,000 effective Infantry on the heights, and 3000 at Balaclava, that our Artillery and Cavalry are done for, you may easily conceive that such a number is small for the effectives of an Army that amounts to 54,000 on paper.

"I am looked upon here as a Cathcart man, and, as I have hit some hard blows in conversation, I believe (you may laugh, but it's true) that I am more feared than loved. Several suggestions I made relative to

Balaclava eight weeks ago, were commenced upon five days back; and since the *Times* has written against Headquarters, some have attributed the attack to me (which is untrue), and I have been invited to breakfast, and made much of. Seriously, since the articles in the *Times*, I have observed much more activity at Headquarters; and they evidently see that sitting in a warm room and writing orders, whilst the men are dying by hundreds, don't suit the British public. I need not tell you that, although a grumbler, I am not disposed to attack people in the dark, . . . but the sooner, now poor old Cathcart is gone, they hand the Army over to Fred Markham, or some other man of his standing, the better.

"Believe me, your Peninsular heroes are of no use nowadays. They who really led the Army in Spain are gone, and those who, as juveniles, served in it, have not caught the mantle that fell from Wellington's shoulders.

"If the weather we have now lasts three weeks, we are gone, my dear Anthony, and, as an Army, ruined.

"I am very well and strong, but see clearly that the climate, mismanagement, and overwork, will bring us to destruction."

January 17*th.*—Cold and snow the same as yesterday, but the sun warm. Rode to Headquarters and saw General Airey, who gave me another letter to Commissary-General Filder about the divisional transport ponies. Went to Balaclava and presented it, when Filder told me that he had no ponies, owing to the ship they had given him for them having been filled with sick. These latter could not be disembarked, and, therefore, his horses could not be embarked.

Thus the Division will have to go without fuel, and everything will have to be fetched by the men.

I hope to God I may never be attached to so helpless an Army again ; once in a man's life is quite enough to have to do with such a set of incapables. I have not seen the papers yet, but understand the attacks on Lord Raglan are most severe. It is now, however, too late.

January 18*th.*—Went down to the trenches, and was glad to find one small shed erected. Got the Artillery to bring nails up from Balaclava.

Rode to Balaclava and saw Mr. Filder again. No use, although I took him a letter from the Quarter-master-General. Went also for charcoal and got a third of a load, or 1200 lbs.; no more landed. Again time and labour thrown away.

January 19*th.*—Wrote to Sir John Campbell, reporting in strong terms the conduct of the Balaclava authorities. I did not specify the Commissariat, for had I, they would have said it was the fault of the Navy, and *vice versâ*.

January 20*th.*—63rd Regiment left us. Went to Balaclava, and saw them settled.*

January 26*th.*—Went to Balaclava to superintend the disembarkation of the drafts. Arrived late in camp, having had to load my mare with the knapsacks of the men, and to walk in my big boots. The drafts consisted of detachments for the 20th, 46th, and Rifles —in all 100 men.

* They were practically annihilated, chiefly by disease and death.— W. H. R.

January 27th.—Made arrangements about the bât animals, and Mr. Balcombe was appointed transport officer.

Saw Lord Raglan in camp this afternoon, and spoke to him on the subject. The ammunition horses are to be cleaned and kept with our bât animals.

January 28th.—At work again about the bât animals. Went on board the *Bucephalus*, and had an interview with Suckling regarding my horse-trough. It is to be finished on Wednesday. (This was a trough for the bât horses of the 4th Division.)

January 30th.—Wrote a letter to Sir J. Campbell for the perusal of the Quartermaster-General, but he galloped off to Balaclava before I could catch him. So I took it with me to Headquarters, and got Wetherall to forward it to the Commissariat. Airey seems to approve highly of the regulations I have written out.

January 31st.—Ponies came up for the first time.

The night before last I sent to Headquarters a young cadet of the Russian Artillery. They seem pleased with his information and manners.

To-night we are warned by Lord Raglan to expect an attack.

February 1st, 1855.—There was more continual firing of musketry and artillery between the French and Russians last night than I remember since the siege began. I have heard a much heavier cannonade, but never so much pop shooting with small arms at the same time. Called up by the corporal of the Battery

Guard at half-past four, as he said the Russians were advancing. Found a strong musketry fire going on, with occasional French bugles. Weather thick.

Waited until the sortie was repulsed. It must have been a heavy one, lasting an hour, and, as the moon was full, or nearly so, the loss must have been serious ;* but the French keep these things very close.

Bosquet's Division paraded this morning, and marched towards Inkerman and back. They evidently expected an attack this morning, and I daresay we should have had one had not the Russians lost all their Artillery horses, which, from what my Artillery cadet says, appears to be the case.

Went to Headquarters and saw Lord Raglan. Heard there that the sortie against the French was a heavy one, and disastrous to them as to loss of men, but that the enemy had not injured their works.

Went on to Balaclava. On the two last occasions of going there I plainly saw that they were acting on the letter I wrote General Airey weeks ago. They might have employed me to carry out the plan I laid down; I could have improved upon it.

However, so long as the work is done, I care not whom it is done by.

February 2nd.—Went to Headquarters on "Inkerman," who, I am glad to say, is better; and, when well, one of the nicest horses I ever rode.

Received more parts of huts, and gave one to the Rifles and one to the 46th.

* The French loss was 16 killed, 30 wounded, and 18 taken prisoners. —Letters from Headquarters.

The worst of the winter was now over, and the following letter to Mrs. Windham gives a more cheerful description of the state of affairs :—

" HEIGHTS ABOVE SEBASTOPOL,

" *February 2nd,* 1855.

" . . . . The Army is looking better, and is more cheerful; the weather has improved, and the Headquarters Staff are at last carrying out the suggestions I made to the Quartermaster-General about ten weeks ago ; so I hope by the warm weather, should peace be declared, we may be able to get the Army down to Balaclava. As to its moving ten leagues before May, it is ridiculous to suppose it possible. No preparations are ever made for what is to happen five days in advance ; and, until dire experience teaches them, they will never give up the system of favouritism that rules supreme. If anyone at Headquarters had an insight into human character, and a knowledge of men, you would have seen very different appointments from those that have been made. However, let us hope that peace will be proclaimed, and then the appointments won't matter a bit. It would be hard on the majority of mankind if fools could not get on, but it is certainly annoying that they should so often have the power of life and death in their hands.

" The Russians made a severe sortie against the French yesterday morning, and inflicted a considerable loss on them, and took a good many prisoners. The French were surprised. I had to listen to the fight for hours, but it was too thick to see it ; but I could hear the shooting and firing as it were under my nose.

" We lost nobody, they not having fired at us.

" I hear good accounts of the nurses here.

" February 3rd.—There is snow again this morning, but it will not last. . . .

" C. A. W."

February 3rd.—Distributed the oranges presented by the " Crimean Fund," and more bits of huts.

I am glad to hear that the transport hut at Balaclava is nearly finished, and I hope that in a week the system will have settled into regularity.

Rode to Headquarters, and saw the prisoner cadet. He seems to be in favour, and is decidedly a Pole. Ordered up the tea (of the " Crimean Fund "), of which the men are fully inclined to avail themselves. Very cold ; snow, wind, and frost.

February 4th (Sunday).—More huts came up, and the " Crimean Fund " tea arrived, and was instantly distributed. No church-parade, owing to the snow and cold.

More assertions that the Russians would attack us again, but I hardly believe it. The town is, however, well garrisoned, and immensely strengthened in batteries.

February 6th.—Blake, who had come to the Crimea to superintend the distribution of the " Crimean Fund," rode to camp on my grey pony. Took him round the trenches, and saw with disgust that the ignorance of the Engineers, and the carelessness of regimental officers, have rendered my felt sheds of little or no use.

The unthriftiness of this Army is something wonderful.

February 8th.—Rode to Headquarters, and found the Quartermaster-General's Staff absent.

This is another instance of the annoyance of the centralizing system; in other words, of the habit they have in this Army of making everyone go to Headquarters for everything, instead of leaving each Division to its own A.Q.-M.G. Why should this be?

As to checking accounts and issues, it could easily be arranged once a week, and endless trouble and delay spared to all concerned.

But I must control myself—even in this journal—although it is unquestionably disgusting to be put under such a system, and to see men rewarded, as those at Headquarters have been, for casting ruin and havoc to the right and left through their ignorance, or rather want of forethought and business habits.

Had they made up for it by any marvellous superiority in fighting, it might have been borne; but this they have not done, though I am far from accusing any of them wanting that commonest of all qualities—a sufficiency of pluck to pass muster.

High and devoted courage is rare and noble, but common pluck is common pluck and nothing else.

February 16th.—I have not written in this book for a week, because things have gone on with so much sameness, that I did not care to do so. I have got up four or five more wooden houses.

Saw Lord Raglan in camp yesterday.

Rode to Kamiesh to-day with Sir John Campbell, and on my return found Codrington and Newton. We were soon after joined by Steele and Leicester Curzon. Gave them some of Payne's curaçoa. Steele gave us a most gratifying account of the disastrous state of the Russians at Bakshi Serai and Simpheropol.

February 18*th* (*Sunday*). — Blew hard and cold almost all day.

No church-parade on account of the parson being sick.

Heard this morning that the Russians had really attacked Omar Pasha at Eupatoria, and had been fairly repulsed.

Also heard that our tactics were to be completely changed. That Niel (the French Engineer) and General Jones are both against an assault, and in favour of an attack on the north side, and a regular investment. I do not pretend to know if this be true or not. Should it be so, it will be singular that we should have been trying for six months to starve ourselves, and should only now prepare to starve the Russians.

Read some of the debates in the Commons and Lords. All too violent against the late Ministers, and if a Committee be appointed, they will, in their present state of feeling, probably commit some absurdity. After all, the great error has been the management of the transport, both as to horses and roads, to Balaclava; and if they try to prove more than this they will fail, except, perhaps, in the matter of "overwork." There the Headquarters are equally blamable, and showed great ignorance of ways and means.

February 19*th*.—Rode to Balaclava. I am glad to say that that beastly place is at last being got into some shape; and I am proud to say that everything

(except the boat canal) which I suggested in the beginning of December last is being executed, almost
to the letter.

The railway is progressing fast, and will soon come
into operation. I heard to-day that the Russian loss
at Eupatoria had been heavy.

Got up the boarding of the last two huts, and I shall
now go on a planking and charcoal expedition with the
ponies.

February 20*th.*—This morning, at two o'clock, Sir
John Campbell came and woke us up, and showed us
a memo. desiring that the troops be kept to their
camps during the day, and the officers in command
at the trenches warned that it was probable that we
should be attacked, as the French and English, under
Bosquet and Colin Campbell, were going out in force
to the right, and the enemy might think it a good
opportunity to try a rush at our batteries.

The morning proved perfectly fearful as to weather;
very cold, much snow, and a regular " poudré," with fog
and a gale of wind.

The weather did not clear up till dark, and no attack
was made.

February 21*st.*—Heard that Sir Colin Campbell had
been out with his Brigade from Balaclava yesterday
morning, and had hit upon the Russians; and, had
the French not been deterred by the state of the
weather, the Russians—to the number of about 1500*—
would probably have been picked up, as they were
unquestionably surprised.

---

* The strength of the Russian force was 7000. The combined English
and French force amounted to 15,000, it being hoped that the Russians
would be surrounded, and would surrender without fighting.

February 22nd.—Wrote to Gordon about some boilers for hot water, that the Division might have a chance of washing themselves. As yet have no positive answer that the blankets may be washed, although I have mentioned the subject four times at Headquarters. There appears to be a perfect paralysis when any plain little common-sense thing is proposed.

February 23rd.—At about 2 a.m. the French assaulted the Russian battery to the right of the Round Tower and failed, losing 240 men and officers.

It was a severe skirmish, and affords another proof of the folly of night attacks, except with a very small force, easily manageable, and well acquainted with one another.

February 24th.—Spoke to the Quartermaster-General about the boilers. He was friendly in his answer, but finding none come, I resolved to send and buy them out of my own pocket.

February 25th.—The washing of the blankets awaits the orders of the Ordnance Department, no one being willing to sanction the outlay of 1s. per blanket for washing, although no hesitation is shown in condemning and burying them by the score after the decision of a Board.

Can anything beat this in the way of childishness?

March 7th, 1855.—Everything has gone on as usual during the last few days. Last night the news arrived by telegraph of the Emperor of Russia's death.

If true, the world will be the gainer for the time, but a loser in the long run ; for I am convinced it would be

I

for the benefit of mankind that constitutional opinions should get the upper hand throughout Europe.

March 12*th.*—A good deal of firing ; and the Russians will soon complete, in addition to their two new batteries to the east of Careening Bay, a strong redoubt upon the hill to our right of the Round Tower, called the Mamelon.   I, of course, shall be called a mere grumbler by any who may read this journal hereafter; but I must say the conduct of the French and English Engineers excites my astonishment in the highest degree.   What the devil they can be about I do not know.   It appears to me that they make it an axiom that it is easier to take a work from the enemy, after it is complete, than it is to take the position.   This appears to be a lively satire on the science of military engineering.

We are now told that everyone knew that the Mamelon was a desirable place for us to get, but that we could not hold it, as we should be shelled out by the shipping.   Now all the talk is that it must be taken.

It appears to me that, as the hill is within range, we could have stopped the Russians from fortifying it as well as they could stop us.   .

But no matter.   This is an age of peace, and not of war, and perhaps so much the better.

March 14*th.*—During the day I watched two guns of Gordon's battery firing at the Mamelon work, and the Russian return fire.   Our practice was, I thought, very good ; the Russians seem to have fallen off.   Probably they have lost their best artillerymen.

Had another working-party, all of the 57th, and very

well they worked, finishing filling in all the tent-holes of the 63rd.

March 17*th.*—About 9 p.m. we were turned out under arms, and were marched to the quarry. It all ended in a French attack.

March 18*th.*—Lord Raglan called at the camp at about 6 p.m. He seemed nervous as to the Russians attacking us. A young officer of the 57th, Lieutenant Mitchell, was, I fear, mortally wounded through the chest this day, in the Woronzoff road.

March 20*th.*—Delivered the ponies to Captain Dick, of the Land Transport Corps, and had from him a sketch of the intended plan. It will be very expensive, and not a bit more effective than the present one. What we wanted was the horses; as soon as we got them we managed our transport well, and everyone was contented.

March 23*rd.*—Last night the Russians made one of the severest sorties they have yet made, but, owing to the wind, we heard but little, though we could see all. The Russians attacked our Left and Right Attacks, and, still more severely, the French Right Attack. In the advanced battery at the Green-hill (Lord West, Field Officer of the trenches), the enemy succeeded in getting in, killing five men and wounding ten. They were driven out before they did any harm, and left two officers and seven men dead in the trenches, and, it is hoped, some outside; but we do not know, as we cannot look up for fear of the rifle-pits. At Gordon's advanced battery seven Russians were found dead.

The English lost three officers — Vicars, 97th; Cavendish Brown, 7th Fusiliers; and Jordan, 34th— killed.

Lieut.-Colonel Kelly, 34th, missing, as is Montague of the Engineers. Major Gordon, R.E.; McHenry, 7th; Godfrey, 34th—wounded. One corporal and fifteen men are missing, and nine are known to be killed.

A very handsome and handsomely dressed Greek, who led the Russians, was killed. They pretended, as usual, to be French, and fought stoutly.

I went all over both attacks this morning, and counted in front of the rifle-pits, and round one in particular, twenty-eight French and forty-nine Russians; inside the French lines, seven French and seven Russians. One Zouave was far in advance— up the Mamelon. The French, I hear, lost 400 men; some say 600.*

Rode to Headquarters, and G——, as usual, refused my requisition, which on this occasion was for planking for the Division.

March 25th.—Went down during the armistice to see the dead buried in front of the advanced battery, and carefully looked at the ground.

I am convinced that from this side we shall not take the place; at any rate, if we do, it must be from a French attack, on the extreme left, supported by the Fleet.

So much for my observation. I have only one thing to add, and that is, that no ground can be more easy to defend than that near our advanced battery.

* Kinglake gives the French loss as 600 killed and wounded; English loss, 70; Russian loss, 1300.

Dined with General Barnard, and met Henry Keppel, who still thinks he could take the *St. Jean d'Acre* into the port, and I firmly believe he could and would do it.

I decidedly agree with him that the Fleet should be constantly under weigh, teasing the enemy, and compelling him to man his sea batteries.

But I will not go on growling.

For my part, I think everything on the part of the allies so slackly performed that I am perfectly disgusted.

March 31*st.*—The siege goes on as usual. More work is required. Very few improvements are made, except such as are produced by the weather

Spoke to Lord Raglan in camp. He appears to be very cheerful, and quite happy about something or other. Whatever errors of judgment he may commit, he may certainly safely be copied by young and old as to manner : no indifferent point, after all.

Hamilton went to Balaclava, and back by Headquarters, where G—— again cut down the requisition (for planking) by one-half, without any apparent reason.

April 1*st.*—Church-parade was ordered at noon, but, owing to the cold, Sir John Campbell sent to the clergyman and told him not to come. I think he was right ; but certainly it is a long time since we have seen a parson.

April 5*th.*—Had a talk with Calvert, the interpreter, who seems to have very considerable military talent. Calvert assured me that every one of the deserters stated that for two days and a half after Alma the Russians positively did nothing—did not even take a spade in their hands.

I look upon the non-pursuit of the Russians after Alma as having cost the country 20,000 men, and twenty millions.*

There is no entry in the Diary of the following day, but some plain speaking in a letter to Mr. Anthony Hudson :—

"HEIGHTS ABOVE SEBASTOPOL,

"*April 6th*, 1855, 10 *p.m.*

"MY DEAR ANTHONY,

"Marianne enclosed me last post a letter from Charlotte, in which I see you have done me another most kind and friendly turn.   Many, many thanks !

Everything goes on here as usual, except the weather, which is now perfectly beautiful, and I only hope it may so continue until we leave this place, which I do sincerely hope may be soon.   I am not a desponding man, or a coward, but believe me that England must not make a point of selecting all the d——dest fools she can find for civil, military, and naval commands, both at home and abroad, if she wants to succeed in a war against Russia.   I have been hammering for weeks at the transport for this Army—when I say weeks, I mean months—and yet here we are, at the opening of a campaign, unable to move five miles.   By God ! it is too bad.   The Crimea would be far easier to take than Sebastopol—40,000 men at Theodosia (cutting off their supplies by Arabat from the Don), and they would soon be done ; but here we go, on the contrary, tugging

* There is no exaggeration in the estimate.—W. H. R.

up shot and shell to fire at this place, which the French *won't* assault, and we *can't.*

"Oh, my dear Anthony, would to heaven that it had pleased Providence to have put me at the head of this Army at Eupatoria on the 15th of September; you may depend you would have seen my round face swinging or sticking over many a pot-house down in Norwich; but now it is too late; we have nothing else for it but to make peace if we can, and take the chance of getting up a central rising in Europe should Russia break out hereafter. I am told here that I am looked upon as a very good officer, which, I suppose, is the reason they do nothing for me at home.

"Love to Charlotte and the girls. I hope Harriet is better.

"Ever, my dear Anthony,

"Yours affectionately (as I ought to be),

"C. A. W.

"We are told every day that we shall open our batteries—if we do, it is all nonsense. They can do nothing—it will only end in a bombardment, an investment, a retreat, or a peace. Take your choice!"

April 7th.—I have received this night an order to prepare for an attack to-morrow, and everything is ordered to be in readiness. For aught I know, it may please God to prevent my seeing either wife or children again in this world; and, therefore, I am writing with serious feelings, and with no levity. Yet I wish to record my feelings; and I do say that the imbecility of the conduct of the Allies, arising from I know not what beyond pure stupidity, surpasses human comprehension.

But no matter: it is clear to me that God puts whom He will at the head of affairs, and arranges all things as He likes.

I hope it may please Him to carry me safely through the battle to-morrow, if there is one, and let me see Pem, and little W——, and the other two, once more. Should He think proper to order it otherwise—His will be done. I leave my love to all my family, and to dear old Anthony, my best and truest friend.

April 8th (Easter Sunday).—Divine Service at eleven. Dined with Sir John Campbell; and after we had returned home, an order came from the A.-G., confirming the afternoon's rumour, that the batteries are to open at daybreak to-morrow. The guards of the trenches to be removed to the ravines in flank.

THE SECOND BOMBARDMENT.

April 9th.—Got up before daylight, and found it raining, and a thick fog besides.

At sunrise we began, except Gordon's battery, which fired but little. The French fire is wonderfully heavy, and up to this (6.15 a.m.) the fire from the town is unquestionably less than in the October opening.

8.45 a.m.—Up to this the firing seems greatly in our favour. I had no idea of the Russians replying so mildly. The truth is, I am fairly puzzled.

11 p.m.—From all I can hear, our loss has been slight. We are now shelling the town like the devil.

April 10th.—The firing continued all night with shells, and this morning the batteries began again. The Russians, as yesterday, scarcely making any reply, except from the Bastion du Mât, which was reported yesterday, at noon, absolutely "*extinct.*" This morning, accordingly, it has fired with greater vigour than ever.

Had a long talk before noon with General Penne-father, who, I think, views the case soundly. His description of the "moral" of the French is certainly not encouraging, and he thinks, and with reason, that the British would be neither wise nor successful in making an assault.

April 11th.—We have kept up a steady fire all day; but I expect this bombardment will prove a failure, as did the October one.

Had a long talk with Steele. We never agree. He holds my opinions cheap (they may be right, never-theless); I hold his cheaper, because they have been wrong.

A young Artillery officer has, I hear, had both legs amputated from a wound received to-day. Poor fellow! I hope that, for his own sake, he will die.

April 13th.—The advance battery, on the left of Green-hill, opened fire with four guns this day, Captain Oldershaw, R.A., commanding. He was quickly overpowered, and nearly all his men dis-abled; but I understand that Captain Oldershaw is quite contented with the parapet, and, as he is promised fourteen guns to-morrow, has volunteered to take the command again.

The enemy concentrated twenty 68-pounders on him. I hear he had about 40 killed and wounded out of his party.*

* The survivors of Captain Oldershaw's party volunteered to a man to serve in the same battery under him on the following day.

April 15*th.*—Yesterday the bombardment continued, but not so heavily as before.

At 4 p.m. to-day I heard that the French were to attack the Bastion du Mât at eight o'clock. They did so, and the firing has just ceased. I hope they have effected a lodgment, and that our week's work of shooting shot and shell will not be thrown away.

A letter to Mr. Hudson gives a somewhat fuller account of the French attack, together with some general comments on the events of the war :—

" HEIGHTS ABOVE SEBASTOPOL,

" *Sunday, April* 15*th,* 1855.

"MY DEAR ANTHONY,

"After church, this day, I was informed that something serious was intended, and thought it very probable that the English would be called on to assault some portion of the works. About 4 p.m. I was, however, informed that the French intended to spring a couple of mines, and then attack the Bastion du Mât after dark. This they have just done, and a short, sharp, angry fight they have had ; but, at present, I don't know whether they have succeeded or not. It is now about half-past ten p.m., and the morning will show. If they have failed, I look upon this business as hopeless, unless some providential accident or other helps us through. How true it is that 'War' is usually a series of mistakes. The conduct of the Allies, since we have arrived in this country, has been one continued piece of blundering stupidity; and our opening our batteries on Monday last was, in my opinion, quite unnecessary.

We have now fired upon the place for seven days, have lost many hundreds of men, and, unless we follow it up with bloody assaults at different places, we shall never take it; and, should we lose a large amount of men in doing so (which is more than probable), we shall have thrown away more life and more money, for a useless object, than was ever done before. For, mind you, with the southern part of this place in hand, you will be no nearer a peace than you are now; for, until you take the northern side (and perhaps not even then), Russia will never consent to the non-reconstruction of the fortifications here; and as they will have, in the course of a day or two, 100,000 men effective within twenty miles of us, it will not be so easy to take the northern side. *N'importe*, if the French have taken the Bastion du Mât to-night, *and can hold it*, a great point is gained *quo ad* the capture of the place. To revert to the question of the mistakes made in war. I believe if General Liprandi's advice had been followed in October last, we should have been done. Take your map (or, if you should have none, I will enclose you a rough sketch). His wish was to make an attack, with 10,000 men, at Inkerman; to have thrown the same number right at Balaclava; and then, with 45,000 men, to have marched straight up the Col de Balaclava, and turned our whole position, a sortie being made against the French Left, the same as it was on the 5th of November. Had he succeeded, we should have been hopelessly lost; and had he failed, they would equally have been done; but the chances were in his favour, particularly if they had never made the attack at Balaclava on the 25th of October, inasmuch as we never dreamt of their having such audacity, and

were only dreaming of entering the town. I shall
now close for to-night, and resume, as the parsons
say, the thread of my discourse to-morrow.

"*16th*, 10 *p.m.*

"Last night was most noisy, unceasing firing,
springing fougasses, &c.; but I have discovered at
Headquarters that, though the French had entered,
and remained in, the Bastion du Mât all night,
they thought proper to withdraw in the morning.
I of course expected a renewal of the attack
to-night, but up to this minute there has been none,
and this night is as quiet as last night was noisy.
Our chiefs seem to do nothing but hold consulta-
tions, and I do not put the slightest faith in any
of them but Omar Pasha.

"I believe the Russians will have 100,000 effective
men at Batchi Serai in a day or two, and that, without immense risk, loss, and luck, we shall never take
the place. I only sincerely hope that I may receive,
by the mail to-morrow, news of peace from Vienna,
and that I may get safely home. I do not expect
ever to get anything for what I have gone through.
I don't eat humble pie enough, or listen with sufficient
humility to some titled or official fool, to get on; but
if I only get back again, and should ever be once more
employed, I must have the devil's luck, and my own
too, if I do not get a better lot over my head than I
have now.

"To revert to Liprandi. It was his intention, after
rising the Col de Balaclava, to have marched straight
upon Sebastopol, and have crushed the left wing of
the French. It would have been an awful hubbub
had he tried it; and had he been worsted he could

still have got into Sebastopol. Had he done this on
a foggy day, like the 5th of November, he would
have succeeded.

"I send you on the other side a small sketch.

"Love to Charlotte and the girls.

"Yours ever affectionately,

"C. A. W."

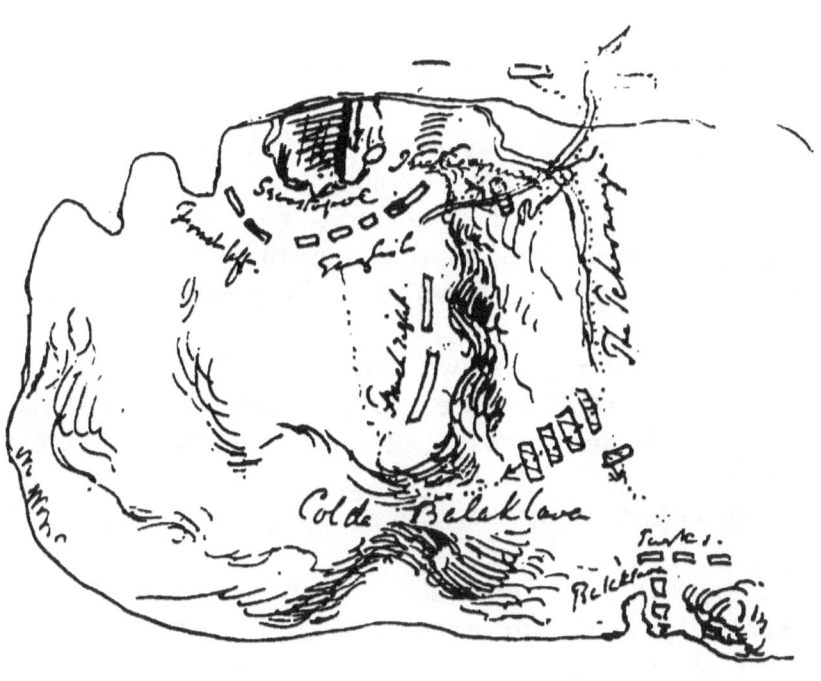

The dotted line shows Liprandi's intended march and attack on
Balaclava and the Allies.

April 16th.—Rode to Headquarters, and found that the French had not accomplished what they had announced that they intended doing, but it appears that they occupied the Flagstaff Battery all night.

I dined with David Wood, and, before dinner, had a long talk with General Pennefather. Touched on Cathcart, and the proceedings of the 4th Division at the battle of Inkerman.

I find he knows as much of our proceedings as I do of his, which is exactly what I thought; but he is the hero of the battle.

What with unintentional and intentional misrepresentations, not once in a thousand times do you come at the truth.

To give an idea of what General Pennefather's notion was of the 4th Division, I will just mention that when I told him *the Division* did not go to the right, although Cathcart did, and that the whole of the men who went down the hill numbered about 380, he said:

"Well, that's pretty well out of 700."

"Why," I said, "Sir, we lost 747 killed and wounded (in the Division), and 51 officers, 29 of whom were killed."

He looked astonished.

April 18th.—I understand that yesterday Lord Raglan proposed to storm, and said he was ready. This pleases many, but does not please me, nor did it the French.

If we stormed we should be beaten.

What we shall do now, I know not. Our transport is not ready, and, in fact, the Army is no army, and is incapable of moving twenty miles. The French are just as badly off as ourselves. In fact, we have not a man amongst us.

April 19th.—At night the Light Division attacked the rifle-pits by the Woronzoff road.

April 20th.—The attack last night succeeded, but we lost 68 killed and wounded; among the former, Colonel Egerton of the 77th, a fine fellow.

April 25th.—Heard that yesterday's unceasing fire by the French on the left arose from their determination to prevent the Russians from occupying the vacant rifle-pits at the head of their advanced sap. Notwithstanding their labours, the Russians occupied the pits, and were in full possession this morning.

If true, this looks as if the French were no match for them at this sort of close work, and I really begin to think that they are not. The Army appears to be dull, and in expectation of nothing. I do not like the idea of assaulting under present circumstances.

April 26th.—In the afternoon rode to the right, and saw a review of Bosquet's Corps and the French Cavalry. The men under arms amounted to 33,000, and looked very well. Canrobert did not.

What a pity it is that we should have no real leader in either Army. The French are, I think, worse off than we are. They have as much prejudice, and more conceit.

April 28th.—Met Morris, of the Artillery, who is attached as A.D.C. to Bosquet. He told me that Canrobert's letters to France are full of complaints as to the English, and the hindrance we have been to him.

He also said that the French were much disappointed in Canrobert as a general.

The French force he states at 55,000 effectives: very small this, and, if correct, shows they must have suffered immense losses.

April 29th.—The French on the left are keeping up an incessant fire (11 p.m.). The perseverance they show in fighting in the trenches is really wonderful, and I must admit I think them quite right in refusing to assault.

There are no entries in the Diary on the two following days, but a letter to Mr. Hudson shows the intense indignation excited in the Army by the partial distribution of rewards, and by the meanness with which the soldier of that day was treated by the authorities :—

> " HEIGHTS ABOVE SEBASTOPOL,
>
> " *April 30th*, 1855, 10 *p.m.*
>
> " MY DEAR ANTHONY,
>
> "The mail from England arrived this morning, but as usual they do not choose to forward the letters to camp, and I therefore shall not be able to answer by return of post, as the mail leaves here to-morrow morning. These delays occur constantly, and are most irritating. I suppose England is not particularly pleased at the failure of the last bombardment, or rather artillery attack ; for my part, I never doubted its failing, and am therefore neither surprised nor annoyed. It is true that I cannot for the life of me understand why we opened fire at all, but I suppose they had their reasons.

" I feel convinced we shall now wait until some large reinforcements arrive, and with these, and time and blood and money, we may take a place that common dash would have carried, after Alma, with no loss at all. I suppose I shall never get promoted—when I see Torrens, who commanded six companies, and was wounded in six minutes, made a Major-General ; when I see Sir John Campbell and General Eyre (the latter a junior Lieutenant-Colonel to me) both made Major-Generals, although they have neither been really under fire with their brigades since they have been here, I must say I think it hard that I, who took Torrens' place and kept it for seven hours (having many more men under me), should be passed over with no kind of notice. The direct act of injustice about the ride to the Katcha I forgive ; but this last case, with both the brigades of my Division vacant, to give neither to either Horn or myself, is too bad.

" It is perfectly true that Colonel G——, who landed three days after the battle, was my senior, and that I have had no junior put over me ; but God bless me, were we not told that merit was to be the order of the day ? If not, upon what principle are Lord R. and all the other generals promoted over the heads of their seniors ? Had the old system been adhered to I would have said nothing ; but I must say that I did expect, having been at every fight, I should have had some consideration shown me ; but really and truly the British Government is not a Government to serve under. Most of the best men in this Army—yea, Egerton (killed the other day), and many others—have got nothing, and I firmly believe never will have.

" If we are to be rewarded, it is a d——d shame not to do so at once. Is it the fault of the Army that

K

Sebastopol is not taken? Have the heads not blundered, and hesitated, and pottered away thousands of poor devils who would a million of times sooner have died in the breach? Why then reward the heads, who have done all the mischief, and decline giving anything to the men, who have done all the work? The Emperor of Russia allows the defenders of Sebastopol to count one month's service in the town during the siege for six months, whereas that old petrified dandy, Lord Palmerston, won't even allow the winter campaign, that has absolutely killed one man out of three, to count for aught extra—this is purely brutal. To-day is cold; the weather is, however, soon going to be hot, and, I am sorry to say, fever is on the increase, and we have a few cases of cholera. I expect we shall await our transport until the heat knocks down the Army; and not until England rises in a towering passion do I see any chance of getting rid of the horrid imbeciles that beset us on all hands. As to the French, they are worse off for Generals than we are; they have as much prejudice, and a great deal more conceit; and I believe their Army here to be thoroughly disgusted with their Generals and Engineers, and well they may be. This is a growling letter; but I am angry at the letters not having arrived, and at everything going wrong. Love to Charlotte and the girls.

> "Ever, my dear Anthony,
>
>> "Yours affectionately,
>>
>>> "C. A. W."

May 2nd, 1855.—Observed about mid-day, with Sir John Campbell's glass—a new and powerful one—

that a large body of Russians were entering the town. At about 3 p.m. the Russians made a sortie upon the French Left Attack. The fight lasted an hour, and the firing very heavy.

Heard to-day that a force of ten thousand French and English troops were to go to Kertch. At last they appear to open their eyes to what is wanted.

May 8th.—Having finished my old book, I have neglected to write my Diary for a week.

On Sunday last I heard at Headquarters that the expedition to Kertch had been recalled by General Canrobert, from orders received from Paris. Here the "worry" has been going on as usual. In fact, this campaign is enough to drive anyone mad— nothing but waste, stupidity, orders, and counter-orders.

May 9th.—Rode to Headquarters, and presented Airey with a calculation of transport animals necessary to move an Army of 24,000 Infantry, 3000 Cavalry, and 3000 Artillery, with fourteen days' provision and ammunition complete.

General della Marmora arrived at Headquarters while I was there—quite a young, active man.

I was yesterday shown a letter from General Yorke to Lord Raglan, informing him that Lord Hardinge did not think it proper to recommend me for an advance of rank. This advance would have given me £200 per annum, and seeing that I have served Her Majesty twenty-nine years, and have never yet received one shilling that I have not paid for, I did think I might have had a chance. As it is, my insurances swallow up my pay, and as those who have not been here during the winter are to be given the good things, I must content myself with the reflection that if I have done but *little*, I have, at any rate, received *nothing*.

The expedition to Kertch, which sailed a week ago, arrived safely at its destination, and was about to disembark, when it was recalled by General Canrobert.

This little pleasing episode cost us £50,000 in coals, and has not a little disgusted those sent upon it.

I have heard various reasons given for its recall, but do not pretend to know the real one. Should it occasion the Russians to strengthen themselves there and at Kaffa, we must hark back, and go over the old ground.

May 10*th*. — This morning at one o'clock, it being very dark, a sortie was made by the Russians on Gordon's Advanced Parallel; it was quickly repulsed, with much cheering, and small loss. I soon saw, from the quantity of shells thrown by the enemy, that they had not succeeded.

(*From a letter to Mr. Hudson, of same date.*)

"Whether my eyes have been blinded by looking at Sebastopol every day, and all day (to say nothing of the nights), is a matter for your judgment; but, supposing they are not, I am free to confess that I do not see how we are to take this side of the town without immense loss of life, time, and money; and when we have taken it, I cannot see what use it will be to us, as we cannot use the harbour until we have conquered the north side as well.

"To do this, *an* Army (either this or some other) must *move*, and I therefore have said, and do say, that to attack this south side by assault, to lose thousands of men in doing so, and to risk a defeat, is pure insanity. If unsuccessful, all the 'prestige' now in our favour will be gone, and many of our men with it ; if successful, we shall have to draw off, and attack the Army on the outside, either by crossing the Tchernaya, embarking at Balaclava for Aloushta, or some place to the eastward—or by going by sea to Eupatoria.

"I am aware that some men think that the north side could be easily and rapidly attacked from the south side ; but I believe they are thoroughly in the wrong.

"The Allies, as I have oft repeated for months, ought to have been ready to move, if wanted, on the 1st of May—they are not : it is of no importance to my argument to know who is to blame for this flagrant error.

"I made a calculation some days ago, for the Quartermaster-General, as to the number of baggage animals it would take to move an Army of 24,000 Infantry, 3000 Cavalry, and 3000 Artillery, with 14 days' provisions, forage, and reserve ammunition ; together with all its camp equipage, and forage, for its bât animals.

"I found that it would require 15,000 mules, or horses, and 5000 transport men, the meat being driven with the troops, and killed as required.

"3500 two-wheeled carts, and 8000 animals, would do better.

"If 30,000 British troops could be moved with this amount of transport, I do not see why others could

not do as much; and as every man can, as we did,
carry, at any rate, two days' provisions on his back,
I think twice the amount of transport I have
mentioned might move an army of nearly 100,000
men for ten days.

"Owing to the withdrawal of the expedition to
Kertch, and its appearance in that quarter having
awakened the enemy, I should be inclined now, all
things considered, to try Eupatoria.

"The greatest mistake the enemy has made since
we landed in this country was the not attacking and
taking Eupatoria, before advancing against us at
Balaclava and Inkerman last year.

"Liprandi's plan of attack, if carried out against
us at Inkerman, would, I think, have succeeded;
but no matter, they made a fatal mistake when
they allowed us to get a firm hold of Eupatoria,
and by it will probably, if the war lasts, lose the
Crimea.

"My plan is to give up the trenches (if compelled
to do so by events), and strengthen ourselves in every
possible way upon the heights; then to assemble
every possible means of transport at Eupatoria, to
collect there all the Cavalry, and every man we can
spare, and make a bold advance straight on
Simpheropol, and bring the campaign to an issue
by one or two great fights.

"I am told that the French have now more than
40,000 men at Constantinople, and nearly as many
more coming.

"We must now have nearly 100,000 men upon
these heights, and when we get the whole of the
Sardinians (4000 have arrived), we surely can hold
this place, and Eupatoria also, safely, in conjunction

with the Turks, and yet advance against the Russians at Simpheropol with 100,000 men.

" If we do this we shall win, but we must not potter away our time here and pertinaciously, like an old Leicester tup, keep butting against the post when the gate is wide open before us.

" If we persist in attacking the Russian Army through Sebastopol (for that is what we are doing), we shall merely play their game, and waste everything that is most valuable, and probably shall not get away from this cursed place before the winter.

" We have had a few cases of cholera, but I hope the heat won't begin in earnest before the latter end of June, and until then we shall, I hope, do well enough.

" You cannot think how disgusted I have been with things here ; and when I read Lord Palmerston's speech, declining to allow this winter campaign to count for anything extra in the way of service, I felt more disgusted than at anything I ever knew in my life.

" Had he consented it would have cost the country next to nothing, for how many will ever live to benefit by it ?

" It was a harsh and cruel decision, and when I look back at the ungrumbling manner in which the private soldier laid down his health and life during the last horrid winter, I feel certain that none but a pampered statesman would ever have made such a speech.

*　　　*　　　*　　　*　　　*

" Yours ever, though wet and tired,

"C. A. W."

May 12th.—Just after I had coiled myself up in my blankets, a sapper came and stated there had been a heavy attack on the Green-hill Advance, and asked for an ambulance waggon.

I turned out and got on my horse (1.30 a.m.), went to Major Grant, and ordered one.

I then returned and went to the trenches, and found there were thirty-six killed and wounded on our side, and about twelve Russians killed in the trenches.

Macbeath was much pleased with the conduct of the men. Shocking wet night, and some of the men severely wounded. Captain Edwards, of the 68th, killed.

May 13th (Sunday).—Sent for early by the Quarter-master-General, and fancied I should, on seeing him, hear something of importance; but it all ended in his sending me to Balaclava to enquire into fuel and ration questions, thus giving me a long ride for absolutely nothing—for how is it possible that I should con-tradict the reports of two gentlemen at the head of their departments?

Alas! it is really painful to see a really good-tempered man like Airey placed in such a position. He would have made a very good brigadier, but is utterly unfit for his present place.

May 14th.—Went this day with Sir John Campbell, and was examined by Sir John McNeil and Colonel Tulloch.

I answered very few questions, for the plain reason that I did not know they were examining us both together. ;

I could see that the examination took a line that

must damage Airey very much; indeed, it is difficult to see how it could do otherwise, or how he can get over the fearful delay in issuing the things sent from England, occasioned by his plan of making everything pass through Headquarters, and not allowing the Divisional Staff to have anything to do with the subject, beyond the passing on of requisitions.

May 19th.—Heard to-day that Canrobert was certainly displaced, and the command of the French given to Pelissier.*

Sent down eight carts for the Rifles' huts, with written authority for their issue, and found there were none left. How annoying are these arrangements.

May 22nd.—Expedition sailed to Kertch.

About twelve midnight a most heavy fire began on the left between the French and Russians, and lasted till near daylight. The loss, I should think, must be severe, and I only hope the French have succeeded in doing what they wanted.

Matters are unquestionably pressed on more vigorously than by Canrobert.

May 23rd.—Heard this morning that the French loss last night amounted to 1200. This, I trust, is exaggerated.

May 24th.—Went to the Cavalry review, near Monastir. When talking to Mrs. Duberly, Omar Pasha came up and spoke to her. He is a soldier-

---

* General Canrobert behaved in a very soldierlike and manly way under most difficult circumstances, and earned the generously-expressed admiration of Lord Raglan.

like looking man, and his appearance by far more military and gentlemanlike than that of the French generals. Pelissier seems, however, to have stirred up the French. Their loss the night before last was between 1100 and 1200 men, but last night the Russians bolted, and the French completed what they wanted to do, and are now very cock-a-hoop. There is much talk of the Mamelon being assaulted to-night.

What I believe is certain is, that a large force will go to-morrow into the valley of the Tchernaya, and stay there.

It is now late, and the shelling is very heavy. What is singular is that the Russians have sent seven steamers to anchor off the Mamelon, which proves their information to be pretty good. The ships, however, seem to have done harm the night before last, having killed a large number of their own men. Their loss is said to have been 4000 men that night.

May 25th.—This morning found that a large portion of the Army had moved from our rear and from Balaclava, and now occupy the heights close to the Tchernaya, immediately in front of the redoubts lost by the Turks on October 25th.

The Russians did not dispute the ground, but made off as fast as they could.

May 27th.—Heard this morning that the expedition to Kertch arrived and disembarked there on the 24th; also that the Russians had blown up their batteries, and deserted the place.

Our men are now at Yenikali, and have captured fifty guns and destroyed a large foundry.

At Headquarters to-day I heard Sir E. Lyons most highly spoken of. Steele says they have information that the Russians acknowledge to having lost 50,000 men out of the 80,000 they had here during the winter. The enemy certainly has had a very bad week of it from the French.

May 30*th.*—No change among the troops outside.

Walked round the trenches with Pakenham and Smith. The guns are unquestionably heavier, the mortars more advanced, and ammunition more plentiful than before ; and people seem to think that something will really be done in the next bombardment.

I nevertheless disapprove of it, and think it perfectly useless. The Army outside should be beaten first, and then both sides taken at once.

June 1*st,* 1855.—After dinner I met Sir John Campbell on his return from dining with Lord Raglan. He told me that we had had very considerable success in the Sea of Azof, had captured or destroyed 240 coasting vessels, four men-of-war steamers, and six millions of rations.

June 2*nd.*—Sir John came this forenoon and showed me a "confidential" memo. from Lord Raglan, by which it appears that we are soon to attack the quarries in front of the Redan. It does not say if the attack is to be made by night or day, but the rest of the plan is plain enough. But I cannot see what we can want to take the Quarries for until the French try the Mamelon, and then I think it would be wiser to attack the whole place at once, instead of losing hundreds of men in these nasty little "bit-by-bit" affairs.

June 3rd.—Yesterday afternoon Sir John Campbell announced that he was ordered off to Kertch, and gave up the command of the Division.* I am sorry for it, as he is a good-tempered and agreeable man, cheerful, kind, and hospitable. Last night he gave me his cave, and to-day made me a present of half his cocks and hens, and his ewe and lamb, besides pots of marmalade, &c.

June 4th.—Sir John Campbell left us, and went to Balaclava. He had not gone long when up came Bentinck, and, though unwell, I stayed some time with him. Ordered a fatigue - party to put the ground in order for his horses, &c. He and his A.D.C., Greville, dined with us. He has very kindly ordered Smith and me to dine with him every day.

June 5th.—Went to Headquarters, and on to Balaclava ; very hot indeed. I cannot find out if the Russians have as yet shown any symptoms of being hard hit by our Kertch operations.

June 6th.—Another very fine day, but did not go out, not being well yet.

At 3 p.m. our batteries opened against the place, and towards evening the Russian fire certainly did not appear strong. Fire continued all night on our part, and the enemy scarcely returned a shot. Heard that the French Cavalry (if not ours also) were to advance

* To Lieutenant-General Bentinck, who had returned to the Crimea from England.

up the country, and that an attack was to be made upon the Mamelon by the French, and on the Quarries in front of the Redan by us, to-morrow.

This I think likely, and I hope it will prove true. Something, I fully expect, will come off, and the sooner the better.

June 7th.—A few minutes after ten a magazine in Gordon's Attack blew up with a very heavy discharge, and I am afraid has done considerable damage. Daniell came up from Balaclava, and called on me. While he was here Bentinck informed me that the intended attack on the Quarries and Mamelon were to take place at half-past five o'clock p.m. An hour later news arrived that, owing to the heat, the French would not attack till half-past six.

At a quarter-past six the signal went, and they attacked the Mamelon, and carried it with little or no opposition.

Previous to the attack I accompanied Norcott and 300 of the 68th to the Woronzoff road, and placed them in reserve and, I hoped, in safety. I took Hamilton with me and left him there. On our way down a 42-pounder came slap into the middle of the men, but, thank God, hurt no one.

After seeing the men safely placed, I returned and reported the fact to Bentinck, and watched the attack.

The French took the Mamelon quickly and gallantly, and with very little loss ; but as soon as they had done so, they (as far as I could see) chose to follow on and attack the Malakoff Tower. Here they were warmly received, and lost, I fancy (I am writing at midnight, and don't know), a great many men.

Somehow or other they appeared to be driven from

the Mamelon, as well as out of the Round Tower, and were positively attacked in their trenches, until a reserve came up, retook the Mamelon, and reattacked the Tower, unsuccessfully.

We could see nothing of the proceedings of the British owing to the dense smoke, but at about 8 p.m. General Pennefather sent to Bentinck, saying he was hard pressed, and wanted two battalions to support him. These were quickly told off, and P. Herbert desired me to march them past Pennefather's tent, and learn where they were to go.

My horse being saddled, and the men not ready, I rode to General Pennefather's (thinking thereby to save time), when I found he thought that I was already at the advanced works.

Now, seeing that I had not had any notice of his distress above five or six minutes before I called on him, I was certainly surprised at his being astonished that I was not already in the advanced trenches. My surprise was, however, increased when, upon my galloping back and going to the 17th lines, a distance of at most 300 yards, to find the men falling in, and Colonel P. Herbert present, who told me that six hundred men I was about to march down should only act as a reserve, and on no account be taken to the front.

No sooner had I sent Earle with this order to General Bentinck, thereby letting him know that I considered that I was no longer under the orders of General Pennefather, but of Lord Raglan, than I received an order to turn in the whole of the six hundred men, and to march down a separate party, previously told off as a second reserve, under Colonel Maxwell, of the 46th, to the support of Colonel Norcott, whom I had originally taken down.

So much for having a variety of "Kings of Brentford."

On arriving on the scene of action I found that Lord Raglan was quite right, and General Pennefather quite wrong, as everything was going on successfully, and there being no appearance of our losing (either French or English) the ground we had taken.

June 8th.—A nasty, blowy, dusty day.

Went early to Headquarters, having been sent for to receive, as usual, the most childish orders. Remained in camp until I marched down Colonel Kirby and the 48th to the Woronzoff road. A mistake was made about a party of 250 men going to the Right Attack; not Smith's fault. They did not leave camp till midnight.

June 9th.—At 12 o'clock there was an armistice to bury the dead. I rode to the Quarries, where I found some thirty of our men dead, or being carried away, and about two hundred Russians.

I went as close to the Redan as the Russian sentries would allow, and I looked both at their officers and men. They looked, according to my opinion, annoyed and distressed. They were captious at officers looking at the Redan; and there was no one, as on the last occasion, to ask us when we intended going away.

I afterwards rode on to the Mamelon, and a very clever, well-contrived work it is, and I hope it will prove a good lesson to our gentlemen of the Engineers. The parapet was immensely thick, and the space in rear of the guns very narrow. The screen in the rear was also very thick—say twenty feet—and the work was mostly built of gabions about eight feet high.

The confusion in it was not so great as the description would have led one to suppose, although there were, of course, many guns upset and broken, and many Russians—buried, half buried, and unburied—lying here and there.

The loss of the French, in taking it, appears to have been very small; and had they not gone on, contrary to orders and without supports, to the attack of the Malakoff Tower, they would have lost few men, and be where they are with many of their best men alive.

June 10th.—Rode to Headquarters, and saw Lord Raglan about Cathcart's monumental inscription in Russian. He asked me to dinner, and I accordingly stayed, and had a pleasant dinner. Had a long talk with him and also with Airey. The latter appears, and is, a much better man in theory than in practice, on paper than in action. In fact, to judge from his conversation, had he had his own way, the whole management of the Army would have been exactly the reverse of what it has been.

He told me that the Russians had 45,000 men in the town, and plenty of provisions; but, upon my telling him that I did not believe the Russians could bring 60,000 men into the field against us, he agreed.

June 11th.—Rode with Bentinck, Smith, and Greville to Kamiesh. The French have nearly, if not quite, finished the ditch and rampart round this town for re-embarkation. It strikes me that it is using rather a superabundance of caution, but as they have lots of hands, it is perhaps as well.

What the devil can Russia mean by not coming to terms? Is it not surprising to see a nation continuing an immense war like this, when she cannot, by any conceivable success, make us do more than we ourselves are willing to do—viz., go away, and remove our Army.

June 12th.—Went to Headquarters by appointment, but Airey had not time to speak to me about the place of attack I pointed out to him on the evening of the 10th. I rode with him, and we selected a place for the 63rd, which regiment will rejoin the Division to-morrow (having been completely reconstituted).

We have made a further advance towards the Redan, and have got two mortars into the battery. It is to be armed with two 10-inch and three 32-pounder guns, and these two mortars.

By a deserter we hear it is asserted that the town is all mined, and that the Russians are ready to spring the mines and quit for the other side as soon as we advance.

This, however, is more easily said than done, unless they are determined to blow themselves up with us. They are certainly in a very considerable funk, and, if I were Commander-in-Chief, I would immediately assault the heights and shut them up, and go at the town on the other side.

The man said that of his regiment of 1500 they had only fifty left.

June 13th.—The 63rd come to-morrow instead of to-day. At about half-past six Lord Raglan rode into camp to call on McPherson, and afterwards came and looked at Sir George Cathcart's tomb, and decided upon the Russian inscription being placed upon the centre. When at the fort, he looked at the town and advanced works through my glass, asked many questions, and remained there for some time. Sir John Campbell also came there, having arrived from Kertch.·

The tone of the Army is decidedly good, and everybody looks upon success as nearly certain. God grant it may be so, and that we may all live to see it.

Four hundred of the 57th were sent to the advance of the Right Attack, having been ordered to join that attack in "After Orders." I daresay there will be nothing for them to do, notwithstanding, as I have great doubts of the Russians making any more sorties in force.

June 14th.—Rode with Bentinck and Smith to Monastir in the afternoon. The General much surprised at the beautiful sea view and the romantic appearance of the place. The day was beautiful, and certainly nothing could look more grand than the high, bold, rocky coast, with the calm blue waves hundreds of feet below, large steamers of 2000 tons looking like little boats.

June 15th.—General Airey came to camp to take a stare from the Fort.* Sir John Campbell arrived from Balaclava late, and dined with the 57th. At 11 p.m. a short, sharp fire of large and small arms commenced between the Mamelon and Round Tower and parts adjacent.

---

* Better known as Cathcart's Hill.

FIRST ASSAULT ON THE REDAN.

June 17th.—Running about all day, preparing for the assault.

Marched off scaling and wool-bag party, under Hamilton, twenty-five minutes past midnight. Perhaps I should say twenty-seven minutes past, there being a difference of two minutes between Sir George Brown's time and mine.

About an hour before, General Bentinck received an intimation that the attack would probably be at 3 a.m. (18th), and that care must be taken to have all the troops down in time. I accordingly told the General that I agreed with him that there was no necessity to alter the orders, but that I would tighten, and not slacken, the cord. I therefore hurried off the party a quarter of an hour before the time named, and left camp, with Sir John Campbell and his party (1750 strong), about five minutes before one o'clock.

Although Colonel Windham was aware that his post would be with the Reserve Brigade during the assault, he thought it possible that it also might be engaged, and wrote the following letter, to be despatched to Mrs. Windham in the event of his death:—

"*June 17th,* 1855.

"MY DEAREST PEM,

"Our batteries opened again this morning, and we have received orders to storm the place in a few hours. I do not anticipate that it will be a very bloody affair; but, as I shall be of the party, it may please God that I shall lose my life. If so, you will bear in mind that my last thoughts will be with you and the children. As I have never received a single thing from the Government during the twenty-nine years that I have served, I hope that the Queen, should I fall, will do something for you and the children. At any rate, petition Her Majesty *direct*, and ask no one else; for, if she will do nothing, you may be sure that no one else will. My commission money will be lost, and you will be badly off; but, my dearest, I can't help it. You must do the best you can with the children, and I only pray that God will protect both you and them when I am no more. Kiss little W—— for me, and tell him he must be a good boy, and not be troublesome to his mother when he grows up; and do the same and say the same constantly to the other two. If they turn out well all will go well. Now give my best love to all my brothers and sisters, and to yours, and do not forget dear Anthony Hudson, the oldest and best friend I ever had. D—— will see about your money affairs, and look to the insurances, &c.

"Give my love to Guy and Charlotte, and also remember me kindly and warmly to the Somervilles and Des Voeuxs, particularly to C. Des V. and Mary S. And now, my dearest, God bless you and protect you and the children, and may He enable me, as heretofore, to go on like a man to-morrow, and assist in bringing this detestable siege to an end. I cannot help thinking the Queen, should I fall, will do something for you if applied to.

"Ever, my dearest,
"Your affectionate husband,
"C. A. W.

"P.S.—It is now 12 (midnight), and I am off to the trenches; so God bless you, my dearest, and the children. To-morrow will, I hope, be a proud day for Old England, and not a sorry one for you."

June 18*th*.—On arriving at the twenty-one gun battery I found no officer of Engineers, although one had been promised me, to give Hamilton's party, of one hundred and ten, wool-bags and scaling-ladders.

When I had been there a minute or two Colonel —— [name illegible] came, made me an offer to direct the working-party, and went, I believe, with Hamilton and the scaling-party.

After seeing all the men file in the trenches, I left to march down the Second Brigade to their place.

On my way back, Cathcart asked me, from Sir George Brown, if the Fourth Division was in its place, to which I replied, "Yes."

Owing to the time I had been detained, I met Bentinck, with the Second Brigade, in the Woronzoff road, and conducted them to the caves, and other places of comparative security; while Bentinck rode to the twenty-one gun battery, to see Sir George Brown.

Shortly after the Second Brigade was settled and comfortable the attack began; and, though I was sent out twice to look at the proceedings, I could see nothing, owing to the smoke and heavy fire; but we soon learnt that the attack had been a failure, and that Yea and Sir John Campbell were killed. At about half-past nine General Bentinck sent to Sir George Brown for orders, and was told that we might march home with the Reserve Brigade. We shortly afterwards returned to the camp, and found the Twentieth there—they had formed the working party.

June 19th.—Rode to Headquarters, and had luncheon with Lord Raglan. Found people somewhat down, more so than I see any necessity for.

The attack was badly planned, and worse executed; and, from the hour being changed, as well as the previous system of attack altered, late at night, everything went wrong.*

I look upon poor Sir John as having been one of the kindest, best-hearted men I ever knew in my life, and as brave as any man could be; but he was a person without the organ of arrangement, and one who thought that "British pluck" would do everything.

Now British pluck is very much like any other pluck, and British soldiers will be found to resemble others most uncommonly, if they are badly managed. Had the covering and wool-bag parties been placed, before daylight, down the hill to the left, and thrown as far forward as the ground would allow, and had the 57th (the storming column) been also placed in their rear, clear of all the works, and the supports to the storming-party placed *in rear of the Quarries*, the men in the advance moving forward to the "re-entering angle" of the Redan, as was ordered, and not to the apex, the attack might have succeeded—at least, they would have reached the place.

Nothing of the sort, however, was done; everything was left to haphazard, and people appeared to think that as soon as a cheer was heard the work would

* The change was made at the request, or demand, of the French, and against Lord Raglan's wish and advice; it must, however, be allowed that the French gave good reason for the change.

be carried. But it was not so. The enemy were prepared and steady; their guns were loaded; and they showered such a fire of grape upon the advanced party, that the whole thing failed.

One way and another we lost a thousand men, killed and wounded, as near as I can guess; and I can see no likelihood of our deriving any advantage from this attack, except that the Allied Commanders may now be induced to take the field, and try their hand at the outside, not the inside.*

The more I look at the matter, the more convinced I am that every man lost in front of these works is pure waste, as we must eventually invest the town; and the sooner we do it the better.

General Bentinck gave strict orders to Sir John not to lead the storming-party, and I too begged him to turn his attention more to direction, and less to leading; but I saw it was of no use, and told Hume, his A.D.C., that I was sure he would make a rush, which was exactly what he did, and accordingly lost his life, and did not win.

Poor fellow, he was as kind-hearted and gallant a man as you would meet with anywhere: but, alas for his wife and family, he thought of nothing but carrying the Redan with his own sword.

The French, if anything, conducted their affairs worse than we did.

June 20th.—Rode to Headquarters, where I heard that 95 officers and 1443 men were either killed or wounded. This is a most severe loss, and, added to those lost in the attack on the Quarries, makes an entire Brigade of our

---

* Windham's opinion on that subject completely changed when he became Chief of the Staff.— W. II. R.

little Army, which can but ill be spared. All this too for nothing, except a couple of houses, and a slight advance to the left of the Left Attack gained by Eyre.

The men, I understand, did not behave well. But this, no doubt, arose from mismanagement of the attack, and is possibly a good lesson for some of our officers, who always seem to think that British pluck has done, and can do, everything. Now British pluck is not absolutely universal. When present it is as good as any pluck, and in some respects better, but without *head* is worth very little.

June 22nd.—Heard to-day that we shall give up the houses that were taken by Eyre's Brigade, and destroy the Russian rifle-pits. What next is to be done seems difficult to say. It is quite clear to my mind that they will try another assault, simply because it is a thing they can do, and whether it succeeds or not seems to matter very little. Oh dear! oh dear! what a wonderful thing is reputation, and what a miraculous thing is discipline.

The French troops attacked better than ours, but both made a disgraceful failure; whereas, had the French stuck to the original scheme, we should certainly have had the Malakoff, and possibly the Redan. It must be admitted, however, that the French got out better (from some cause or other), and attacked in large numbers, and with greater spirit, than we did; but their supports were badly arranged, and Pelissier seems to have made a considerable mull of it.

A letter to Mr. Anthony Hudson gives some particulars of the assault, and shows how it failed :—

"HEIGHTS ABOVE SEBASTOPOL,

"*June 22nd,* 1855.

"MY DEAR ANTHONY,

"You will long ere this have received an account of our failure on the 18th, as well as that of the French; by it we have lost ninety-five officers and 1453 men, and the only little bit of advance we gained costs us daily so many men, that we give it up to-night. The truth is, the original plan was bad, and made worse by the hour of attack being changed at a late time of the night. The Russians were perfectly prepared, and I am by no means sure that, as soon as 'shelling' the different points for three hours previous to our storming was abandoned, we could ever have taken the Redan; acting as we did it was impossible.

"The Redan is an arrow-headed work, supported by other works in the rear, and may be represented thus :—

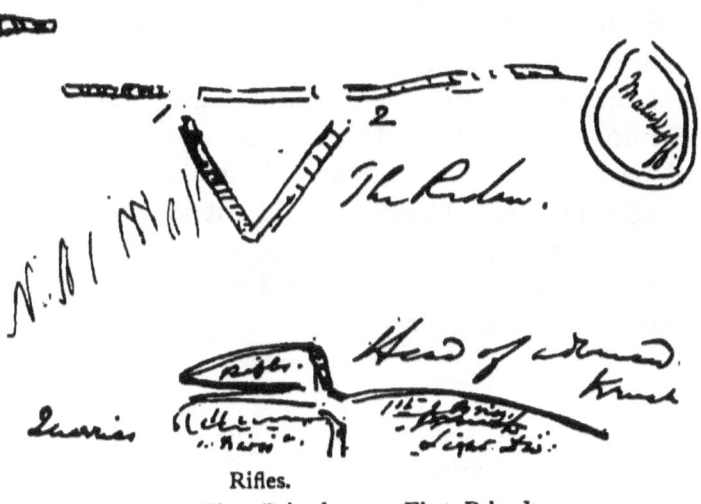

Quarries.   Rifles.

First Brigade,   First Brigade,
Fourth Division.   Light Division.

"The 4th Division was ordered to go at No. 1, the Light Division at No. 2, and they were formed at and in the advanced works, where they were so crowded that they could not have very easily been got out under 'no fire,' and where it was most difficult to make them do it under lots of grape, and after one has been trying for months to make them stick to their trenches. The 1st Brigade of the 2nd Division was to have assaulted the apex of the Redan as soon as the 4th and Light entered it by the two re-entering angles. In fact, a brigade from each Division was told off for the purpose, consisting of 1760 men each. Sir John Campbell, with our 1st Brigade, was told by me, from my previous knowledge of the ground, to keep down the hill to the left of his advanced party, so as to drop the Redan, and be invisible to all save the two batteries upon its proper right. This he did not do, and he made hardly any arrangements, or thought of aught save being the first in. He was as brave and as kind a fellow as ever lived, and during all this arduous, long winter he was never once unhappy or depressed, or did I ever have a word with him, poor fellow. He was hit right through the head by a grape shot, and poor Yea, who commanded the Light Division Attack (an old friend of mine), met the same fate from a rifle, and the whole thing became a perfect failure. I am too tired to go on. Love to Charlotte and the girls.

"Yours ever,   C. A. W."

June 23rd.—It seems positive that General Pennefather goes to England, and that General Estcourt is better. The Guards having come to the front, the duties are greatly lightened.

June 24th.—It is positive that General Pennefather goes to England, but not positive that poor Estcourt is better, as he died this morning.

I am sorry for this, as he was a talented, gentle-manlike man, superior in intelligence to most at Headquarters.

I cannot make out what is going to be done next. I fancy the Malakoff Tower will be tried, and cannot for the life of me understand why it should not be taken. But alas! what is the good of forming opinions as to what will be done by a sort of disjointed command, such as we have.

In my opinion, Napoleon III. would do much better to appoint Lord Raglan Commander-in-Chief of the Armies. He is an amiable man, the oldest soldier, and, I believe, if left to himself, the best.*

At any rate, if the original plan of attack had been carried out on the 18th, we should have done something more respectable than we did, and not have made a disgraceful failure.

June 27th.—Heard this morning that Steele and Lord Raglan have both been very ill (cholera).

Rode with Bentinck to the Maison d'Eau, and took a good survey of the town from that point. Afterwards went on to Headquarters, where, I am glad to say, we heard that Lord Raglan was better, and saw Steele looking quite fresh. A great deal of sickness, however, appears to be about, and there is some talk of Lord Raglan being obliged to go away for a short time. Codrington will, I believe, and I am glad of it, rejoin the Army to-morrow.

* This remark should be set against some harsh criticisms of Lord Raglan which occur in the Diary. Windham frequently remarks that he, of course, did not know what difficulties Lord Raglan had to contend with.

June 28th.—A Medical Board assembled on Sir George Brown, and he goes home.

At half-past six Bentinck returned, and informed us that, at half-past four p.m., Lord Raglan had been taken much worse; and at about half-past nine Ed. Somerset * rode to the Cave, and informed us that he had died about an hour previously.

Poor Lord Raglan. I am most deeply sorry for it. His age, his previous position with the Duke, his rank and excellent manner made him admirably adapted to deal with the French. Looking to the extreme difficulty of finding a successor to him, I cannot help thinking his loss a serious one.

June 29th.—Morris, of the Artillery (Bosquet's A.D.C.), told me last night that the cause of Canrobert's resigning was that Lord Raglan would not raise the siege and go forth against the enemy. Bosquet called Sir George Brown to witness the truth of his statement, who, by his silence, admitted it.

" *Il faut prendre une partie,*" was Canrobert's expression, and his arguments were the same that I have often used. Would to God that his advice had been followed.

Heaven alone knows what we (the Allies) shall do now. Lose 10,000 more men at the Malakoff, I suppose.

July 3rd, 1855.—Among the many rewards distributed I find I have got nothing, and suppose I never shall have, so I will not grumble.

Heard that General Simpson was appointed Commander-in-Chief, and that another Chief of the Staff was coming out.

* Lord Raglan's nephew, afterwards General E. A. Somerset, C.B.

July 5th.—Dined on rice soup and tapioca, having been unwell since the 2nd.

July 6th.—Ditto.

(Colonel Windham was ill for eleven days, but remained at his duty.)

July 7th.—Major Harrison, of the 63rd, was killed by a round shot in marching with the relief to the trenches, or rather in riding down, for he was mounted. Hard luck this, considering that the day was so thick that it must have been a chance shot. Such is fate.

July 10th.—I have still been kept in by this nasty diarrhœa and fever, but think I am decidedly better. Yesterday I heard that Calvert* and Vico† were both taken desperately ill at Headquarters with cholera.

Calvert died last night, and Vico to-day. There has been a great uprooting of the Staff there.

July 12th.—All right, but not quite strong.

July 13th.—Rode to Headquarters, and found Arthur Hardinge‡ unwell. That young fellow ought to go home, or his father will lose him.

Barnard told me that his appointment, and others, were in abeyance, by a telegraphic despatch. The truth is that everything is unsettled; the French very down in the mouth; and future proceedings of all kinds uncertain in the highest degree.

* Mr. Calvert was the Russian interpreter at Headquarters.
† Le Commandant Vico, the very popular French Military Attaché at Headquarters.
‡ he late General the Honble. Sir Arthur Hardinge.

July 18th.—A sortie was made last night, about midnight, against our attack (centre of it). It was quickly repulsed, with a loss on our side of three killed and two wounded. Much yelling on the part of the Russians, but no very daring advance. Garrett was down there, and the 48th had to receive the attack, and, I understand, behaved steadily, although from the want of a banquette the men can never fire properly.

July 19th.—Rode to Headquarters, where everything looks as dull as ditch-water. Saw Airey and Steele—the latter not looking well. Spoke about some bricks for the ovens, and was told that it was what Lord Raglan had wanted ever since he came here. This, I suppose, was the reason that no one ever tried it until I took the matter in hand.

There is no entry in the Diary on July 20th, but a letter to Mr. Hudson may still be read with advantage by those whose duty it is to write despatches. Medals are still issued when most of the men entitled to them have left the Army:—

> " HEIGHTS ABOVE SEBASTOPOL,
> "*July 20th*, 1855.
>
> " MY DEAR ANTHONY,
>   " This old bruin, Pelissier, keeps everything to himself, and gives us nothing but a grand and overpowering example of bad manners and bad language. I hope he may have something beyond this in him —time will show. As for me, I am very well; and if we succeed in taking this southern side of the town without getting my head knocked off, I shall return to England, as I clearly see that I have no chance of getting on with such a lot as we have at

home and here. I think Lord R.'s despatch of the business of the 18th as absurd a document as was ever written; and until Commanders give up the habit of undistinguishing praise, the sooner they leave out men's names the better. It was an ill-arranged and worse executed plan, and deserved to have been passed over in silence at the best, merely mentioning the poor fellows who went gallantly to the front and fell. Singular to say, the regiment that with us deserved the most praise is scarcely mentioned; and an officer of the 17th (Captain J. Croker), who was killed, and who was as fine a fellow as ever stepped, was not mentioned;* and others who behaved very unlike him got puffed, as did Sir G. Brown and the Generals of Division, who deserved about as much credit as you did at Norwich. The whole system, my dear Anthony, is purely rotten, and nothing else. I am in hopes that I may live yet to see one other good fight, well commanded, and where those who do . the work shall get the credit   The British Government is certainly a pleasant Government to serve, and always so handsome and rapid with their rewards: by God, they would sicken almost any-one, let alone such an intemperate one as I am. My best love to Charlotte and the girls.

"Nothing will occur before August on our side, and then, I suppose, the same sort of thing again.

"Ever, my dear Anthony,
"Yours affectionately,
"C. A. W."

"I am really and truly sorry for poor Caledon." (Who had recently died.)

* This is a mistake; Captain Croker was mentioned.

July 23rd.—Bricks for a new oven came up from Balaclava. Last night there were two heavy affairs between the French and Russians, one on the right, to seaward of the Malakoff and Mamelon, and one on the left, at the Bastion Centrale. Very heavy shelling, but we were left perfectly quiet.*

On my return to-day from Headquarters with Percy Herbert, agreed to go with him to the French Right Attack, from the Mamelon to the advance; some grape, round shot, and rifle balls flew over us, but the shooting was very moderate. The heat was most oppressive.

The French have certainly done a great deal since the 18th June, in advancing towards the Malakoff and Little Redan. The more I see of the attack the more convinced am I of the folly of attacking a place that we could not properly invest. However, I am always met with a host of absurd objections, proving—if anything—that perseverance in error is better than beginning again.

July 24th.—To-day has been distressingly hot, and I gladly bring this volume to a close.

I am in very good health.

July 29th (*Sunday*).—I finished the last volume on the 24th, and, from idleness, have neglected to write in this till to-day. The last mail brought out the appointments to the Bath, and I see I am a Companion; much good may it do me.

To have withheld these honours until now, and to have given the great dissatisfaction that the Ministry

* This was generally the case at the close of the siege. Todleben gives, as reason, that we were not so dangerous as the French.—W. H. R.

have given in their distribution, certainly required the united talent of a British Cabinet. If Alma, Balaclava, and Inkerman were the test of merit, why not have given the Bath after those battles? If the winter were to be the test, why exclude those who served through the winter? As it is, many cannot see why they are included; others, why they are excluded; and many are naturally and properly most annoyed.

In fact, the Government wanted to make more than it was worth of a bauble; and those who, like myself, think they fairly earned it in November last, do not thank them for their tardy gift; and those who have since gone through hardships and dangers think, with reason, that they are fully entitled to it, and are disgusted at its not being given to them.

I speak plainly. Our Government is a disgusting one to serve, and rewards men according to anything but merit and hard work.

Was introduced to the Duke of Newcastle at the Old Fort (Cathcart's Hill).

Rode out with Airey, who was accompanied by Colonel ——, who is a fool, if ever I saw one. What selections they have made in this Army! They are enough to frighten horses from their oats.

July 31*st.*—Yesterday I dined, as usual, with the General, and met the Duke of Newcastle, with whom I had a long talk concerning last winter, preparations for this winter, &c.

I think him, and always have thought him, an ill-used and much-abused man. Had he been well seconded here, I firmly believe all the outcry would have been saved; but I see now that this year we shall have very nearly the same result as last, unless

M

the Q.M.G. and Commissariat are made to do something else than dream.

I think the Duke one of the most reasonable and sensible men who have come out here, and I am sure that in his explanation in the House of Lords he took as much blame upon himself as he was entitled to.

August 3rd.—In general orders, I see that Assistant-Surgeon —— is dismissed the Service; and, as the proceedings of the Court of Enquiry* will be published, I shall be held up as a time-server and worshipper of the powers that be. This will certainly be rather a new character for me to appear in, never having been supposed to have the bump of veneration very strongly developed.

August 8th.—I dined yesterday with Wilbraham; and for the last five days, I own, have not written in this book, although during that time I have been put in orders to command the 2nd Brigade of the 2nd Division. I yesterday saw it for the first time, and a very fine brigade it unquestionably is, and I only hope I may live through the campaign to command it.

At seven yesterday morning I paraded with it, for the first time, to see General Markham distribute medals for distinguished conduct to two N.C.O.'s and a private of the 47th.

To-day I have quitted the old 4th Division, where I have been for nearly a year, without having a disagreeable word with a soul.

---

* Colonel Windham had been President of this Court of Enquiry, which made investigations as to the authorship of a letter published in the *Times*, bringing false charges against the Army Medical Department.

August 9th.—I attended the parade of the 47th this morning at half-past ten ; was introduced to the officers of that regiment, and had a little talk with the different sergeants and men that I came across.

I went yesterday with Markham and the Duke of Newcastle over the Right Attack, and got caught in a heavy shower and thoroughly ducked. A shell also fell in the trench about two or three yards from us, and I had just time to slip out of the way.

The firing last night was heavy ; they threw three shells up to the Old Fort (Cathcart's Hill), and seemed determined to hunt out the Duke of Newcastle.

August 10th.—Dined early, and rode down to the trenches at about half-past seven. Lieutenant-Colonel Cuddy,* 55th, commanded in the advance ; heard a good character of him, and, from what I could see, he deserved it. Went over all the works, and then visited the Reserves, and established myself in my hut. No musketry, but increasing shell, shot, and grape from 9 p.m. till 2 a.m., when it slackened for an hour, and then went on till 4 a.m.

August 11th.—On visiting the advance this morning, I found that the casualties amounted to about twenty, four or five of whom were dead or dying. Captain Elton, 55th Regiment, was wounded.

Poor Coppinger, of the Commissariat, died to-day.

August 12th.—Went to church at eleven, and afterwards, with Markham,† to see the hospitals of the

---

* Killed at the assault on the Redan, September 8th, 1855.

† Lieutenant-General Markham had joined the Army from India, and had taken command of the 2nd Division, in succession to Sir John Pennefather.

Division. Early in the morning I was called upon by Sir William Eyre, who desired to have a talk with me upon Quartermaster-General's matters.

At 5 p.m. attended the funeral of poor Coppinger, as strong as a horse, and only twenty-eight, and yet taken off quickly by fever and diarrhœa. He came out with me in the *Harbinger.*

7.30 p.m.—General Markham came and told me the result of the conference at Headquarters.

It appears that 24,000 of the Russian Imperial Guard have arrived, and that a false attack upon our trenches, and a real one on the Tchernaya, are expected.

Sir Colin Campbell has gone to the Right Attack with the whole of his Division, and we are all ordered to be in readiness throughout the night, and to be under arms at 3 a.m. to-morrow.

This is all right, but I feel very uncertain whether this will be more than a false alarm, and for this reason : I do not see how 24,000 men will enable the Russians to force the attacking party. If they are able to do so, we cannot be warranted in besieging (as we call it) Sebastopol. However, let them come on. I shall be glad of it, for if we beat them (and we shall, please God), I think they will give up the defence.

Their real point is the Mamelon, and I cannot but think the French will hold it, in spite of all the Russians can do.

August 13*th.*—The whole Army of the Allies was under arms from 3 a.m. till daylight. The Russians did not move.

August 14*th.*—Heard that Sir R. Airey was very unwell.

August 15*th.*—Heard Airey was worse, and, from what was said to me, I think it possible that they will offer the post to me, if he is obliged to leave. If so, I shall take it; but I fear we are very much behind with everything.

Young Hardinge is ordered to England.

August 16*th.*—This morning Wilbraham came and told me to have the brigade in readiness to fall in, the Russians having attacked the line of the Tchernaya in force, somewhere near the Aqueduct Bridge at Tchorgoun, at about half-past eight.

The reports were somewhat contradictory, some saying the Russians were falling back, others that they were advancing in great force. Our Cavalry was all out on the plain, and our Artillery in places taking part in the fight.

The cannonade appears pretty smart.

5.30 p.m.—I have just heard that the Russians have been heavily repulsed, with a loss of upwards of 2000 men killed, probably an exaggeration. However, David Wood, who has been down into the plain (we—the Infantry—were all kept in readiness to turn out), says he thinks the enemy must have lost 6000 in killed and wounded.

Went, as General of the Right Attack, to the trenches, and was informed that a sortie might fairly be expected.

Went all round the advance, and saw that Colonel Hume (95th) had everything in place. On returning from the advance, received a despatch from Airey informing me that both attacks would open fire at daybreak. Settled everything on that head, and then went to my hut.

Some particulars of the battle of the Tchernaya are given in a letter to Mr. Hudson :—

"HEIGHTS ABOVE SEBASTOPOL,

"*August* 16*th*, 1855.

"MY DEAR ANTHONY,

"I am for the trenches to-night, and as I think it very likely the enemy will begin in the morning, I do not know what will be the result to me personally, so I take up my pen to write to you. I have written to Marianne, but of course not this sort of letter, as it would merely frighten her. The Russians are now descending in great force to the Tchernaya, and, as they are pushing on their waggons and heavy artillery, I do not doubt they mean business, and before long I expect we shall have a heavy fight. I should say they are from 30,000 to 40,000 men (visible), and, from all we can learn, they are in much greater force on the Belbek. Omar Pasha, I am sorry to say, is at Constantinople, for without him I do not rank the Turks very highly. We have, however, now on the Tchernaya :

Sardinians	10,000
Turks	20,000
French	20,000
English Cavalry	2,000
French Cavalry	4,000

And about 100 guns.

"If these men fight as they ought, the Russians cannot get across, and, for my part, I don't know that they would if they could, for we have fully 60,000 men up here. One thing is, however, clear, and that is, from some cause or another, ever since the flank march, the Russians have always taken the initiative, and may do so again.

"I have no expectation of anything serious occurring before the morning of the 18th, and I firmly believe, from the nature of the ground, that the Russians never will go down into the plain, unless they are 80,000 or 100,000 strong. If they come it will be a noble fight, and if we win it, which by God's help we will, it will be a crusher to the pride of the Autocrat. The English and French have 8000 sabres (effective) in the field, and the Turks and Sardinians 1000; so we ought to do something if once the Russky come into the plain.

"I hope my brigade may be there, as it is one of the finest in the Army, and 2500 real good Miniés are not to be sneezed at, supported and assisted by a good steady battery of 12-pounders; besides, my men led at Alma and Inkerman, and are fully convinced that they can lick the Russians, and they are, moreover, healthy and cheerful. If the Russians really make an advance into the plain (which I doubt), it will unquestionably bring matters to a crisis, a consummation devoutly to be wished. In fact, although the affair will, I fear, be bloody, yet, should the Philistines come down into the plain to give us battle, I do hope the ' Lord will deliver them into our hands,' and that we shall make a better use of our advantage than we did at Alma. I hear we intend opening our batteries this afternoon, but doubt the truth of the report; but as I do not close this until my return to-morrow morning from the trenches, I may have many things to add. I have just heard that the Russians have left 2000 dead and wounded about Tchorgoun ; if so, the Sardinians and French must have done well."

August 17th.—In the trenches all day. The batteries opened fire at daybreak, and, for a quarter of an hour at least, the Russians made no reply; after that they kept it up well for about two hours, and occasioned us much loss.

On my return to camp I found that Captain Hammet, R.N., had been killed; poor little Dennis (of the Buffs), who was with me in the Right Attack, mortally wounded by a shell (both legs and one arm shot away); together with fifty-eight others killed and wounded. This does not include Artillery, Sappers, or Sailors. We had five guns disabled, the Left Attack many more — twelve, I believe. Oldfield * was killed on the Left, and Henry † lost his arm.

The continuation of Colonel Windham's letter to Mr. Hudson follows:—

"10 *p.m., August 17th,* 1855.

" I have just returned from a twenty-four hours' bout in the trenches. Our batteries opened this morning at daylight, at the request of the French; our loss in the Right Attack was fifty killed and wounded, and on the Left I should think about half. I was the General of the Right, and am very tired.

"I hear the battle of yesterday was much more than was at first thought. Report here says that the Grand Duke Constantine was present. Gorchakoff commanded the reserve, Liprandi one of the wings, and General Reid the other; this latter was killed, and we have all his plans and papers. The Russians lost full 5000 men, and were really and truly hand-

---

* Captain Anthony Oldfield, R.A., who had frequently distinguished himself during the siege.

† Brevet-Major C. S. Henry, R.A.

somely licked; but then again they, as usual, were not followed up. There was our Cavalry all drawn up in rear, and yet nothing done. I am so tired that I will not finish this to-night."

August 18th.—This morning at daylight, though after a bad night's rest, I rose and started with Roger Swire* for the Tchernaya. I see plainly that the fight was a severe one, and the Russian loss heavy. Returned home quickly, as the battle-field was decidedly unpleasant. I saw at least a thousand bodies at the *Tête-de-ponts.*

I understand that the Sardinians gave a good account of the enemy, who were fresh troops from Warsaw.

On my return, rode to see Eyre concerning his bakery for the 3rd Division. I saw General Simpson, who told me that he thought the Russians would again try the Tchernaya, as their orders from St. Petersburg were most positive. I cannot see why they attacked it before, still less do I see why they should again. It appears to be merely playing our game.

I hear the garrison of Sebastopol is much demoralised, and believe it; otherwise, why did not they sally, as directed, on the morning of the 16th? The French may do something soon at the Malakoff, as we help them by keeping under the fire from the Redan.

August 19th.—General Markham still very unwell, though somewhat better. Up to 7 p.m. I heard no account of poor young Dennis's death. He was with me in the trenches on the night of the 16th; the day following he, unfortunately, would not take the advice

* Lieutenant in the 17th Regiment, and A.D.C. to General Windham.

of a sapper as to the safety of the place he was in, nor take warning from one shell that lit and burst near him, but persisted in eating his breakfast in the same place, when a second shell came and broke both his thighs and one arm. Yet he is still alive, though dying.

August 20*th.*—Markham, I am glad to say, is looking better, and when I spoke to him this morning, was as fresh again as yesterday.

August 21*st* (1.30 *a.m.*).—Thesiger has just come in to let me know that the brigade must be under arms at 3 o'clock, as a row is expected.

Our information lately has been better, and so it may on this occasion prove correct. Should it be so, I only pray that God may give us a complete and glorious victory, should the enemy come out in force, and that our being in a state of preparation may enable us to deal him a severe blow.

God grant that "Crapaud" and ourselves may do it well, and that the Russians may catch it even hotter than they did in the Tchernaya.

August 22*nd.*—In the evening, whilst at dinner, a round shot came through Markham's stable and killed King's horse. Went down to the trenches at 7.30 p.m. After going all round and through the advance, and having been very nearly caught by a shell, I returned to my old quarters, the hut; and had not been long there before a telegraphic message came to order me to throw out sentries about the white rifle-pits, and to take special care that the Russians did not turn the left of the French Right Attack.

I went down and did so. Tyler, of the 62nd, is active, and, with practice, will make a good trenchman.

August 23rd.—Musketry sharp at 4 a.m., as I went round the advance; but there was no attack, and I am glad of it, though I think Tyler would have done very well.

August 24th.—Forwarded the Field Officer's report, and am sorry to see that the casualties amounted to seven killed and thirty wounded.

Markham informed me that a severe attack was expected on the Tchernaya, and that if it were unsuccessful, the enemy was expected to withdraw altogether. *Tant mieux*, say I ; I only hope he will get a good thrashing, as he did on the 16th.

August 25th.—No attack from the enemy, but we are still ordered to be on the look-out; and so thoroughly convinced are the people at Head-quarters that something serious will occur on the right, that Sir C. Campbell and his Highlanders are to be sent to Balaclava.

Poor young Dennis is still alive.

August 26th.—Went to church, and walked after-wards with Bentinck and visited him in his cave.* I should be grievously sorry to see us make peace now, unless the Russians consented to terms that really proved us to be victorious. If we carry on now we must before next spring bring them to their senses, no matter what the size of their Army may be.

---

* This was a very curious and comfortable excavation, close to Cathcart's Hill.—W. H. R.

Heard to-day that the 6th Parallel was opened to aid the French. This is the only reason that could be given for such an absurdity; for, as regards our attack, it is as useful as the fifth wheel to a coach, and will cost us many men. The enemy appear to be working very hard on the north side, and at the bridge. What means the latter? Is it for retreat, or advance, or both? I cannot help thinking it looks like a preparation to withdraw, and I sincerely hope it may be so, for I am convinced we do not shine as besiegers.

Heard to-day that poor Torrens had died in Paris. Poor fellow! I am very sorry for it. I suppose it was from the effects of his dangerous wound at Inkerman.

August 27th.—An investiture of the Bath took place at Headquarters. I did not go, as I was ordered to remain in camp in readiness to turn out, should the Division be wanted. No French officers were decorated, which I consider a great mistake.

The Russians finished and opened the bridge across the harbour, and I expect that as soon as the moon wanes we shall find out what they intend doing.

August 28th.—Intended to ride to Balaclava, but found that the other Brigadier had gone. As General Markham does not wish us both to be absent for any length of time I curtailed my ride, and merely looked over the heights to the right, then on to Inkerman, and the Light Division look-out.

Heard yesterday from Howard, of the 20th, that three spies had been executed by the French.

Owing to the Highland Brigade having gone to Balaclava, duty falls very heavily upon our men.

The worst of it is that no arrivals ever seem to do more than make good our losses. The 56th have joined us in this attack.

A letter to Mr. Greville, written on the following day, fills a gap in the Diary :—

> " HEIGHTS ABOVE SEBASTOPOL,
> "*August 28th*, 1855.

" Many thanks for your letter of the 6th. I agree to almost all you say, but I think you underrate the losses and difficulties of the Russians. We have all been continually confined to camp, expecting daily that some important move will be made by the enemy, either on our trenches or our right.

" For my part, I believe the much talked of attack that *is to be* was begun and ended on the 16th August. The Russians advanced very firmly on that day, but they got a severe thrashing, and, from what I saw, I cannot put down their loss at less than 5000 men, which, I think, is more than they would lose for the mere purpose of reconnoitring. However, the impression here is that they will attack us again somewhere, and, if that fails, cut off for good.

" They have finished the bridge across the harbour, which of course gives them great facility of bringing troops into the town ; and they have also been working immensely hard on the north side in throwing up defensive works, which looks as if they meant to use the bridge in decreasing, and not increasing, their garrison. A few days, I really think, must bring matters to something like a crisis.

" We cannot go on throwing away life and time much longer in the way we have done.

"The last three times I have gone as General to the
trenches I have lost 33, 27, and 97 men; in fact, we
lose in casualties upwards of 250 men in a week.
The attack with which I am connected is the largest
and, I believe, the most dangerous; but they lose men
in the left one too.

"The moon is now at the full, and I do not expect
an 'hooroosh' at us until that is passed; but as soon as
we come to the dark nights, I fancy the enemy will
have a try. If they do not they will have made their
minds up to abandon the south side, and will probably
look to peace, for I am convinced that their loss during
the winter will be awful, and ours ought not to be so;
although, from the carelessness and want of method
of our people in authority, I dread it beyond measure.
Pray do not think that I wish to cast dirt at others, but
I assure you there is a slackness and a constant looking
to home for all the common necessaries, that makes
me dread the passing the winter here. In the first
place, they put faith in the railway—a perfect absurdity;
then, again, in the 'Army Works Corps,' not much
better; and, lastly, in the Land Transport Corps—
a corps as ill managed and as badly started as anything can well be. I do not say we shall be as badly
off as last winter. Our men themselves are better,
as are our regimental officers, but still I think there
will be much misery, and much unnecessary misery,
from the want of method at Headquarters. I am
writing to you *in private*, but you may believe me when
I tell you —— is *a fool* plainly and simply, and all the
greater one from his having a certain quantity of
specious paper talent, that induces people at home to
believe that he knows what he is about.

"I have for some time had the command of a

brigade, but I suppose they will not make me a Brigadier-General, as it costs the Government a few shillings a year; and as a younger son, I am, of course, bound to be shot for nothing.

" Yours very truly,

" C. A. WINDHAM."

August 29th.—The French magazine in the Mamelon exploded last night, by which they lost forty killed and a hundred wounded. We lost five killed and fourteen wounded. The magazine contained twelve hundred barrels of powder.

The French have certainly been very unlucky, or very careless, with their magazines.

August 30th.—I have been waiting in pretty nearly all day, expecting a visit from the Field Officer of the trenches; I being the General of the Right Attack to-night, and a very unpleasant duty it unquestionably is.

Called on Markham, and begged that he would use his exertions with the Engineers to get them to make a banquette to the 5th Parallel, and put the whole parapet into a proper state, which it sadly wants.

Walked up to see Bentinck, who saw Bosquet yesterday, and received a true account of the French losses from him. They are certainly very great, at least 250 men a day, from death, wounds, and sickness.

I hope I shall get through this with safety and credit, and that God will spare me as he has often done before.

I am free to admit that I have no desire to be attacked in the trenches where no generalship can be exhibited, and where the confusion is such that you are as likely to be shot by friend as foe.

The French are certainly getting very near the Malakoff ditch, and if they ever mean storming, will do so in a few days.

August 31st.—I came off duty at six this morning. Passed a most unpleasant night, when in my hut, from a superabundance of fleas.

At about 11.30 p.m., the moon being very bright, about fifteen or twenty Russians attacked the working-party in front of the 5th Parallel. The advanced sentries ran in without a moment's hesitation, and the working-party ran away, leaving everything behind them, which allowed the Russians to upset all that had been done. A sharp skirmish then took place between the —th and —th and a party of the enemy, in which the Russians were ultimately driven back. We lost some twenty-three men, four of whom were officers; Lieutenant Preston was killed on the spot.

I was not present, nor did I hear anything until it was all over, but it appears to have been a bad business. Had our sentries behaved well, there would probably have been no fight.

September 1st, 1855.—Received the Field Officer's report, and am sorry to see by it that the casualties on the night of the 30th amounted to fifty-nine.

Rode to Headquarters, and saw General Barnard about the transport arrangements for the winter, and also spoke to him about the 5th Parallel.

He wished me to go to General Simpson, which I did, and told him what I thought of it in plain and strong language. He referred me to Colonel Chapman, with whom I had a long talk.   He admitted its being very incomplete, and promised to apply for fifty additional miners, and to do his best to complete it.

After Chapman I saw Bentinck, and advised him to apply for 12,000 saplings to hut the 4th Division, as I am convinced no number of huts will arrive for the troops before winter is upon us.

Hear that was a more ruinous business last night than the night before.   Captain Fraser, of the 95th, killed ; the Adjutant of the 30th since dead ; and an officer of the Buffs killed ; besides several men killed, and some taken prisoners.

September 2nd (Sunday).—The anniversary of old Cromwell's death, and of the "crowning mercy of Worcester."   I have always fancied this day an historical one as regards England, and, therefore, have fully expected an attack.

Went to church at 11.

After dinner I received a "confidential" letter from General Barnard to General Markham, announcing an intended attack in great force by the Russians to-morrow upon the Turks at or near Baidar, the French at the Tchernaya, and ourselves in the trenches. Owing to the numbers being specified, and the places marked, it looks like business, and we are all ordered to be in readiness.   Yet I can hardly think the enemy can make a successful move upon so extended a line. Surely, if he makes the reverse, we can turn it to some profit.

I hope that we may be given the victory, as I am convinced that if the Russians fail they will abandon Sebastopol altogether, and will be more likely to make

N

peace than if we took the Malakoff and the Redan without their having this last throw of the dice.

Gave Bentinck a calculation of the number of saplings requisite to hut his Division.

Went round the hospitals with Markham, who told me I was to take his place upon a Board at 11 a.m. to-morrow, in connection with Soyer* and his soup. Heard to-day that poor young Dennis was dead.

September 3rd.—Sat at a Board as Markham's representative, in the First Division Camp, to take into consideration a letter from Lord Panmure relative to the soldiers having some hot soup before going on and when coming off duty in the trenches.

In one respect it was a most pleasant Board, as M. Soyer gave us a most excellent luncheon, of which General Eyre partook most heartily, although he disapproved of the principle of Soyer's cooking, &c.

Another order from Headquarters about being prepared for the enemy, but no enemy came.

September 4th.—Rode to Headquarters, and saw the Quartermaster-General relative to getting poles for the 62nd to hut themselves. He consented, and I rode on to Balaclava to arrange for their being sent up to camp with as little delay as possible. Found a great deal of shot and shell still coming ashore and going up to the front; so I expect to hear of our opening again, and then, I suppose, we shall assault.

At dinner an order came to hold ourselves in readiness.

* The French cook who came to teach our men how to prepare their food, and did some good. He published his experiences under the title, *A Culinary Campaign.*—W. H. R.

September 5th.—Got up to-day before daylight, and, to my surprise, the French Left Attack opened fire at sunrise with severity, aided very slightly by our batteries and their own right.

I don't think I ever saw anything more beautiful than the commencement. The morning was clear and lovely; from some condition of the atmosphere, the smoke did not disperse.

The flashes of the guns and the ships at sea could plainly be seen under a curtain of smoke; and the town, too, was brightly lighted up by the just rising sun. I never saw anything so perfect. None of the other bombardments were half so beautiful to look at.

Heard that Anderson,* of the 31st, was killed last night at that beastly sap, and a great many men hit, in trying to hold the rifle-pit in front of our right. Captain Rowlands, of the 41st, with twelve men, got into it easily enough; but seeing himself about to be surrounded by the Russians, and being heavily shelled by the Malakoff, he retired again to the trenches.

We lose about twenty men a night in this absurd business, which, if the Malakoff were taken, would be ours at once, and which cannot be held at all until the Malakoff is taken.

Rode to Headquarters, and called on Chapman on my way back. Heard from him what was intended to-night. In three or four hours I shall be in the trenches; and I thought of writing to Pem, knowing it to be a service of danger, but I shall not—it would only frighten her if I were not hurt, and do her no good if I were.

A long conference to-day at Headquarters: General Pelissier, Omar Pasha, Sir E. Lyons, and Simpson.

* Captain Charles Anderson, 31st Regiment, Assistant Engineer.

The bombardment has been continued by the French all day, but ·not very spiritedly; it is now half-past three o'clock.

At 5 p.m. Charles Woodford came and had a long talk with me; and from what he and the Engineers told me, I directed Lieutenant-Colonel Hancock,* of the 97th, the Field Officer of the trenches, to post his men for the protection of the sap, and of the right of the 5th Parallel.

Left for the trenches at 6.20 p.m.

September 6th.—The posting of the sentries and the sap both got on very well. The Engineers reported most favourably of the whole proceedings.

We had a quiet night, whether owing to the arrangement of the sentries, or to the previous bombardment, I don't know. One thing is certain, the sap progressed well, and the working-party only had two men very slightly wounded.

The whole casualties during the night did not exceed ten.

During the greater part of the night we were illumined by a Russian ship, set on fire by the Allies.

Have been employed for some time during the day in explaining to Colonel Daniell the nature of the ground where the right sap now is—in front of our right. Buckley, and afterwards Scarlett, came to ask me how the sentries were to be posted, they then being on their way to the trenches. I then found that Lewis was the General of the Right Attack, and not Daniell, so my plans and lecture have been thrown away for to-night.

* Lieutenant-Colonel the Honourable H. R. Hancock, killed three days later at the assault on the Redan.

September 7th.—Saw Lewis on his return from the trenches, at 6 a.m. He told me that they had had a bad night of it, and that poor Buckley* was killed.

The batteries kept up a tremendous fire all night, and to-day they are doing the same. A conference is being held at Headquarters, which, I suppose, will receive the final intentions of the Allied Commanders.

If my brigade is ordered to lead the assault against the Redan, it is a hundred to one that I am killed ; but better far die so than get ignominiously hit in the trenches.

At one time to-day the firing was quite tremendous ; at other times they have slackened or nearly ceased.

Erecting my stable hut, which, with a wall outside my house, will make, I think, a good job of it.

At ·about half-past ten I was sent for by General Markham, and I was informed I was to lead the storming-party against the Redan to-morrow.

I look upon the attack as certain to fail, unless the Russians give way as soon as the French have got the Malakoff. We know nothing of the obstacles we have to meet with, and all we do know is that there is a very deep ditch, over which we must get somehow or other.

God's will be done. I pity poor dear Pem, and deeply regret the prospect of not seeing her and dear little W—— again. I must, however, do my duty, and do my best ; and hope that God will have mercy upon my many sins, and have pity on me and my children, and preserve my poor dear wife to take care of them.

* Captain D. F. B. Buckley, Scots Fusilier Guards.

Asked the Duke of Newcastle to interest himself, on behalf of dear Pem and the children, with the Queen, which in the kindest way he promised me to do.

I like that man.   He is honest, kind-hearted, and sharp-sighted.

Before entering into Colonel Windham's account of the storming of the Redan and of his proceedings on that occasion, it may be well to remind the reader that Colonel Windham was not responsible in any way for the arrangements made.

Sir James Simpson, the British Commander-in-Chief, entrusted the command of our troops which were to form the assaulting force to Lieutenant-Generals Codrington and Markham.

It will be seen from the detailed account of the assault, written by Windham for his children, that he was not told that he was to lead the storming-party of the 2nd Division, until all the arrangements had been made.

Foreseeing a probable disaster, Windham protested strongly against the narrow front (20 files only) on which the storming-party was to advance.

His protests were, however, unavailing, and he retired to make all the arrangement of his affairs that was possible, fully expecting to fall in the assault, but determined (in his own words) to do his duty as a Christian and a soldier to the last breath.

Among other letters written before the assault was the following, to his wife :—

> "CAMP, 2ND DIVISION,
>
> "HEIGHTS ABOVE SEBASTOPOL,
>
> "*September 7th,* 1855.

"This may possibly, ay, and probably will, be the last letter you will ever receive from me. Your last only reached me this day, enclosing dear little W——'s drawings 'to please Papa' (God in His mercy bless him!), and also a kind scrap from dear ——, and my oldest and best friend, Anthony.

"It is now late, and I am ordered to-morrow to lead the storming-party of the 2nd Division against the Redan, an operation, my dear, of great difficulty and great danger. I shall probably fall, but I have spoken to that kind-hearted man, the Duke of Newcastle, who is now here, and asked him to interest himself for you and the children, should such be the case.

"That I may return to see you all again is my most earnest prayer, but should I not, I hope God Almighty will, in His mercy, give me a clear head and resolute heart to do my duty as a Christian and a soldier to the last breath. Give my love to all your brothers and sisters, as well as to mine, and my blessings, dearest, upon you and the children. May they be a happiness and comfort to you, and may we all meet together in the world to come.

"No soldier ought to marry—the ties of this world ought not to have so strong a hold on him. I have left this letter in the hands of Mr. Baudiere (son of the Vicar of St. Mary's). I shall read prayers with him to-night, and hope to go to-morrow to the assault with a light and cheerful heart, and God grant we may succeed.   Love to Guy and Charlotte.

"Yours, my dearest Pem, most truly,

"and your affectionate husband,

"C. A. W."

"The Duke of N—— promised to make a personal request to the Queen in your behalf, should I fall —most kind—and the Queen will, I think, help you and the children, in consideration of what I have done and shall do. This feeling has made me quite happy."

SECOND ASSAULT ON THE REDAN.

September 8th.—Awoke and rose this morning before six, having slept very well.   I dare not think of Marianne and that dear little boy W——, and my comfortable little home at Myton, as it unmans me quite.   But God help them, and by His mercy, for their sake, may I get through this day.

If the Russians stand an assault, I have no expectation of beating them, but quite the reverse; and yet, wonderful to say, with these opinions, I really do not feel nervous, and never slept better.

And now, my dear Pem, this journal I have ordered to be sent to you, provided I am never to write in it again.   It is written hurriedly, and in some places violently, but always honestly.

Mind, if I die, you must live for the boys, and you must get help from the Government.

Do this by properly applying for a pension. This application, made direct to the Queen, will, I am sure, succeed, as she is a kind-hearted woman.

Kiss the children for me, and remember me to the Somervilles, Hudsons, and Des Vœuxs.   And now, my dear, again God bless you ; I shall soon march down to the assault.

The following short account of the assault seems to have been written on the night of September 8th :—

The assault took place at one, and I went over the Parallel at the head of the 41st.   The Grenadiers followed me pretty well, but not in the best order.   I went straight at the ditch, and did all that man could do to get them into the centre of the battery, but it was no go.   I ran out into the middle of the battery with my sword over my head, but it was useless. They would stick to their gabions and to firing, and not come to the bayonet ; so, after holding on to it for near an hour, and having sent back Swire twice, a young officer, Lieutenant Young,* of the 19th, and Colonel Eman,† to tell Codrington that he *must* send me the supports *in some formation*, I went back myself and asked leave to have a fresh battalion.

This was granted, and I put myself at the head of the " Royals."   Whilst Codrington was considering whether he would let me go on or not, the whole attacking force fell back, leaving behind numbers of killed and wounded.

If I could have got the men of the storming-party to make a rush, I should have carried it ; but I never could.   They were all in disorder, and each looking out for himself.   The officers behaved well, and so did the men as individuals, but not collectively.

* Ensign W. W. Young, who was severely wounded.
† Lieutenant-Colonel J. Eman, C.B., 41st Regiment, killed.

Came back very hoarse. Poor Roger Swire is badly wounded.

Dined with David Wood, and after dinner was sent for to Headquarters, where I told General Simpson the same as I had told Codrington—that there was nothing to stop good troops, and that if the Highlanders, who were not tired and overworked in the trenches, were let at it, they would be sure to carry it.

September 9th.—The whole of last night loud reports were heard, and large fires blazing, and everything clearly prepared for abandoning the town.

This morning it was found evacuated, and so ends the memorable and bloody Siege of Sebastopol, the greatest ever known in ancient or modern times.

September 11th.—Early in the morning Barnard came and offered me the post of Commandant or Governor of that part of Sebastopol surrendered to the English. I was much surprised at this, seeing that the attack on the Redan had failed, and knowing that, with most men, success is the criterion of merit.

I accepted it most willingly, for certainly it is a great compliment.

God knows I did the best I could, and I believe the Army here think so; but after all, it is not pleasant to be a beaten cock.

A few more entries were made in the Diary, principally allusions to Windham's work as Governor, which was arduous and unpleasant

A letter to Mr. Greville, written a few days later, throws further light on the failure of the assault:—

> "DOCKYARD, SEBASTOPOL,
>
> "*September 14th,* 1855.

"This is the anniversary of our landing, and here I am, at last, resting myself in that town which I fully expected would have taken some time longer to have got into.

"And when you consider that two out of the three French attacks, and our one, all failed, you will probably agree with me in thinking we have, on the whole, been very lucky.

"'Except to assist the French,' by giving occupation to some thousand Russians, the attack on the Redan was thoroughly useless, as it is completely commanded by the Malakoff.* It was badly planned, and I firmly believe (from the fact of our men never having advanced a yard since the 18th of June) that, until a very few hours before the assault took place, it never was intended. That part of the above paragraph marked by inverted commas, was the reason given out here. Only look at it! To have been good for anything, the attack ought to have taken place at the same instant as the attack on the Malakoff, whereas it was ordered that none of the other attacks should be made until a *succés assuré* had taken place at the Tower. In other words, the other attacks did not take place until they were useless. I told all my Generals that I was convinced that, unless the Russians bolted on the loss of the

---

* The capture of the Redan would have caused the surrender of the bulk of the Russians, as they could not have used the bridge to the north side.—W. H. R.

Malakoff, we should never succeed. And why did I say this? Simply because I agree with Napoleon, that troops should not be exposed to grape for 300 yards. Under a severe fire it is impossible to *form men*, and as they had to get over a high parallel, they were perfectly sure to be broken at the very start. Men 'in formation' may hold it under fire with a fair start and good discipline, but, once broken, the thing is hopeless. The result was that I went straight at the battery, followed by a few Grenadiers and officers, crossed the ditch, and went through the third embrasure on the proper left, and found myself alone, or nearly so, in the battery.

" Hartnady, a Grenadier of the 41st, was the first over after me, wounded ; Kenealy, ditto, the second ; and Dan Mahoney the third, immediately shot through the head ; as was an officer of the 90th. I did all I could to get them on by advancing and cheering in my own person, by turning round, patting them on the back, telling them to look to their bayonets, &c., but it was useless. Those who had got between the parapet and screen were of many different regiments, unacquainted with me or each other, and could not be got on ; and I have heard since that their great stumbling-block was their conviction that the whole battery was 'mined.' It is odd, but nevertheless true, that their great fear of gunpowder was the cause of their halting directly over the magazine. There was a great deal of individual pluck, particularly in the officers, and many of the old soldiers behaved well ; but there was no 'united pluck,' and without that how can you act against numbers.

" . . . So, although I have been handsomely spoken of by both officers and men engaged, I suppose I shall meet with my Inkerman fate, and, after having borne the brunt and dangers of the day, be thanked by my inferiors, approved of by my conscience, and be un-rewarded. . . .

" I have been made Governor of the English portion of Sebastopol, and am therefore a sort of little Osten Sacken.

" The first thing I had to do was to clean out the hospitals, in which there were about 500 dead, and every species of dirt. I am sure I wish, with you, this war was over ; but if it continue, I do hope that we may have to act alone, and in a country where there is no electric wire, and under a man who is not obliged to wait every day for orders from home.

" The three Generals you mention are the best here, and the first* the best of the three. Markham's health, I am sorry to say, is too much broken, and Eyre's bad temper too intact.

" In fact, until the Home Government make up their minds to choose a proper person, without fear of the Army or the Press, we shall never get on as we ought to do. For my part, I do not dislike General Simpson ; he has been very kind to me ; but he is too old, and has no weight, and in fact does not 'command' the Army. It is lucky for —— that the town is taken, for his arrangements for the winter were so absurd that we must have come to a standstill.

" Sebastopol must have been one of the handsomest places in the world. It is now one heap of ruins. I cannot put down the Russian loss at the last bombard-ment and attack at less than 15 to 20 thousand men. The Allied Cavalry (10,000 sabres) and the Light Artillery ought ere this to have been at Eupatoria, or on the Alma, whereas we have not moved.

* Sir William Codrington.

"So now farewell; show my letters to whom you like, but do not, as an old friend, use them to my detriment. To you I write the naked truth, which of course ought not to be published until the world is good enough to hear it.

"Yours ever,

"C. A. WINDHAM."

A month later, General Simpson called on Windham for information required by Lord Panmure, the Secretary of State for War.

The *unofficial* and *official* letters to General Simpson merit attention, as does the private letter to Mr. Greville.

"*To General Simpson.*

"CAMP, SEBASTOPOL,

"*October* 13th, 1855.

"MY DEAR SIR,

"After our conversation this morning, I should like to place before you my opinions; but as to the propriety or impropriety of the attack on the Redan I shall remain silent, as also upon the details of the attack, and shall confine myself to that which came under my notice. The whole character of the fight at the Redan would have been changed had the leading party never stopped at the salient, but gone, without halting, at the second line of defence; and from the gallantry of their advance to the salient, who can say they would not have done this, had not their leaders been killed. Had they done so the fight would have been at the second line, not at the salient; and the supports would have arrived inside, instead of outside, the battery. I arrived after the Light Division, and attacked on their right. I went through the third embrasure (I think) on the proper left of the work, but was not followed by any numbers, as the men clung to the salient. This again would not have happened had we gone straight at the second line without halting. It is true that I (and others) tried to get the men out of the proper right face of the work (to which I had crossed from the left), without success; but, in justice to all parties, it should be remembered that, what with traverses and screens, the men were necessarily cut up into small bodies (to say nothing of being of different regiments), and a simultaneous rush was, therefore, almost impossible when once file firing began. Without a certain body of men, it was useless to attack the second line; but how get them out of these little chambers, in which they were necessarily separated into small parties? I have no hesitation in saying that the men I came across did hang back, but I do not say it was altogether from want of courage: *want of mutual support* was the great thing; this the intermixture of the regiments rendered difficult, and the construction of the battery almost impossible; it could have been avoided by a rapid and continued advance from the first, but could not be overcome. I stated ·at the time (and think so still by my subsequent observation), that one united battalion, thrown on the proper left face of the work, would have carried the second line, provided they could have kept clear of the men upon the salient; this I told Sir W. Codrington at the time, and I was then sanguine as to the complete success of such a move. But since I have cooled, and calmly looked at the battery, I am not sure that we could have held it; but we should, at any rate, have brought the question to a fair trial.

"Sir William waiting for a few minutes to see what the French were doing was the wisest plan of the two.   Had the Royals (the regiment I got from General Markham) run to the salient, I am positive it would only have added to the slaughter, as there would have been no means, under such a fire, of preventing them from intermingling with the others. The failure of our attack, particularly at such a moment, was very unlucky, but it does not follow that if renewed it would have succeeded; and it should be borne in mind that the French failed in all their attacks against the works open in the rear, and that the Russians, after their defeat at the Malakoff, turned greater weight on us.

"As to the ladders, they were long enough, and I cannot see what use Field Artillery could have been to us.   I have only now to request that you will not suppose for a moment that I attribute our failure to the Light Division men, as individuals. I only think that had their leaders not been killed, the men would probably have *gone* into the battery with a rush, instead of firing into it; and it would have remained to be proved whether or not we could have held it.   At any rate, we should, under these circumstances, have tried the question fairly.

"With regard to the belief held by the men as to the work being mined, I saw no explosion during the time I was there; but I think I should have, had we succeeded."

Letter to Mr. Charles Greville, enclosing a copy of the official letter to General Simpson :—

" SEBASTOPOL,

" *October* 15*th*, 1855.

" This is very nearly the letter I have to-day for-warded to General Simpson for Lord Panmure's perusal, and it contains my honest opinion. I declined saying anything as to the attack of the Redan being wise or unwise. I have all along been against it. The attack, if made anywhere, should have been made between the Karabelnaia Ravine and Malakoff, which would have aided the French more, and put us more within reach of one another; but no matter as to this. What I wish you to do is to stop any enquiry into the conduct of the troops. If any man ought to know what that conduct was, it is your humble servant; and yet, I assure you on my honour, if before a court, I could not bring home a case to anyone of my own knowledge. The regiments were so inter-mixed (and I had thirteen different regiments, or parts of them, in the scramble), the men strangers to me and one another, and to the officers who addressed them, that I am quite sure it would only create an immense deal of bad feeling, and do no atom of good. The country ought, in justice, to remember that we called on the men to attack a work that was perfect, and defended by more men than we could bring against it, to say nothing of the protection of distant batteries; and so they ought not to allow their national pride to come down too heavily upon the men who 'stood' probably better in the Redan than many would have done who complain of them.

o

" I much regret the strong attacks against General Simpson. They are not fair; he is by no means a bad man. . . . We all know he is not the 'personage' Lord Raglan was, that there is not for him, with the French, the same amount of 'prestige' that there was for the friend and secretary of 'Vilainton,' the man who had lost his arm at Mont St. Jean, and had gone through the wars of the Empire; all this is true, and it is also true that he cannot speak French nearly as well as Lord Raglan.

" I am told, but I know not if it is true, that the French strongly opposed our going to Eupatoria; if so, they have prevented the Russian Army from being cut to pieces. One of the great dislikes I have always had to the attack on the south side has been the certainty that we should lose 10,000 men, and the equal certainty that we must afterwards go to the north before anything could really be done against the Russian Army.

" Des Salles has fallen back from the Belbek, and all idea of turning their left is abandoned. I always thought it would be. The authorities do not seem to have made up their minds where the Cavalry are to go, but the general opinion is to the Bosphorus.

" If this war lasts, everything will depend upon the early opening of the campaign before the enemy can receive his reinforcements. We ought to have six weeks start of him, and in that time crush him. But for this purpose everything should be prepared at Eupatoria, ready for a start the first fine weather; but I am afraid this will not be done. We shall be looking to the Russians retiring (which I think they will do) and to the diplomats.

" I would look to nothing but God and the sword,

and would smite them hip and thigh, from the rising to the setting of the sun.

" There is one good thing in rest, we shall be able to touch up our recruits a little ; and, had these roads not been going on, we should soon have had them tidy soldiers, and it must be admitted that the trenches have done them much harm.

"Only think of my having a Division ! As to the newspapers, they seem to make me the greatest hero that ever was, which is purely and simply ridiculous. I am too old, however, to have my head turned by that sort of nonsense, and am well aware that this day fortnight I might be just as much in their black books as I am the reverse now. I have no belief in the Russians attacking us again, notwithstanding the advice from Berlin. I think they can hardly be so foolish ; yet fighting is, of all things, the most uncertain.

" Pray do no harm with my letters, particularly this one, and do what you can to stop the 'nagging' the Army and 'hitting it in the raw.' When we meet the Russians in the open field I hope to see a different account of old ' Brickdust.'

"Yours very truly,

"C. A. WINDHAM."

Official report to Lieutenant-General James Simpson, Commander-in-Chief in the Crimea :—

" SEBASTOPOL,

" *October* 15*th*, 1855.

" SIR,

" I have the honour to inform you that I have no remark to make upon the first portion of Lord Panmure's despatch.

"The conduct of the troops in the attack upon the Redan, on the 8th September, was good in their advance to the salient; after the unfortunate halt there, it was characterised by hesitation and want of unity of purpose, which I attribute (1) to the regiments becoming intermingled; (2) to the construction of the battery (the face being divided into small chambers); (3) the difficulty of getting any simultaneous movement; and (4) the dread of the work being mined.

"The leading Division having lost its leaders and not going at once to the second line, but commencing firing, is enough to account for our want of success.

"Had there been no halt until we arrived at the second line, my party and the supports would have 'brought up' inside, instead of outside, the battery.

"Whether we could have held the work is a matter of doubt; at the moment I thought we could, but upon reflection, and considering the fact of our Allies having failed against all works open in the rear, I am not so confident as to the correctness of my first opinion.

"At the time I thought that an entire battalion thrown over the proper left face of the work, clear of our men then fighting, would have carried the second line, and I think so still.

"But had the 'Royals' (which regiment was granted me for this purpose) joined the men at the salient (and who can say they would not have done so), their attack would only have added to our losses.

"I saw no reason to complain of the length of the ladders.

"I do not see how Field Artillery could have been brought advantageously into play. I saw artillerymen present for the purpose of spiking the guns.

"I beg to enclose a letter from Captain Rowlands,

of the 41st, who led the Grenadiers of that regiment on the 8th September, touching the men's opinion as to the work being mined.

" I saw no explosions during the fight, but, from what was observed next day, I think it fortunate that no second attack was made, as I should probably have seen many.

" I enclose a sketch of the work, and, for the information of Lord Panmure, wish to say that what I call the second line of defence was simply a ditch, perfectly easy to pass over both ways, in which the Russians were placed, their heads only being visible.

" I have the honour to be, Sir,

" Your obedient humble servant,

"C. A. WINDHAM,

"Major-General Commanding 4th Division."

A letter to Mr. Charles Greville, written a few days later, gives some interesting particulars of the assault :—

" CAMP, SEBASTOPOL,

" *20th October,* 1855.

" Many thanks for your two last letters : both reached me yesterday. What a curious thing is a popular cry ! If my head was inclined to be turned I might fancy myself a hero ; but, after all, I really did but little. Praise ought only to be given to me for trying to remedy an error, and quickly seeing the only way it could be done with any chance of success. Not liking to set a bad example by retiring in my own person, I sent four times to let them know what I wanted, which was, ' Soldiers in formation and under obedience.' No number of scattered men joining the rear of an already disjointed lot has any chance of moving it, or restoring order; as well might you hope, by doubling the rear of a riotous mob, to make them more rational in front. By the enclosed sketch you will see that our men, having got into those little chambers numbered 1, 2, 3, &c., were by necessity cut up into small parties; and as the Russians held in force the proper right and the four flanking guns, the only thing to do was to get our men out of that position and take the second line—an easily-traversed ditch— by a dash, which would have induced all followers to come into the battery, instead of into the salient.

"This I found impossible. I tried it three times. Many of the men could not see me, others were busy firing; two only came out with me when I went forward, and took a shot, by my order, at a Russian officer, where I have put a cross. But in spite of the most approved theatrical attitudes, and *strong* language, I could never succeed in getting attended to, the more so as I found myself with the Light Division (who were the leaders), and not one man in fifty knew me. All this time, when I was at work in the chambers and in the battery, the men on the salient kept up firing at the Russian heads visible in the second line, and at the re-entering angle upon the proper right. Having failed, I immediately sent for support, and, as the men looked shaky, called upon them to hold on to what they had got: that supports were coming; and some officer (very wisely) had the 'advance' sounded lustily on the outside by a bugler of the 62nd. I kept eagerly watching for some *number of formed men with officers*, that I might lead them over the ditch of the second line. The guns of the whole battery, bar the flank ones, had been abandoned, and therefore it is probable that, with a battalion of men in order, I should have taken the second line. I *might* have held it, especially if the enemy had contented himself with firing at us from the third line until our working-party had secured us. I say I *might*, but I do not think I could, unless—which is possible— the Russians should have bolted upon seeing both Redan and Malakoff lost. As soon as ever the fresh battalion had mounted the parapet on the proper left, the men on the salient, outside the ditch, would have joined their comrades, and we should have had a hell of a rough-and-tumble fight before we had given way; for I much question if the enemy would have held the battery on the proper right (four guns) with my troops in possession of the second line, and if they had not, the men in the trenches would have come out much more freely. It was these guns that helped to cut us up so in the advance, together with the mass of riflemen placed there.

"You will probably now understand why I wanted *soldiers in formation.* It was because I wanted to make a move, and, by *attraction*, obtain what I could not get by *propulsion;* that is to say, to lead the men out of the chambers and off the salient and parapet into the second line, thereby bringing the taking and holding of the battery to a fair trial.

"As to the town, except the store-houses in the dockyard, everything is in ruins (but Fort Nicholas). The inhabitants consisted of some used-up soldiers, and the hospitals, houses, and streets were full of dead bodies.

"Gortchakoff's despatch described very correctly the state of the town. If the Russians can hold on through the winter (why they should try to do so is to me marvellous), it will come to what I told you, namely, a loss on our part of 10,000 men to get us out of our difficulties; for, if the Russians can feed themselves, nothing will drive them out so easily as an Army acting from the Eupatoria coast. I believe the weather difficulty could be yet overcome; and a battle fought on the head waters of the river running westward, or anywhere near Simpheropol, if decisive, would seal the fate of the Crimea. Long before the assault, I told the Duke of Newcastle that the first step to take, *previous* to attacking the south side, was to have Horse Artillery, Cavalry, and every spare thing in the shape of transport and provisions sent to Eupatoria, so as to be ready to follow up success, if such were granted us—and it will now have to come to this: and it is on this account that I would, if possible, have all the English Cavalry, &c., that could be spared sent there now, and not to the Bosphorus, that they might be ready in the spring to act before the Russian reinforcements could arrive. If this had been done in connection with the Turks, and 55,000 Infantry had been collected, it would have settled Russky's hash, because had he denuded this part of troops, those left here of us would have taken the north shore, and our object would have been gained.

"The only Russian woman I have seen is a one-eyed one of fifty (used as cook at Headquarters), since the 8th of September.

"Yours very truly,

"C. A. WINDHAM."

It has been decided to include in this book the following paper, although it was not written for publication, as the discussions anticipated by General Windham have arisen recently :—

"ACCOUNT OF THE ATTACK ON THE REDAN

"ON THE 8TH SEPTEMBER, 1855.

(Written in 1857.)

"As I think it quite possible that hereafter discussions may arise as to the attack on the Redan on the 8th of September, 1855, I am determined to write a short account of the matter, for the satisfaction of my children ; in this account, which is not meant for publication, I will, as far as I am able, speak the whole truth, and only hope that I may not state anything unfair of any party concerned.

"On the afternoon of the 7th of September, 1855, I was sent for to Markham's hut, and informed by him that my brigade would furnish the storming party of the 2nd Division; and that the attack was to take place the next day at twelve o'clock, provided the French met with success at the Malakoff.

"The attacking-party told off for the Redan was as follows :

1.	200 men .	.	Covering-party.
2.	320 „ .	.	Scaling-ladder-party.
3.	1000 „ .	.	Storming-party.
4.	400 „ .	.	Working-party.

"This force was to be drawn equally from the Light and 2nd Divisions. The first and second parties were to go abreast, and the storming-party was to toss up which should lead (to prevent jealousy, I suppose). I accordingly tossed up with Colonel Unett, who on that day was in temporary command of Shirley's Brigade, owing to his (S.'s) absence.

"Percy Herbert flung up a Napoleon; I lost the toss, and Unett chose the lead.

"I now think it right to state, as nearly as I can, my impressions at the time as to the ultimate fate of the attack. There were a good many officers present; amongst others, Brigadier-General Warren, Colonel Mauleverer, Colonel P. Herbert, Colonel Wilbraham, and Markham himself. Unett, as soon as he had chosen the lead, went out of the hut.*

"Having heard that the ditch was revetted, and twenty-five feet deep, I honestly stated that I did not see how it was possible to carry the work in the way we were going to attack it. Our ladders were reported to us as being twenty-four feet long, and I naturally asked how it was possible to pass over any number of men with rapidity with such short ladders.

"I also strongly objected to going out twenty file abreast from one given point, stating that I felt sure the rear of the column never would, or could, keep up; that the proper way to attack was to rush from the whole length of the 5th Parallel, and then to be backed up by men in order from the rear.

"I also objected (after the experience of the 18th June) to there being no 'banquette,' stating that I felt sure some of the men really would hang upon the gabions and not be able to get over, whilst others would pretend to do so. To these objections I met but with one reply from Markham, and it was always to this effect: 'It is no use talking, Windham, all that

---

* He was mortally wounded in the assault.

is settled, and you must do it as directed.' I succeeded
in nothing but getting a promise of some tubs and
planks to form a ' banquette ' along that portion of the
5th Parallel from which we had to get. I was told
that Warren's. Brigade would support me, and I here
firmly state that I went to the attack looking upon
myself as immediately under *Markham*, and relying
upon the 2nd Division to support me. In proof of
this, I solemnly declare to having shaken hands with
Markham after my long discussion in opposition to
the proposed plan of attack, and said, 'Well, you
may depend upon my going into the battery, if I
keep upon my legs; but if I ever get to the second
line, *mind*, I will not quit it for the white buildings
until you or Warren come up.' Having retired to my
hut, I made my will, wrote my letters, &c., and sent
for the officers in command of the two regiments from
which the storming column was drawn, namely, the
41st and 62nd (Eman and Tyler).* Having given
them my directions, particularly as to the men not
fixing their bayonets (for fear of their tumbling on
to one another in the ditch) until they were absolutely
in the work, I lit my cigar, and passed my time as
usual until the evening, when I went with Swire, my
A.D.C., to Baudiere's hut, and had him read prayers to
us; after this I went to bed, and slept soundly till the
morning.

"I thought we were under arms a great deal too
soon—but that perhaps is a fault on the right side.
I remember the morning was both cold and windy. I
marched my party to the head of the Light Division
ravine, and there I saw Codrington, who asked me if

---

* Colonel Eman was killed, and Colonel Tyler severely wounded in the
assault.

I knew the details of the attack, to which I replied—Yes.

"I was on horseback, and rode down the front of the company of the 41st, and told them that although the service they were on was one of danger, that we should no doubt do it well and successfully. That I begged they would be cool and quiet, and *not fix their bayonets* until they were over the ditch of the Redan. That there would then be plenty of time for that, as the Light Division would be ahead of us, and that I wished to avoid accidents in descending the ladders. It was only after seeing Codrington that I found out Shirley had come back, which put me more out of joint as commanding the storming-party, and made me hold my tongue when in the trenches, and refer everyone to him for orders. I, however, took upon myself to see that Maude was all right with his ladders; and I sent back an order to Dr. Alexander, of the Light Division (without consulting Shirley), upon finding out that the Medical Officer at the Quarries had been there upwards of twenty-four hours, and had used up all his lint, bandages, &c., of which he then had none. This was about two hours before the attack.

"I had two men of the leading company of the 41st killed (one next to me) before the attack, and the Russians kept shelling us heavily; one portion of the shell that killed the right-hand man of the Grenadier company of the 41st next me, also struck Captain Hood, of the Buffs, in the stomach, and obliged him to withdraw.

" As soon as the flag was up I was ready, and ordered my men to follow me along the trench until I came to the proper place to cross. I then jumped over, and the first thing I did was to collar the man next me and make him unfix his bayonet; when I got up to the advanced sap (having my back to the Redan, and facing my own men), I observed some were inclined to make for the shelter of this sap, and I accordingly ordered Roger Swire to place himself there and prevent their entering it.

" I proceeded on to the Redan with the Grenadier company and Eman. Upon coming up to the work I diverged slightly to the right, to clear the Light Division, and went at once into the ditch, which, thank God, was not revetted for above six feet; and was the first man of the 2nd Division storming - party that crossed the ditch. I was accompanied by Privates Hartnady, Kenealy, and Mahoney—the rest of the company I thought slow, and I called to them loudly to hurry on; as soon as I got a dozen or fifteen men over, I turned and entered the work at the second or third embrasure to the right, the first being on fire, and went straight into the middle of the work. *I was followed by no one, to the best of my belief.* I crossed the work, and went into the chambers upon the proper right face of it, and patted many of the men upon the back, and tried to get them out of both the openings towards the second line—it was of no use: I was never followed but by one man of the 88th, and two men of the Rifles. The man of the 88th came out most gallantly, and was abreast of

me ; the first rifleman also came out well, and it was to
these two men, who unfortunately would fire and not
charge, that I said, " Well, if you will fire, shoot that
(a strong expletive)," pointing to a Russian officer, who
was kicking away the gabions in his front to give his
men a good shot at us.   Finding, notwithstanding my
cheering and doing the theatrical, that these three men
were all that came, we fell back ; and, on my getting
upon the parapet, the men were nearly taking a panic.
I accordingly ran upon the top of it (amongst their
muskets), and assured them that there was no cause for
fear, and implored them not to fall back ; the men on
the salient gave me a hearty cheer, and all seemed
right.   I then sent Roger Swire back for the supports
(having recrossed the ditch), and returned on to the
parapet of the Redan.   In a short time another panic
came on, and I thought they would all be off ; but I
shouted to them to stand firm—a bugler of the 62nd
sounded the advance, the men cheered, and all was
again quiet.   I now, after having hit a man of the 62nd
with my fist for firing through the burning embrasure,
tried my best to get the men away from the salient,
where they were crowded, along the proper left face
of the work ; but beyond a dozen it was no go.   I
accordingly crossed the ditch, and young Swire having
returned, I sent him back immediately to desire that
our batteries would keep up a heavy fire upon the
Redan, no matter whether they hit us or not.   I also
sent back another officer (I have heard it was Major
Rickman, of the 77th, but I cannot say from my own
knowledge that it was) to request support ; until this
time I had received only a few scattered men, and I
think it was about this time that a fair-sized party of
the 23rd came out, and also some riflemen, under

Captain Hammond* and Major Ryder. A sergeant of the Rifles would have been of great service to me, as he was active, cool, and brave; but he was killed whilst I had my hand upon his arm, being shot through his black belt, and the blood spurting quite out from his body.

"A sergeant and party of the 23rd also behaved tranquilly and well; and I cannot help thinking I might have succeeded in getting at this time fifty men to have followed me to the proper left of the work, had this sergeant not told me distinctly that the last words of Sir W. Codrington, on sending them out of the trenches, were, 'Mind and not go to the *right*.' The sergeant was so cool and collected that I could not but believe him, and replied, 'Well, I suppose he sees something there that I cannot see.' At this time a tremendous volley of grape and musket balls came, and certainly must have knocked over at least twelve or fifteen of the party, and the rest soon dispersed from the heavy fire. Having again been thwarted, I had nothing for it but to send again to hurry on the supports, requesting they might be sent in a mass, and some sort of order. This time I employed Lieutenant Young, of the 19th Foot, who was wounded. No numbers, however, came, and ammunition began to run short, and the men to get slack. I accordingly called Colonel Eman to me, and said, 'Now, Eman, you are a man of high rank; you ought to have some weight with the General, whoever he may be. Go and tell him, that if he cannot send or bring me some real support, and in some order, I would rather, *by God*, he sent me none.' I was angry.

* Captain Hammond was killed.

"Stones now began to be thrown, and the ground was thickly strewed with dead and wounded; but I still thought the fire at the Redan was by no means insupportable; and if I could only have got a fresh battalion over, at the proper re-entering angle, on the left of the work, I *felt* convinced I could get the second line. Seeing that Eman's message had apparently no effect, I at last turned round to a young officer, standing close to me, and asked him his name. He replied, as I understood, Graylock (it was Crealock). I then said to him, 'I have sent five times for support; the last man I sent was Eman. Now, bear witness that I am not in a funk (at which he smiled), but I will now go back myself, and try what I can do.'

"I accordingly called out to the man on the salient to hold on till I got up the support; and then, running back to the 5th Parallel, I saw Codrington standing in the trench. Without going from the top of the parallel, I said to him, 'If you will only send me a fresh battalion now, and help me out with it, I can carry the work.' His answer was, 'Come down, Windham, you'll only be killed there. Why, my good fellow, they won't go, and I have no number to send.' Seeing the trench filled with wounded and disheartened men, I immediately asked for Markham; and hearing he was in the Quarries, I ran across, a distance of fifty or sixty yards, and found he was not there, but at the old advance. I ran to him, and found him in company with Richard Wilbraham, Percy Herbert, young Thesiger, and King. The first thing I said to him was, 'Only give a battalion, and help me out with it, and I will carry the work at once.' He said, 'Can you? then take the Royals.' I asked

Wilbraham to order the batteries to keep a heavy fire upon the Redan, and immediately, without a second's delay (and I appeal to Markham's Staff on this point), I marched the Royals to the front. As soon as I got to Codrington I halted the regiment, jumped on to the parallel, spoke to the men, telling them to stick to me, and not mind the others now on the salient of the Redan ; and then, turning to Codrington, said, 'Now, sir, I am ready; give the word, and help me.' He pulled me down from the top of the parallel, and said, 'Come down, Windham, don't be in such a hurry; let me see what the French are about.' Having been stopped, I argued the case as quietly as I could. He (C.) asked me if I thought I was sure to succeed; if it were possible to get men out steadily under such a fire. I admitted the difficulties and uncertainties—I admitted that if I failed on the left the loss would, of course, be great. At this time Williams, of the Artillery, ran back from the Redan, and said to me, 'Sir, if you will only now come on, Major Maude says he will open out and let you through.' To this I offered all the opposition I could. I told Codrington that if the attacking-party once joined the men on the salient, it was all over ; and, beyond file firing and logs, you would get nothing; that the only thing to do was to keep clear of the other, and try the proper left of the work. At this time a panic seized the men at the Redan, and the day was lost. Upon reviewing my own conduct up to this point, I think very highly of it; and had I only replied to Codrington when he pulled me down from the top of the parallel, when at the head of the Royals, 'Well, sir, do as you like about the attack—I will rejoin the men at the salient,' I should have abandoned my

P

plan of attack on the proper left (the only thing to have been done), but I should have given my most bitter enemy no chance of saying one word against me.

"I have heard it said that I ought to have returned (and so I should in a minute or so, had not the repulse occurred); and people seem to insinuate that an exposed position at the 5th Parallel was a place of comparative comfort; but it was not so, nor did I seek it on that account.

"I was now desperately tired and hoarse, having been in great excitement and continued exertion for eight hours, but, after having assisted in stopping the men from abandoning the 5th Parallel, I strongly recommended Codrington to send to Simpson and ask him to attack again with the Highland Division, adding, 'I am, as you know, a married man with children, but having been three times into the work, and the old flag not being where it ought to be, I will volunteer to lead them and show them where they ought to go over.' I believe that orders were sent to the Highland Division, because I have heard Rokeby express his surprise at Sir Colin Campbell declining to attack *unless the orders were sent in writing.**

"No further attack being intended, and being hurt by a gabion and greatly fatigued, I asked Markham, as my brigade was reduced to nothing, to allow me to go home, which he did; and I went and dined with Colonel David Wood, at that time commanding the Artillery attached to my old Division, the 4th. I of course talked over

* General Simpson says in his Despatch, "The trenches were, subsequently to this attack, so crowded with troops, that I was unable to organise a second assault, which I had intended to make with the Highlanders, &c."

the attack without disguise, and said that so convinced was I (notwithstanding David Wood's opinion) that the place could be taken, that I was determined if I went to Headquarters I would tell them so, recommend it, and offer to lead it. Hardly had I said these words when Barnston, of the Quartermaster-General's Department, came in and said, 'General Windham, you are wanted at Headquarters.' David Wood lent me his pony; I got up from table and rode off immediately. Upon entering the great room at Headquarters, I saw at table General Simpson, Sir Colin Campbell, Airey, Steele, de Suleau, &c., &c.

" I told the General I had come according to orders; he seemed surprised to see me, saying he had not sent; to which I replied that Captain Barnston had ordered me there, and that I had left my dinner on purpose to come. He then asked me to sit down, and said, ' How comes it we failed at the Redan?' I told him bluntly, 'From want of pluck and method.' That there was nothing in the work itself to stop anyone. Seeing that he did not much like this answer so openly given, I stopped, and afterwards said to Airey, who sat between me and the General, sufficiently loud for the latter to hear, ' Tell the General he ought to attack again at once with the Highland Division.' The General heard me, and asked again what I had said. I repeated my advice, to attack again immediately, and that I was quite sure I could carry the work in half-an-hour. To this, Simpson's reply was somewhat curious. (Sir Colin sat next him and *heard* all I had said.) 'Well, may be you're right, but I must see Pelissier about it in the morning, first.' So strong were the opinions I expressed as to the whole attack, that I received next day a letter from Steele (which I now have), deprecating my plain speech. The next day I saw General Simpson after he had visited the works the Russians had abandoned during the night, and I then asked him whether he thought my impressions and opinions wrong; his reply was kind and frank. He said, 'Eh, mon, but ye have spoken the truth; ye have gallantly won your spurs, and I hope you will get them.' Upon giving me my Major-General's commission, on my birthday, the 8th of October, he said, 'Here's your General's commission, Windham; the spurs have not yet come, but I hope they will later.' And I will just add that they have not come yet, although I have been in England months.

"I daresay people will like to know whether I still believe that the Redan could have been taken had I gone on with the Royals. All things considered, I think it would not; the men looked disheartened, the trenches were filled with wounded, over whom they had just passed (which always must have a bad effect), and instead of going forward in one continued stream, they would have met almost as many coming back as going on. If I had to do it again *from the beginning*, I think it unquestionably could be carried, but I am not so certain, as I was at the time, that anything would have turned the fight when once the men began to hang in the chambers."

CONCLUDING REMARKS: CRIMEA.

As has already been stated, Windham was, on the 11th September, 1855, appointed Commandant of the British portion of Sebastopol; but he only held this appointment for a month, as, on the 14th October of the same year, he was specially promoted to the rank of Major-General, for his distinguished conduct on the occasion of the assault on the Redan.

General Simpson had warmly and generously recommended Windham's claims, but the knighthood, which he considered that Windham had fairly earned, was not bestowed till many years had elapsed.

General Windham was gratified by being given command of his old Division, the 4th, which knew him so well, and which owed as much to his exertions, in camp and on the line of march, as to his gallant leading in battle.

Still higher honour, and duties of even higher responsibility, were, however, in store for Windham ; and on the 17th November, 1855, he was appointed Chief of the Staff to his friend, Sir William Codrington, who had succeeded General Simpson as Commander-in-Chief in the Crimea.

In Windham's hands this office became a useful reality, and it was on the condition that it should be such, that Windham accepted it.

Fully supported by his chief, for whom he felt both respect and affection, General Windham now entered on what was probably the happiest period of his life. Incessantly busied with plans for the improvement of the Army, and daily seeing the troops improve in health, efficiency, and mobility, Windham was in his element.

It is natural that the letters written by him at this period are, in some respects, less interesting to the general reader than were those written in the days of battle and adversity. Windham's official position now tied his tongue, and, moreover, there was little to find fault with.

So, trusted and respected by his chief, by the Army

in the Crimea, and by the public at home, General Windham worked loyally to the end, "sticking to the ship" in the final dull and uneventful days as he had in that dark and gloomy time when she seemed likely to founder.

Peace came at last, and on June 30th, 1856, he embarked for home—one of the last to quit the Crimea, as he had been one of the first to set foot on its shore.

There must still be many who can remember the enthusiasm with which Windham was received in England, and with which, much to his gratification, his native county of Norfolk heaped honours upon him.

The gift of a Sword of Honour and the Freedom of the City of Norwich were followed by the triumphant election of the distinguished soldier to Parliament, in which unfamiliar scene General Windham fulfilled his promise to his constituents—to speak only on matters with which he was acquainted.

It should here be mentioned that Mr. Anthony Hudson, the old and dear friend to whom so many of the letters in this volume were written, lived to welcome General Windham to England, and to rejoice in his honours, but died while Windham was on his voyage to India.

THE INDIAN MUTINY.

ON the outbreak of the Indian Mutiny Major-General Windham at once offered his services, which were eventually accepted, owing to the numerous casualties in the higher ranks. The General arrived at Calcutta very shortly after the fall of Delhi, the capture of which place was completed on September 20th, 1857.

General Windham applied immediately for a command in the field, and finding that there was no immediate intention to employ him, volunteered to keep open the lines of communication, if placed in command of some of the disarmed regiments of the Bengal Army.

This offer was not accepted, and shortly afterwards he was ordered to take command of the Sirhind Division, a district which had been denuded of troops, and which was far removed from all chance of active service.

Windham was, however, suddenly relieved from the depression and disappointment caused by this order, as Sir Colin Campbell, the new Commander-in-Chief, who was about to march from Cawnpore to withdraw the garrison of Lucknow (now commanded by Outram), placed Windham in command of his base of operations.

Sir Colin marched from Cawnpore on the 9th November, 1857, leaving Windham in his first independent command. That independence was, however, but very partial; and it is evident, both from the instructions given him and from the manner in which

215

he acted under them, that Windham had little freedom of action.

His garrison was a small one (about five hundred Europeans and a few Sikhs), and he was directed by the Commander-in-Chief to place his troops within the entrenchment which, on the re-occupation of Cawnpore by Havelock in July, had been hastily constructed on the river.

His further orders were—not to attack any enemy unless by so doing he could prevent the bombardment of the entrenchment; to send to the Commander-in-Chief all detachments of European Infantry that arrived from down country; and, further, he was ordered not to detain troops, even if seriously threatened, without first asking for instructions.

It appears, in fact, that Sir Colin Campbell was so intent on the second relief of Lucknow, an object certainly of vital importance, and a task of great difficulty, that he disregarded the danger of Windham's small force being attacked and crushed by the Gwalior troops.

Sir Colin persuaded himself that no such attack would be made before his return from Lucknow, and grievous was his miscalculation. Moreover, he had not the excuse of want of warning, for the chivalrous Outram wrote to him in good time, pointing out that it was "obviously to the advantage of the State that, before Lucknow was relieved, the Gwalior rebels should be first effectually destroyed," and stating that the Lucknow garrison could hold out till the end of November.

The Commander-in-Chief having marched away from Cawnpore, Windham prepared at once to carry out his instructions. He took measures to clear the 'glacis' of the entrenchment, and the country beyond it; to strengthen the works; and to train men to work the guns.

There was no time to be lost, for the error of the Commander-in-Chief was promptly exposed; Tantia Topi, the most capable leader produced by the Mutiny, was already advancing against Cawnpore, and marched from Calpi on the day following Sir Colin's departure.

Windham's responsibility was now very great, for the defeat and destruction of his small force would leave the Commander-in-Chief without a base, and with a victorious enemy acting in his rear. Windham saw clearly that he would be attacked, and made an urgent application to Sir Colin for permission to retain such troops as he might think absolutely necessary for the defence of his position, continuing, meanwhile, loyally to send on reinforcements to his chief.

On November 13th, the Chief of the Staff, Major-General Mansfield (afterwards Lord Sandhurst), wrote Windham the warm letter of thanks for his co-operation given in the *Observations*, and on the following day gave him autharity to detain certain troops. By this means Windham's force was gradually increased from the original strength of 500, until on the 26th November, when his first action was fought, he had about 1400 bayonets in the field, together with about 300 men left to guard the entrenchment.

Before this date, however, the situation had become more and more critical; the Gwalior contingent was approaching him rapidly, and all communication with Lucknow suddenly ceased on the 19th. To add to his difficulties he learned, on the 22nd November, that the enemy had surprised and defeated a police force at Banni, on the high road to Lucknow.

Windham at once resolved to weaken his small force, with the object of restoring communication with the Commander-in-Chief; and at 3 a.m. on the following morning sent a wing of the Madras Infantry Regiment, with two guns manned by Europeans, to re-occupy the Banni Bridge.

Then, having to choose between an active and a passive defence, his decision was quickly formed. That it was to attack, rather than to be attacked, will surprise no one who has read the preceding pages.

Such is ever the best course of action against an Asiatic enemy, and it was also the most congenial to the bold and resolute Windham.

Early on the morning of the 24th November he broke up his camp, and marched six miles south-westward to meet the advancing enemy; two days later he attacked and defeated a force of 3000 men with six heavy guns. The fight was severe, and the enemy left half his guns in the hands of the 34th Regiment when driven from the field.

The British loss on this day amounted to ninety-two killed and wounded, six of whom were officers.

The troops then returned to Cawnpore in excellent spirits, and took up a position, previously selected, from which Windham hoped to be able so to act against the enemy as to defend the city and bridge from his attack.

A letter had been received from the Commander-in-Chief's camp to the effect that all was well, and that the Army was marching back towards Cawnpore.

Tantia Topi now showed the instincts of a real general, and taking advantage of his great superiority, both in numbers and in artillery, endeavoured to crush Windham before the Commander-in-Chief's arrival.

Two days' severe fighting followed (November 27th

and 28th), during which Windham's small force suffered heavily, partly from the great strength and the determined action of the enemy, and partly from an untoward incident to which further allusion will be made presently.

Such were the odds against him, and such the difficulties caused by this incident, that Sir Colin Campbell, on his arrival (on the evening of the 28th November), found Windham's force on the point of being driven into the entrenched position.

General Windham's conduct of affairs, during his three days' fighting before Cawnpore, has been freely criticised, both by competent and incompetent writers ; by those acquainted with all the facts of the case ; and by those who obviously are not acquainted with them.

He has been blamed for taking up too extended a position for his small force ; but this, it should be remembered, he did in compliance with the written instructions of the Commander-in-Chief ; perfectly proper instructions they were too, or they would not have been issued by that experienced and cautious soldier.

As for Windham's choice of method in his defence of Cawnpore, the opinion of Colonel Malleson should justify him.

" That Windham," he writes, at the conclusion of his description of the fighting, " was justified in deciding to make an aggressive defence cannot, I think, be questioned. It is the opinion of those best qualified to form an opinion, that, regard being had to the enormous superiority of the rebels in artillery, a purely defensive system would have ensured the destruction of his force, and the occupation of Cawnpore by the rebels, with consequences—Sir Colin and the women and children of the Lucknow garrison being on the other side of the river—the evil extent of which it would be difficult to exaggerate.

"Windham, by his military instincts, saved the country from this disaster."

The circumstance previously alluded to as causing the worst of General Windham's difficulties, was one happily of very rare occurrence in our military history ; one which the General could not have provided against, and for which he was in no way to blame.

There is both official and private testimony establishing the fact, as appears from a letter addressed to H.R.H. the Duke of Cambridge by Sir Colin Campbell, as soon as the latter discovered that he had been guilty of an unintentional injustice to General Windham.

Sir Colin, in this letter, mentions the "remarkable forbearance" of General Windham towards the person who had caused his discomfiture, and adds that the true facts of the case had come to light without pressure on Windham's part.

General Windham's conduct had indeed been most generous.

The official despatches follow :—

"The Right Honourable the Governor-General in Council has received the following despatch from his Excellency the Commander-in-Chief, and hastens to give publicity to it.

"It supplies an omission* in a previous despatch from his Excellency, which was printed in the *Gazette Extraordinary* of the 24th instant.

"Major-General Windham's reputation as a leader of conspicuous bravery and coolness, and the reputation of the gallant force which he commanded, will have lost nothing

---

* This omission was that of a favourable notice of the name of General Windham and of the officers who had served under him.

from an accidental omission, such as General Sir Colin Campbell has occasion to regret.

" But the Governor-General in Council will not fail to bring to the notice of the Government in England the opinion formed by his Excellency of the difficulties against which Major-General Windham, with the officers and men under his orders, had to contend.

" *To the Right Honourable the Governor-General.*

" HEADQUARTERS, CAMP, NEAR CAWNPORE,
" *the 20th of December,* 1857.

" MY LORD,

" I have the honour to bring to your Lordship's notice an omission, which I have to regret, in my despatch of the 2nd December, and I beg to be allowed now to repair it.

" I desire to make my acknowledgment of the great difficulties in which Major-General Windham, C.B., was placed during the operations he describes in his despatch, and to recommend him and the officers, whom he notices as having rendered him assistance, to your Lordship's protection and good offices.

" I may mention, in conclusion, that Major-General Windham is ignorant of the contents of my despatch of the 2nd December, and that I am prompted to take this step solely as a matter of justice to the Major-General and the other officers concerned.

" I have, &c.,
" C. CAMPBELL, *General,*
" *Commander-in-Chief.*"

Seldom has an act of injustice been more frankly and honourably undone, but it is, unfortunately, the fact that the slur on General Windham's reputation, cast by Sir Colin Campbell's hasty condemnation of the operations before Cawnpore, has made a far deeper impression on public opinion than has his subsequent attempted reparation.

It seems desirable, therefore, to complete General
Windham's exoneration, and to make it as widely
known as possible, by the republication of a pamphlet,
privately printed by him in 1865, entitled, *Observations,
supported by documents ; a supplement to Colonel
Adye's " Defence of Cawnpore."*

THE OBSERVATIONS.

" By those who only read the title-page of this
pamphlet, it may be asked—Why, after the lapse
of many years, publish anything relative to the
proceedings at Cawnpore in November, 1857? Why
trumpet a work, well and ably written, it is true, but
composed by one who served with you, who was
your friend, and who wrote to do you justice? I
reply, that Colonel Adye had not permission to
publish certain letters and documents which prove
the correctness of his statement, but that I have.
Also, I may add that, having now been graciously
rewarded, without application on my part, I can
appeal to public intelligence as to my proceedings
under very trying circumstances, without my intentions being misrepresented.

" Moreover, although a man may—nay, in this country
often must—bear in silence the hasty comments of the
daily Press, it does not follow that he is called upon to
be equally reticent when he has reason to suspect that
certain transactions in which he was chiefly concerned,
and in which his conduct has been criticised, are about
to appear in a work which, from the known ability of
its author, is likely to descend to posterity.

" The reader will find, should he condescend to
peruse these few remarks, that I have carefully

avoided giving my own impressions and wishes, without at the same time giving proof of their correctness; that I have likewise avoided entering into minute details, or the description of individual actions, knowing the almost utter impossibility in such cases of doing justice to all parties.

"Difficult is it fairly to represent the quiet actions of daily life—more difficult far to detail with justice those that happen in the excitement of a fight.

"I shall avail myself, however, of this opportunity, not only to strongly recommend Colonel Adye's work to those desirous of knowing the truth as to the proceedings at Cawnpore, but also to explain why, in my opinion, he was justified in selecting those well-known lines of Addison for his motto:

'T is not for mortals to command success;
But we'll do more, Sempronius—we'll deserve it.

"In adopting this couplet, it might seem at first sight as though the able statement which follows had been drawn up by Adye with a view rather of describing difficulties which excused a 'failure,' than of recording measures and movements which, despite all difficulties (and they were great and many), led to a 'success.'

"That the latter is proved by his narrative will be obvious to the reader, who shall bear in mind the nature of the duties entrusted to me.

"These were twofold:

"1. The forwarding from day to day, as they should arrive, troops, material, ammunition, &c., to the main Army, under Lord Clyde, at Lucknow.

" 2. The defence of the entrenchments, hospital, and
  bridge at Cawnpore, and the watching of the
  Gwalior Contingent.

"The first of these duties, though involving no small
amount of labour and anxiety, was of routine character.

"That it was performed efficiently, and to the
satisfaction of His Excellency, is proved by the
testimony of the Chief of the Staff in the following
handsome letter :—

"CAMP, ALUMBAGH,
" *November* 13*th*, 1857.

"MY DEAR WINDHAM,—Your official and private letters
of yesterday have both just come to hand, and I lost no
time in reading them to the Chief. He desires me to thank
you warmly for all you are doing to support him. The
impulse you have given to everything is immense, and his
expression to me is, 'I cannot be too thankful for having
him at Cawnpore just now.' The troops you have sent on
will be of incalculable advantage to us, as we shall be
compelled to leave so many posts as we go along.
Crawford's guns will keep our batteries undiminished
after providing for the proper armament of those posts.
The trans-Goomtee scheme will not do, I am afraid (it
was followed next time) and we must proceed deliberately
with the big guns and the sappers, clearing our road as
we go along, and saving the troops from musketry fire as
much as we can. I think, with management, we shall
be able to accomplish this to a great extent. I understand there are some troops just arrived into camp, which,
I suppose, is Colonel Welles' party.

" Yours truly,
"W. R. MANSFIELD.

" To Major-General Windham.

"P.S.—You were quite right about the camels, and Sir
Colin entirely approves your decision."

" This letter, I think, proves that the first part of my duty was satisfactorily performed up to that date ; and I think I may add, without any fear of contradiction, that it continued to be so performed to the end. The other duty was of a far more serious and responsible nature. As Colonel Adye has truly said, 'the safety of the position at Cawnpore was at that time a matter of the highest importance.' It is with no intention of unduly enhancing the value of my own service that I call attention to that remark ; for it is still my opinion, taking into consideration all the circumstances of that time, whether as regarded the condition of our own forces or those of the enemy, that the one point in all India on which, at the moment of the relief of Lucknow, the Queen's supremacy in that country chiefly depended, was the position I had been appointed to protect. Had the enemy once carried the entrenchments, and secured or destroyed the bridge over the Ganges into Oude, it is difficult to over-estimate the consequences that would have ensued.

" The hope was that he would not make the attempt ; this also was the opinion of the Commander-in-Chief, founded upon information that he had received previous to his departure for Lucknow.

" The Gwalior Contingent was the force from which alone an attack was to be apprehended.

" But though a maiden force, and better equipped, organised, and commanded than any other body of men in the rebel armies, yet it was considered that, numbering, according to General Havelock's calculation, under 5000 men, it would be reluctant to hazard an assault upon a fortified post defended by British troops. I fancy its numbers were underrated, for I

Q

was subsequently informed by Major Grimes, who was its paymaster when the mutiny broke out, that at that time it was 8500 strong, and its ranks were after-wards largely reinforced. In addition to this, it is said that large numbers of men from Lucknow, who, by a preconcerted arrangement, abandoned that city after the arrival of the British Army there, crossed the Ganges between Futtehpore - Choorassie and Sheorajpore, and joined them. I think this was the case. But be that as it might, the enemy which threatened Cawnpore in the last week of November, 1857, joined as it certainly was by the Dinapore mutineers, was no longer of small account. It had become a large and formidable army. Nor did its intention of attacking us long remain proble-matical. It advanced boldly with 700 scaling-ladders, six or seven batteries of artillery, a large siege-train, and 23,000 rounds of ammunition for guns. The very attempt I was appointed to watch was now at hand. How the attempt was made, and how it was resisted —under what disadvantages on the one hand, and with what desperation on the other—Colonel Adye's pages graphically and truthfully describe. But that it was resisted successfully, that the vital point entrusted to the guardianship of my force was held in security, that the all-important entrenchments and bridge were saved, and the Commander - in - Chief's movements with his charge from Lucknow unmolested, the same pages likewise show.

"Now, as this was the duty entrusted to us, it is clear that we not only 'deserved' success, but we obtained it. But, judging from some criticisms, I am rather called on to prove that, though I did obtain success, I did not deserve it, because, forsooth, I myself created the very difficulties under which the contest was waged !

 " 1. It is said that I took up a position outside the town when I ought to have remained in the entrenchment, and have kept the town between myself and the enemy!

 " 2. It is said that, having taken up that position, I advanced to meet the enemy, when I should rather have waited to receive his attack!

 " These criticisms are somewhat singular. Had I failed to accomplish the task assigned to me, they might, perhaps, have been looked upon as plausible, though even in that case they would have been far from just or reasonable.

 " But the issue being what it was, they hardly call for an answer.

 " It may be fairly assumed that if a general gains his object, his tactics could not have been very much in fault. I am prepared, however, in the present instance to go further, and to assert that, had I adopted measures in accordance with the views of my critics, I should most probably have lost the position instead of holding it, and have brought on the bombardment of the entrenchments and the destruction of the bridge, which it was my particular duty to prevent.*

 " Remain in the entrenchment, indeed ! Why, it had been so hastily constructed, and was so weak and unfinished, that it could not have resisted a bombardment from even half the mortars the enemy had brought with them. Crowded as it was with sick,

* *Vide* paragraph 9, Appendix.

powder, stores, and men, even if the troops under me had been picked veterans, accustomed to act together, I question their standing the 'pounding' they would have had in that confined but yet unprotected space.

"Again, How preserve the bridge but by keeping the enemy from getting within range of it? What better evidence can be given of the inadequacy of the entrenchment to protect the bridge than the fact that as soon as we entered it, on the night of the 28th, the enemy planted his guns, and opened fire upon the bridge at daylight next morning?

"Again, How could I keep the town between myself and the enemy without holding the town? The enemy must have it, or I must. It must harbour one side or the other. Hence the view I chose to take, and which, moreover, was strictly in accordance with my instructions, as far as those instructions went.

"2. Then in regard to my going out to meet the enemy. How did this prejudice the defence? I attacked the centre of three parties that were separately coming down to meet me. It had approached to within three miles of my position on the canal, and was still advancing. Surely a handsome thrashing— the loss of three guns and many men—did not make it advance quicker. I did not go to meet it until it had absolutely started to meet me. I determined to strike the first blow; and in doing so, I do not hesitate to say, contributed in no small degree to the attainment of the end in view, having gained at least twenty-four hours in time and three guns, to say nothing of the prestige.

"Then if all this be so, why should Colonel Adye have chosen such a motto?

"Simply because there is a sense in which its application is both just and appropriate. 'The position' (viz., the entrenchment and bridge,) could, in my opinion, be better defended by holding the town and its outskirts than in any other way. But I desired not only to use the town as a cover to the entrenchment, but also to prevent the town itself from being pillaged.

"To show that this was a long-cherished idea of mine, I wrote on the 10th November to the Chief of the Staff, pointing out certain brick-kilns just without the town as offering the best line of defence. In his reply to me he says (extract of letter dated 11th November, 1857)—'Having not had a moment of time to spare, when I was at Cawnpore, I am not able to give an opinion on the military position there. But it appears to me that if your retreat is secured, it is a great advantage to prevent the pillage of the city.'

"Although this was no order to undertake its defence, it surely allowed me to do so if I thought I could do it with safety.

"I had pointed out the same position to Colonel Adye. I had had everything cleared away between these brick-kilns and the advancing enemy, and had fully made up my mind a fortnight before the enemy arrived where I would meet them. This Colonel Adye knew. He and others who, like him, ably supported me, were, of course, grievously disappointed in not having succeeded in gaining that, which, though not the main point, was one that we wished much to gain. We fought hard for it. Only those who have worked well and fought bravely for a desired object, and with well-grounded hopes of obtaining it, can appreciate the disappointment caused by seeing that object frustrated. Colonel Adye shared this disappointment, but he knew, at the same time, that the result, which, in common with myself, he deplored, was placed beyond my control.   Hence the motto on his title-page, which, as referring to this part of our proceedings, was no less happy in its selection than just in its application ; for in this case, though we could not 'command' success, we did ' deserve' it.

"I now come to a criticism that I consider well worthy of an answer.   It is this—' Why did Windham not send his baggage to the rear on the morning of the 27th ?   It was an error his not having done so.'   It is curious that, amongst the many accusations that have appeared against me in print, this should never have been amongst the number, to the best of my recollection.   It is still more curious that it should never have been made to me in conversation ; for, in my opinion, it is the weakest point of my case.   The question, as it stands above, was reported to me by an old friend as having been asked by an officer of high rank in England, shortly after the news of the fighting at Cawnpore arrived here.

"My reply is very short and simple, namely—' I think it was an error.'   It must not, however, be supposed that I *forgot* to do this ; on the contrary, I had, at three o'clock that very morning, issued an order directing all the baggage and camp equipage to be taken to the island in the Ganges, just abreast the entrenchment.   I deeply regret having rescinded that order shortly after its issue.   I discussed the order at the time with several officers, and the following were my reasons for rescinding it :

" 1. I did not wish to alarm the friendly, or to encourage the adverse, part of the population of the town in my rear by showing any intention of retiring.

" 2. Colonel Bruce's russeldar of police, a native officer in whom he had much confidence, stated through him to me, that if we only remained quiet, the enemy, after the defeat he had experienced the day before, would not advance at all.

" 3. By my instructions (*vide* paragraph 8), I was ordered to show a bold front, and to make the most of myself, provided my retreat was secure.

" 4. I felt sure that I could, as soon as the enemy was reported as crossing the canal, have my baggage and camp equipage removed, and cover its removal (so short a distance had it to go), by holding the village of Sesamhow.

" I rescinded that order with much doubt and hesitation ; and I deeply regret I did so. Had I not done so, I should at once have posted my force, as I originally intended, behind the before-mentioned brick-kilns, and the misconduct that produced the confusion of that day would probably never have occurred. Having thus frankly admitted my own error of judgment (as proved by the result), allow me to add, in justice to myself, that I feel convinced I could, under ordinary circumstances, have accomplished all I aimed at—namely, ' to show a bold front to deter the advance of the enemy ; but should he cross the canal, then to cover the removal of my baggage, and take up my intended position. In this I was frustrated;* I hope no other officer may ever meet with the same hard fate.' I have said that we 'deserved' success; and this assertion is not made without substantial evidence to support it.

"By the kind permission of His Royal Highness the Commander-in-Chief, I am enabled to refer to a letter written to him by the late Lord Clyde, on the subject of the proceedings in question, now published for the first time, and which more than bears out what I have said :—

"Camp, Sherajpore,

"*December 25th,* 1857.

"Sir,—Your Royal Highness is aware that there was much, at the time of my arrival in Cawnpore, to cause me to think very gravely of the occurrences which had previously taken place.

"In justice to Major-General Windham, C.B., I have the honour to bring to the notice of your Royal Highness, that certain facts have lately come to my knowledge, which placed that officer in a most difficult and unfortunate position.

"Lieutenant-Colonel . . . . misconducted himself on the 26th and 27th November in a manner which has rarely been seen amongst the officers of Her Majesty's service ; his conduct was pusillanimous and imbecile to the last degree, and he actually gave orders for the retreat of his own regiment, and a portion of another, in the very face of the orders of his General, and when the troops were not seriously pressed by the enemy.

"The consequence was, the men became excited, and

---

* The village of Sesamhow, in my immediate right front, was given up without a struggle, the strength of the position lost, and endless confusion created, by one man, who, by-the-bye, had no right to be there, as I had displaced him from his command hours before the fight began, for his misconduct on the 26th.

a state of things arose which Major-General Windham could not control, though he used his best efforts to meet the difficulty.

"Major-General Windham, while treating this officer with remarkable forbearance, deprived him of the power of doing further mischief. *

"After some correspondence, a Court of Enquiry was held, and the facts above stated are in evidence.

"Painful as much that has occurred must have been to the Major-General, it cannot but be now a matter of great satisfaction to him that, without pressure on his part, these facts have come to light, and now serve to explain so much of what might otherwise have been injurious to his reputation.

"I have further to remark that the troops at Cawnpore consisted, for the most part, of detachments *en route* to join their regiments, the headquarters of which were employed elsewhere.

"This was another serious disadvantage to the Major-General, which, ensuing as a consequence of the difficulty of the times, was also beyond his control, there having been no sufficient opportunity of organising the detachments in battalions.

"Your Royal Highness will well appreciate how much the moral strength of the garrison would be shaken by such a contingency, and, I trust, will be pleased graciously

---

" * *December 2nd,* 1857.

"MY DEAR WINDHAM,—Pray excuse me for not having answered you sooner. With regard to Colonel ——'s case, I think no one could deny that you have acted with the utmost propriety towards the service, and great forbearance to a man whose conduct on a very trying and difficult occasion, did you such terrible injury. I am confident the Chief thinks as I do.

"Believe me, yours very truly,

"W. R. MANSFIELD."

to afford the full benefit of the circumstance to the Major-General.

" I have the honour to be, Sir,

" The very humble and devoted servant of

" your Royal Highness,

(Signed)   " C. CAMPBELL, *General,*

" *Commander-in-Chief, East Indies.*" *

" The circumstances which occasioned that letter are somewhat singular, and serve to illustrate, in a remarkable manner, the chances attaching to the fortune of an officer in command of a British force. Lord Clyde reached Cawnpore from Lucknow on November 28th ; on the 2nd December following he sent home a despatch relating to the state of affairs as he found them on his arrival there. In that despatch he saw fit to omit all favourable mention of my name, and of the names of those officers who had served under my orders during the arduous operations in which we had been engaged. Why was this omission made ? It could not have been by accident ; and, certainly, it was not because I had failed to hold ' the position ' which had been entrusted to my charge, for the entrenchment and its contents, together with the bridge, were handed over in safety.

"* The above letter was forwarded to me by General Mansfield with the following :—

" *December 25th,* 1857.

" MY DEAR WINDHAM,—I believe this is the best Christmas-box I could send you. I conceive that the Court of Enquiry on Colonel —— is one of the most happy circumstances of your life, and I very sincerely congratulate you on its result. It explains everything in official form, after careful investigation, which was quite unintelligible before.

"Yours very truly,

" W. R. MANSFIELD."

Then, why was my name omitted? I ask the question, as the Commander-in-Chief never told me, and I do not know to this day. I *suppose* it was because I attempted to do more than was required, and that my attempt had not succeeded ; that, having endeavoured to protect the town from pillage, as well as to protect the entrenchment and bridge, the town had, nevertheless, been penetrated by the enemy; in one word, that British troops had, from whatever cause or accident, retreated before the enemy. The fact of this retreat, together with the loss of some camp equipage, appeared, to the Commander-in-Chief, ' disastrous.' I do not complain of this view of the case. Though I had been fighting with less than 2000 men (and these composed greatly of detachments), against 25,000 ; with eight* light guns, drawn by bullocks and manned by natives, against sixty or seventy pieces of artillery, many of them well horsed ; with no permanent staff (and the officers employed by me on such duty new both to the work and the ground), I quite allow that Lord Clyde had reason to look gravely on the matter when he saw the smaller force retiring before the larger on the evening of the 28th. Such a view of the case is perhaps only a necessary consequence of that prestige which the British arms have earned in many a well-fought field, and which it was especially essential to sustain in India at that moment. The only question to be decided in circumstances of that kind, so far as I was individually concerned—and it was not enquired into at the date of His Excellency's first despatch of December 2nd—was

---

"* The two 24-pounders, drawn by elephants, were only got into action once, and, from the usual intractability of these animals, were of more trouble than they were worth.

this: 'Was the result supposed to affect British prestige owing to me as General in command?'

"It would seem, judging from certain expressions in his private letter to His Royal Highness, as well as in his supplementary public despatch to the Governor-General of India, that this was Lord Clyde's first impression on his arrival at Cawnpore, though I am bound to admit that he neither then nor afterwards ever uttered a syllable to me upon the subject.

"At the end, however, of seventeen days subsequent to the date of his first despatch, after a painful and patient enquiry, instituted, be it observed, not at my instigation, but, in consequence of rumours that had reached him, by desire of the Commander-in-Chief himself, His Excellency then arrived at an opposite conclusion.

"He then found that 'difficulties,' over and above those necessary 'difficulties' inseparable from the inferiority and composition of the force under my command, had so embarrassed the operations I conducted as to hinder the attainment of that full measure of success which might otherwise have been anticipated from them. Of those difficulties I have no desire to speak further. They have always been to me a most painful subject, as the like of them must ever be to a soldier who has his country's honour at heart. Lord Clyde has characterised them, and the occasion of them, in language which cannot be misunderstood, and will not be deemed unmerited. He shall be my witness whether, in the face of those difficulties of which he makes mention, I claim too much when I say that I deserved the success which they had so great a share in rendering impossible.

"The reader may agree with me in thinking that the

great wonder was, not that the town, after a long struggle, was penetrated by a daring enemy, but that the vital point was not wrested from my grasp.

"I am told, indeed, that the question has been asked, What if reinforcements had not arrived at the moment they did, on which side would the victory have been then?

"In reply to this let me ask—If I risked losing the entrenchment by entering it on the 28th, should I not have been more likely to do so by entering it on the 25th? One thing is clear—it took the enemy three days and nights to get me *into* that which he came to get me *out of;* and, as I never was got out of it, I shall decline to argue the question.

"Lastly, I have heard it said that 'I was surprised at Cawnpore'; that I had been 'careless, and took no pains to prevent it.' In answer to these assertions, I have to remark that they are simply untrue. Had they been true, I should have had to blame General Carthew, as I requested him to look to this whilst I remained in Cawnpore carrying on the telegraphic and other correspondence between Lucknow and Calcutta. I selected him for that duty, not only from his good sense and ability, but from his knowledge of the language; and I had no reason ever to regret my selection, as no one at Cawnpore did better service than this officer. Let his letters speak for themselves :—

"CAMP, NEAR CAWNPORE,

"*November 22nd,* 11.5 *p.m.*

"MY DEAR SIR,—Your order has just been received, and arrangements are being made to carry it out.

"I have outlying pickets round the camp, furnishing a complete chain of sentries all round; but I have no inlying pickets beyond the quarter-guards of regiments. Those pickets are about 200 yards in front, and the chain of sentries 100 yards in front of them. I will establish the inlying pickets as desired.

"Yours faithfully,

"M. CARTHEW.

"CAMP ON CANAL, NEAR CAWNPORE.

"MY DEAR SIR,—I have just received your note (8 p.m.), and will do all in my power to prevent the enemy coming upon us unawares. I will patrol frequently, both with Infantry and Cavalry. The bridge to the right is blocked up with carts, and guns are mounted on the left bridge.

"I remain, yours faithfully,

"M. CARTHEW, *Brigadier.*

"*November 23rd.*

"MY DEAR SIR,—Your orders shall be attended to immediately; some have already been carried out.

"The intelligence received to-day has induced me to strengthen the bridge with the loose wood lying about. The wood will not be destroyed.

"I remain, yours faithfully,

"M. CARTHEW, *Brigadier.*

"CAMP AT BRIDGE ON CALPEE ROAD,
NEAR CAWNPORE,
"*November 23rd.*

"MY DEAR SIR,—The encampment has been completed. All tents are up and pitched. Our right is near three-quarters of a mile from the Baree Bridge. I have therefore a picket of twelve hussars there now, and will have one consisting of an officer and thirty men out immediately. I have intelligence that a large body of the enemy, amounting to

2000, are at a place called Dhurmungulpoor, about three coss from this. This information was given me by a man on his way to Cawnpore, to report to Captain Bruce, having his nose cut off, and made his escape from them this morning. Captain Gordon, of 82nd, has been good enough to give his services in erecting a log breastwork at the head of the bridge on our left. I will also have the bridge further protected by placing several empty carts across it; and, with a picket well to the front on the Calpee road, I hope we shall be well prepared for the enemy if he should come this way. The officer in charge of the Cavalry visited some of the neighbouring villages this morning. At a place called Kulenpore, on the Delhi road, he learnt that at Choukeypore twelve sowars and a duffadar of the enemy are posted, and eight miles further on, at Shuley, the main body of the enemy is stationed, being sixteen miles from Kulenpore, and eighteen from this camp.

"I remain, yours faithfully,

"M. CARTHEW, Brigadier.

" *To Major-General Windham, C.B.*

"CAMP, NEAR CAWNPORE,
" November 25th.

"MY DEAR SIR,—A scout, who was sent out early this morning from the sowars' camp (but not a sowar), has just come in, and reports as follows:—A small advance picket of the enemy is now at Punkee, 18 guns at Chichoundee, 18 at Dhurmungulpoor, and about 18 have gone off towards Segounlee, with the view, I imagine, of coming on the Delhi grand road. There are at Chichoundee 200 horsemen; of Infantry he can give no idea, but says the topes and gardens are filled with them. The guns are large—some drawn by six and five pairs of bullocks.

"Their advance in this direction, I think, leaves no doubt but that they intend their attack upon us and Cawnpore, and probably the guns which have gone off to Segounlee are for that purpose. Another scout is expected in at three o'clock.

I shall keep the whole force in camp ready accoutred throughout the night, and patrol without ceasing, both Cavalry and Infantry.

    "I remain, yours faithfully,

        "M. CARTHEW, *Brigadier.*

"It was this last letter that made me at once proceed to the camp on the canal ready for the proceedings of the morrow. I myself reconnoitred the enemy, and, finding him absolutely advancing, determined to follow the advice of the 'Great Duke,' and attack him on the move.

"I remained immovable on the morning of the 27th from design, firmly believing that I could cover the removal of my 'impedimenta' should the enemy think proper to cross the canal; and I wish to reiterate that it is still my opinion that I could have done so had I not been met by conduct I little expected, and which is explained in Lord Clyde's letter of December 23.

"I have little more to add, having answered, I hope, temperately and fairly, the main drift of those criticisms which have come under my observation.

"In conclusion, I beg to recommend Colonel Adye's volume, together with these notes and documents, to the impartial consideration of the public. His statements are correct, and, if duly weighed, will vindicate my professional reputation from the aspersions that have been cast upon it by certain parties. Though conscious that they were undeserved, I will not say that those aspersions have caused me no pain. It would be mere affectation to make any such assertion. But I may truly say that they were not expected, at least from the quarter whence they chiefly proceeded.

"My career in India was attended by much mortification ; for having been sent to India, at no little personal sacrifice and inconvenience, for the purpose, as I believed, of taking the command of a Division in the field, I had no sooner landed at Calcutta than I was informed that this could not be, and that I was destined, on the contrary, to the charge of the troops stationed at Umballa (a few invalids), distant some 500 miles from the seat of operations. Yet this was a mortification I had to endure in common with nearly every other officer of my rank in India at the time ; and, coming in the ordinary course of service, must, I suppose, be reckoned as one of the varied mischances of a soldier's fortune.

"The very last mortification I expected was being misjudged by my countrymen at home during my temporary employment. No doubt that this was so is to be ascribed, in a great measure, to those facilities of telegraphic communication to which many a false impression owes its origin, as well as the sort of necessity which is in a manner forced upon the public Press of this country, in these impatient days, to comment upon current events without the materials necessary to form a correct judgment. But this does not diminish the sense of injustice to a public man who may happen to be the subject of it.

"However, I will say no more, but be content to abide the issue of a calmer reflection than my case possibly has hitherto received, recognising much truth in the remark of a distinguished Foreign Minister long resident amongst us—a remark made in reference to the very proceedings to which these notes relate—that 'though this country is the hardest of any for a public man to serve, in consequence of the habit which pre-vails among its people of pronouncing judgment on

R

imperfect information, yet that in the end it is the most just nation upon the face of the earth.'

"C. A. W."

The instructions issued to General Windham by the Chief of Staff were as follows :—

"BY ORDER OF THE COMMANDER-IN-CHIEF.

"*Memorandum by the Chief of the Staff, for the guidance of Major-General Windham, C.B.*

"HEADQUARTERS, CAWNPORE,
"*November 6th*, 1857.

"1. Major-General Windham, C.B., will assume command of the Cawnpore Division, as a temporary arrangement, in pursuance of the General Order issued this day.

"2. His attention will be immediately directed towards the improvement of the defences and of the entrenchment which now covers the Commissariat, two of the hospitals, &c., &c.

"3. He will communicate daily with Captain Bruce, the police magistrate, who will furnish all the intelligence to the Major-General which it is in his power to collect.

"4. A careful watch must be maintained over the movements of the Gwalior Force, which, it is supposed, will arrive at Culpee on Monday, the 9th instant.

"5. If this force show a real disposition to cross the Jumna, the garrison of Futtehpore* should be withdrawn to Cawnpore, and execute the march in two days, bringing their guns with them, and destroying the entrenchment.

"6. A post† should be formed in such case at Lohunda, the terminus of the railway, to consist of not less than (5) five Companies of Infantry and (4) four guns.

"* Officer in command at Futtehpore must communicate this, but quite confidentially, to the chief district authority.

"† To be furnished from Allahabad.

"7. Parties proceeding from Lohunda to Cawnpore should, if the contingency alluded to take place, be of the strength of a battalion. But the bullock-train parties are not to be discontinued till positive information respecting the movement of the Gwalior Contingent renders such precautions absolutely necessary.

"8. Supposing this to have taken place, General Windham will make as great show as he can of what troops he may have at Cawnpore, leaving a sufficient guard in the entrenchment, by encamping them conspicuously and in somewhat extended order, looking, however, well to his line of retreat.

"9. He will not move out to attack unless compelled to do so by the force of circumstances, to save the bombardment of the entrenchment.

"10. For the present the garrison of Cawnpore will consist of the detachments of H.M. 5th Fusiliers, 84th Regiment, and recovered men of various corps, and of the Headquarters of H.M. 64th Regiment, amounting in all to about 500 men.

"The British Infantry, which will be arriving from day to day, will be sent forward into Oude by wings of Regiments, unless General Windham should be seriously threatened. But, of course, in such case he will have been able to take the orders of the Commander-in-Chief.

"11. General Windham may retain the small Madras Brigade under Brigadier Carthew for a few days, until the intentions of the Gwalior Contingent are developed. This force will arrive, with convoy, on the 10th.

"12. He will direct Brigadier Campbell, commanding at Allahabad, and the officers commanding at Futtehpore, to report to him, and communicate so much of these instructions to those officers as affects them.

" By order,

" W. R. MANSFIELD, *Major-General,*
" *Chief of the Staff.*"

"BY ORDER OF THE COMMANDER-IN-CHIEF.

"Memorandum by the Chief of the Staff, for the guidance of Major-General Windham, C.B.

"HEADQUARTERS, CAWNPORE,
"*November 8th,* 1857.

"In continuation of former instructions, Major-General Windham is requested to direct his attention to the general position of the stations threatened or affected by the Gwalior Contingent.

"Assuming that force to have arrived at Calpee, it is apparent from the map that, besides the Jumna, there are, between that place and Cawnpore, the Rind Nuddee, and the Pandoo Nuddee.

"Supposing the enemy to contemplate an advance on the line of the Ganges from Calpee, he would proceed either to Akburpoor or Ghatimpoor.

"In either case, measures would be taken to destroy the bridges on these streams.

"If the enemy proceed to Akburpoor, it is tolerably evident that he would be bound either for Cawnpore or to Sheorajpoor; there would be ample time then to take urgent measures at Cawnpore, supposing the bridges to have been destroyed.

"If, on the contrary, he makes for Ghatimpoor, it may be presumed that his aim is Futtehpoor.

"When he is at Ghatimpoor, it will be time enough to think of abandoning the post of Futtehpoor, which is to be avoided as long as possible, consistently with the military safety of the garrison.

"Assuming that he is bound for Cawnpore, it will be for General Windham to exercise his discretion in calling up the Futtehpoor garrison as a reinforcement. This should only be done as a last resource, government having been fully restored in the Futtehpoor district, the interests of which would be sacrificed by an abandonment of the post.

"General Windham will have at his disposal about 500 rank and file British troops, including a detachment of the Naval Brigade left to work his guns.

"The Madras force will give him 550 rank and file, with six field guns.

"(2) 24-pounders have been added to his ordnance in the last three days, making in all nine guns for the entrenchment, besides the Madras guns above alluded to. There are in addition (2) 9-pounders and (1) 24-pounder howitzer, with ammunition in their waggons, available for movement, but for which there are no gunners.

"There are now in course of arrival, at very early date, at Cawnpore—

> 1 Company Reserve Artillery, R.A.
> 1 Horse Field Battalion, R.A.
> Military Train.
> 5 Companies H.M. 23rd Foot.
> Detachments H.M. 82nd do., and
> 2 Madras H.A. guns.

"The 23rd, and the Military Train, and the Royal Artillery will pursue their march towards Lucknow without delay, with convoys of ammunition, Engineers, Park and Commissariat stores. The detachments of the 82nd will remain at Cawnpore till they reach the strength of a wing, when they will make the distance to Alumbagh in two marches.

"Major-General Windham will have the goodness to send due notice of the arrival and departure of every detachment and convoy, to and from Cawnpore, to the officer in charge of the Quartermaster-General's Department at Headquarters.

"By order,
"W. R. MANSFIELD, *Major-General,*
"*Chief of the Staff.*"

"OFFICIAL DESPATCH.

"*From Major-General C. A. Windham, C.B., to His Excellency General Sir Colin Campbell, G.C.B., Commander-in-Chief.*

"CAWNPORE,
30*th November*, 1857.

"SIR,

"In giving an account of the proceedings of the force under my command before Cawnpore during the operations of the 26th, 27th, 28th, and 29th instant, I trust Your Excellency will excuse the hasty manner in which it is necessarily drawn up, owing to the constant demands upon me at the present moment.

"Having received, through Captain H. Bruce, of the 5th Punjaub Cavalry, information of the movements of the Gwalior Contingent, but having received none whatever from your Excellency for several days from Lucknow, in answer to my letters to the Chief of the Staff, I was obliged to act for myself.

"I therefore resolved to encamp my force on the canal, ready to strike at any portion of the advancing enemy that came within my reach, keeping at the same time my communications safe with Cawnpore.

"Finding that the Contingent were determined to advance, I resolved to meet their first Division on the Pandoo Nuddee. My force consisted of about 1200 bayonets, and eight guns, and 100 mounted Sowars. Having sent my camp equipage and baggage to the rear, I advanced to the attack in the following order:

"Four companies of the Rifle Brigade, under Colonel R. Walpole; followed by four companies of the 88th Connaught Rangers, under Lieutenant-Colonel E. H. Maxwell; and four light 6-pounder Madras guns, under Lieutenant Chamier; the whole under the command of Brigadier Carthew, of the Madras Native Infantry.

"Following this force was the 34th Regiment, under Lieutenant-Colonel R. Kelly, with four 9-pounder guns; the 82nd Regiment in reserve, with spare ammunition, &c.

"I had given directions, in the event of the enemy being found directly in our front, and if the ground permitted, that Brigadier Carthew should occupy the ground to the left of the road, and that Lieutenant-Colonel Kelly, with the 34th divided into wings, and supported by his artillery, should take the right. It so happened, however, that this order, on our coming into action, became exactly inverted by my directions, in consequence of a sudden turn of the road. No confusion, however, was caused. The advance was made with a complete line of skirmishers along the whole front, with supports on either side, and a reserve in the centre.

"The enemy, strongly posted on the other side of the dry bed of the Pandoo Nuddee, opened a heavy fire of artillery from siege and field guns; but such was the eagerness and courage of the troops, and so well were they led by their officers, that we carried the position with a rush, the men cheering as they went; and the village, more than half-a-mile in its rear, was rapidly cleared. The mutineers hastily took to flight, leaving in our possession two eight-inch iron howitzers and one 6-pounder gun.

"In this fight my loss was not severe; but I regret very much that a very promising young officer, Captain H. H. Day, 88th Regiment, was killed.

"Observing from a height on the other side of the village, that the enemy's main body was at hand, and that the one just defeated was their leading Division, I at once decided on retiring to protect Cawnpore, my entrenchments, and the bridge over the Ganges. We accordingly fell back, followed, however, by the enemy up to the bridge over the canal.

"On the morning of the 27th, the enemy commenced their attack, with an overwhelming force of heavy artillery. My position was in front of the city. I was threatened on all sides, and very seriously attacked on my front and right flank. The heavy fighting in front, at the point of junction of the

Calpee and Delhi roads, fell more especially upon the Rifle Brigade, ably commanded by Colonel Walpole; who was supported by the 88th Regiment and four guns (two 9-pounders, two 24-pounder howitzers), under Captain D. S. Greene, R A., and two 24-pounder guns manned by seamen of the *Shannon,* under Lieutenant Hay, R.N., who was twice wounded. Lieutenant-Colonel John Adye, R.A., also afforded me marked assistance with these guns.

"In spite of the heavy bombardment of the enemy, my troops resisted the attack for five hours, and still held the ground, until, on my proceeding personally to make sure of the safety of the Fort, I found, from the number of men bayonetted by the 88th Regiment, that the mutineers had fully penetrated the town; and having been told that they were then attacking the Fort, I directed Major-General Dupuis, R.A. (who, as my second-in-command, I had left with the main body), to fall back the whole force into the Fort, with all our stores and guns, shortly before dark.

"Owing to the flight of the camp-followers at the commencement of the action, notwithstanding the long time we held the ground, I regret to state that, in making this retrograde movement, I was unable to carry off all my camp equipage and some of the baggage. Had not an error occurred in the conveyance of an order issued by me, I am of opinion that I could have held my ground, at all events, until dark.

"I must not omit, in this stage of the proceedings, to report that the flank attack was well met, and resisted, for a considerable time, by the 34th Regiment, under Lieutenant-Colonel Kelly, and the Madras Battery, under Lieutenant Chamier, together with that part of the 82nd Regiment which was detached in this direction, under Lieutenant-Colonel D. Watson.

"In retiring within the entrenchments, I followed the general instructions issued to me by Your Excellency, conveyed through the Chief of the Staff; namely, to preserve the safety of the bridge over the Ganges, and my communications with your force, so severely engaged in the important operation of the relief of Lucknow, as far as possible. I strictly adhered to the defensive.

"After falling back to the Fort, I assembled the superior officers on the evening of the 27th, and proposed a night attack, should I be able to receive reliable information as to where the enemy had assembled his artillery.

"As, however, I could obtain none (or, at all events, none that was satisfactory), I decided—

"*Firstly*.—That on the following day Colonel Walpole, Rifle Brigade, should have the defence of the advanced portion of the town on the left side of the canal, standing with your back to the Ganges. The details of the force upon this point were as follows:

"Five companies Rifle Brigade, under Lieutenant-Colonel C. Woodford.

"Two companies of the 82nd Regiment, under Lieutenant-Colonel Watson.

"Four guns $\begin{cases} \text{Two 9-pounders} \\ \text{Two 24-pr. howitzers} \end{cases} \begin{cases} \text{Under Captain} \\ \text{Greene, R.A.} \end{cases}$

"(Two of these guns were manned by Madras Gunners, and two by Seikhs.)

"*Secondly*.—That Brigadier N. Wilson, with the 64th Regiment, was to hold the Fort, and establish a strong picket at the Baptist Chapel on the extreme right.

"*Thirdly*.—That Brigadier Carthew, with the 34th Regiment, under Lieutenant-Colonel Kelly, and four Madras guns, should hold the Bithoor road in advance of the Baptist Chapel, receiving support from the picket there if wanted.

"*Fourthly*.—That, with the 88th Regiment, under Lieutenant-Colonel Maxwell, I should defend the portion of the town nearest the Ganges, on the left of the canal, and support Colonel Walpole if required.

"The fighting on the 28th was very severe. On the left advance, Colonel Walpole, with the Rifles, supported by Captain Greene's Battery, and part of the 82nd Regiment, achieved a complete victory over the enemy, and captured two 18-pounder guns.

"The glory of this well-contested fight belongs entirely to the above-named companies and Artillery.

"It was owing to the gallantry of the men and officers, under the able leading of Colonel Walpole, and of my lamented relation, Lieutenant-Colonel Woodford, of the Rifle Brigade (who, I deeply regret to say, was killed), and of Lieutenant-Colonel Watson, 82nd, and of Captain Greene, R.A., that this hard-contested fight was won and brought to so profitable an end. I had nothing to do with it beyond sending them supports, and at the end, of bringing some up myself.

"I repeat that the credit is entirely due to the above-mentioned officers and men.

"Brigadier Wilson thought proper, prompted by zeal for the service, to lead his regiment against four guns placed in front of Brigadier Carthew. In this daring exploit, I regret to say, he lost his life, together with several valuable and able officers. Major T. Stirling, 64th Regiment, was killed in spiking one of the guns; as was also that fine, gallant young man, Captain R. C. M'Crea, 64th Regiment, who acted as Deputy-Assistant Quartermaster-General to the force here. Captain W. Morphey, 64th Regiment (the Brigade Major), also fell at the same time. Our numbers were not sufficient to enable us to carry off the guns.

"Captain A. P. Bowlby, now the senior officer of the 64th Regiment, distinguished himself, as did also Captain H. F. Saunders, of the 70th Regiment, who was attached to the 64th, and is senior to Captain Bowlby, whose conduct he describes as most devoted and gallant; as was also that of the men of the regiment.

"Brigadier Carthew, of the Madras Native Infantry, had a most severe and strong contest with the enemy from morning till night; but I regret to add, that he felt himself obliged to retire at dark.

"During the night of the 28th instant, the enemy occupied the town, and on the morning of the 29th commenced bombarding my entrenchments with a few guns, and struck the bridge of boats several times.

"The guns mounted in the Fort were superior in number to those of the enemy, and were well manned, throughout the day, by the officers, non-commissioned officers, and men of the Royal Artillery, seamen of the *Shannon*, Madras and Bengal Gunners, and Seikhs.

"The chief out-work was occupied by the Rifle Brigade, and in the course of the afternoon, by Your Excellency's instructions, they were advanced, and gallantly drove the mutineers out of that portion of the city nearest to our works, under the command of Lieutenant-Colonel Fyers, who was supported by Colonel Walpole.

"Throughout the short period I have had the temporary command of this Division, I have received, both in the field and elsewhere, the most important assistance from Captain H. Bruce, 5th Punjaub Cavalry. Without him I should have been at a great loss for reliable information, and although I am aware that Your Excellency is not ignorant of his abilities, courage, and assiduity, I think it my duty to make this mention of his service to the country.

"Pressed as I am by the operations now going forward, I am not able to specify the services of every individual who has assisted me, where all have behaved so well. I have no Staff of my own, except Captain Roger Swire, of the 17th Foot, my A.D.C., who has behaved with his usual zeal and courage.

"I therefore hope I may be allowed to thank, through Your Excellency, the under-mentioned officers for the great services they have voluntarily rendered me during this trying time :—

> Major-General J. E. Dupuis, C.B., commanding Royal Artillery in India.
> Lieutenant-Colonel John Adye, C.B., Assistant Adjutant-General, Royal Artillery.
> Lieutenant-Colonel H. D. Harness, commanding Royal Engineers.
> Major Norman M'Leod, Bengal Engineers.

Specially.

Lieutenant-Colonel John Simpson, 34th Regiment.
Senior Surgeon R. C. Elliot, C.B., Royal Artillery.
Captain John Gordon, 82nd Regiment.
Captain Sarsfield Greene, Royal Artillery.
Captain Smyth, Bengal Artillery.
"There are several other officers in addition, who I fortunately found detained here *en route* to join Your Excellency's force, and I beg to submit their names also, viz. :—

Captain R. G. Brackenbury, 61st Regiment.
Lieutenant Arthur Henley, 52nd Light Infantry.
Lieutenant Valentine Ryan, 64th Regiment.
Captain Ellis Cunliffe, 1st Bengal Fusiliers.
Lieutenant E. H. Bugden, 82nd Regiment (to whom I
    gave the command of the 100 mounted Sowars).
Captain C. E. Mansfield, 33rd Regiment.
Lieutenant P. Scratchley, Royal Engineers.
Lieutenant W. C. Milne, 74th Bengal Native Infantry.

"I beg to inform Your Excellency that I have called for nominal returns of the killed and wounded, and I have also directed all officers commanding corps, regiments, and batteries, &c., to forward to me the names of any officers, non-commissioned officers, or soldiers, who may have especially distinguished themselves by gallantry in the field, which shall be forwarded to Your Excellency without delay.

"In conclusion, I hope I may be permitted to express my sincere thanks to all the regimental officers, non-commissioned officers, and men, for the zeal, gallantry, and courage with which they have carried out my orders during the four days of harassing actions, which have successively taken place in the defence of this important strategic centre of present operations.

"I beg to forward the enclosed Despatch, which I have received from Major-General Dupuis; and I have called upon the various officers commanding corps, &c., to forward me the names of any officers they may wish to recommend, which I will send to Your Excellency as soon as I receive them.

"I have, &c.,

"C. A. WINDHAM, *Major-General.*"

General Windham's share of the troubles and trials of the great Indian Campaign was now to come to an abrupt end.

He had landed in India on the 6th October, and saw no more of the enemy after the battle in which—exactly two months later—Sir Colin Campbell defeated the Gwalior Contingent.

In this battle Windham took but a minor part, for, much to his distress, he was placed for the occasion in command of the troops who occupied the entrenchment, which he had successfully defended against such heavy odds.

Immediately afterwards he was ordered up-country by the Commander-in-Chief, and was directed to assume command of the Lahore Division.

From this uncongenial place of banishment he made several attempts to return to active service, but with no success.

The following passage in a letter from Sir Colin Campbell gave him genuine pleasure :—

> "CAMP, CAWNPORE,
>
> "*February* 15*th*, 1858.

"MY DEAR GENERAL,

"I have been putting off from day to day answering your last letter to me till I feel that it is almost too late to do so.

"Pray believe me when I say that my first feelings of pain have been obliterated by that communication.

*   *   *   *   *   *

> "Believe me,
>
> "Very faithfully yours,
>
> "C. CAMPBELL."

The following was Windham's reply, and with it we will close this record of an unfortunate episode in the life of a good soldier, an episode which shows on what a precarious basis the reputation of a commander may sometimes rest :—

"MEEAN MEER,

"*21st February*, 1858.

"DEAR SIR COLIN,

"It is with unfeigned satisfaction that I acknowledge the receipt of your letter of the 15th from Cawnpore.

"I do not wish to trouble you or put myself in the way, but should the Siege of Lucknow, from adverse circumstances, drag on (God grant for all our sakes it may not), and vacancies occur, I hope you will remember that I shall be happy and proud to join the force under you.

"Believe me, dear Sir Colin,

"Yours faithfully,

"C. A. WINDHAM."

It is much to be regretted that Sir Colin's "amende" did not go beyond words, and that he was not disposed to avail himself of the services so frankly offered. Nothing short of again entrusting General Windham with a command in the field would have atoned for the wrong inflicted by Sir Colin's hasty condemnation of the operations before Cawnpore. Words count for little, particularly official words ; and ninety-nine men out of a hundred remember that the successful soldier Lord Clyde condemned Windham's operations before Cawnpore : the hundredth may be aware that the condemnation was withdrawn.

On the termination of the operations near Cawnpore, General Windham was directed by the Commander-in-Chief to leave the Field Army and to proceed to Lahore, and assume command there.

Windham retained command of the Lahore Division

until March 1st, 1861, when he returned to England, a saddened and disappointed man.

In June of the same year he was appointed Colonel of the 46th Regiment, and on February 5th, 1863, he became a Lieutenant-General.

In 1865 the long-delayed Knighthood of the Bath was bestowed upon him, and on the 3rd October, 1867, he received command of the forces in Canada, which appointment he held to the day of his death.

Lieutenant - General Sir Charles Ash Windham, K.C.B., died at Jacksonville, in Florida, on February 4th, 1870.

APPENDIX

s

"December 9th, 1895.

"MY DEAR CHARLIE,

"I return your printed cutting. You must not think me lukewarm about the character of your gallant father and my dear old friend.

"I have spoken to many old generals, and none of them seem ever to have read the article to which you allude.

"Few people had a better opportunity than I had of seeing the way in which your gallant father led the assault on the Redan. We all knew the straits to which he was reduced.

"Holding rank as Brigadier-General when in the Crimea, I was present at the Council of War, held on the 7th September, the day before the attack. When it was announced from the chair (Simpson sat in the chair, moved back and did not speak) that two thousand men were told off for the assault on the Redan, I exclaimed, '*ten* thousand you mean!'

"I was at once checked by some general, and told I was there only out of compliment.

"I had been four months attending the trenches daily.

"We were completely outwitted in the *time* selected by the French; *they* knew that 11 a.m., the time selected for *their* assault, was that when the Russians took their rest.

"We were not to assault the Redan until the French flag was hoisted on the Malakoff tower; in fact, when every Russian was in his place to defend it.

"I was ordered on no account to leave our guns. I made my men leave their arms behind them. I had a magazine blown up in one battery, the men tore the stakes out of the gabions, and it was as much as I could do to prevent the men, so armed, rushing in to your father's assistance.

"Always your sincere old friend,
                    "HARRY KEPPEL.

"CAPTAIN CHARLES WINDHAM, R.N."

" DEAR CAPTAIN WINDHAM,

"I was much pleased to hear that you were engaged collecting matter and correspondence relating to your father with a view to publication.

"He was an old and early comrade and friend, staunch in his attachments, and without, I believe, a foe in private life. He was remarkable for his unruffled calmness and complete disregard of danger, as the very charges trumped up against him would serve to show. I rode a part of the way down with him the day he led the attack upon the Redan at Sebastopol.

"He was perhaps too out-spoken to please the Head-quarter Staff, who ill-brooked censure or suggestions.

"He was beloved by all who served with him and appreciated his frank and upright nature.

"I could write at great length, but must not trespass on your spare time. His fault perhaps was, that he was too sanguine of success, and thought no obstacle was too formidable, as his feat in riding 'Major A' would serve to show, with odds (I believe 100 to 1) against him.

"I wish your publication that success which the subject merits. As Cato says in Addison's representation of him:

'' T is not in mortals to command success,
We will do more, Sempronius, we will deserve it.'

"Command me, if I can at any time help you further.

"Yours most truly,

"DORCHESTER.

" FOLKESTONE, 10*th February*, 1896."

"27, WEST CROMWELL ROAD,
"SOUTH KENSINGTON, S.W.,
"*27th November,* 1896.

" DEAR WINDHAM,

"It is a pleasure to me to know that in the forthcoming volume on your father's career, you have quoted the opinion I have recorded on the battle fought by him at Kauhpur during the Indian Mutiny. I adhere to all I wrote in my latest edition of that book (the Cabinet edition) regarding the consequences—the fatal consequences—which would have overtaken us had your father hesitated for a moment. His decision saved India from a terrible disaster. There is one thing, however, that I regret; and that is, that I did not bring more prominently forward the fact that the letters written by your father to Lord Clyde, whilst every moment was of importance, were withheld from that officer until it was too late to take action on them. This neglect, whilst it damns some one, only increases your father's merits; for left alone in a position of great responsibility, and badly supported by some, he yet saved the position. Your father's reputation really required no vindication. No one out of India knew half the difficulties he had to contend with : yet, if I may quote Napoleon, 'he left a reputation without spot,' the best inheritance he could leave to his children.

"Yours very truly,
"G. B. MALLESON.

"CAPT. C. WINDHAM, R.N."

FELBRIGG HALL

SUNSET is the hour of sadness, and the time of Nature's
mourning over the decline of the sun in his splendour, and
the advent of the chilly night.   Sunset in autumn, when the
crimson of the western sky harmonizes with the reddening
leaves, and when the bare branches of the trees seem like
arms upstretched beseeching an inexorable Fate in an agony
of fear, is the time to visit Felbrigg, with its memories of an
ancient house whose sun has gone down in gloom, and whose
wide-spreading lawns now echo to the tread of the stranger.
Felbrigg is a lovely place, the park being a perfect picture
of sylvan beauty at all times, while near at hand is the wide
expanse of Aylmerton and Runton Heaths, and, beyond, the
long blue line of the ocean.   The approaches from Cromer
are of a peculiarly picturesque character—the road winding
through strips of woodland of surpassing beauty, the umbra-
geous foliage above and the wealth of green bracken and
the banks of wild flowers beneath making it a favourite walk
of the visitors at the seaside a mile or two away.   It is not
often that the park is open to the public, but the church
stands within its borders, and thither the way is always free.
If the hall is not available, the church where its lords have
worshipped for ages is full of memorials of their departed
greatness.   There lie the old Felbriggs.   Simon, who died in
1351, is pictured in brass; with his wife Alice, who was buried
at Harling, in effigy at his side.   Close by is the figure of
Roger de Felbrigg, who died abroad in 1380, and beside him
that of his wife Elizabeth.   But the finest memorial of all

is that of the gallant Sir Simon de Felbrigg, Knight of the Garter, and Standard-bearer to King Richard II., whose great brass fills the whole width of the centre aisle. He is in magnificent armour, with the standard in his hand, and the garter upon his knee; and beside him, in a flowing cloak, is his wife Margaret, daughter of Primeslaus, Duke of Teschen in Bohemia, and *domicella* to the Queen of her spouse's Royal master. She died in 1416, and her husband married again; and both he and his second wife were buried, not at Felbrigg, but at Norwich, in the chancel of the Church of the Black Friars, now known as the Blackfriars' Hall. A glance at the inscription below the figures will show that the date of the knight's death has never been filled in. Then there are memorials of the Windhams, one—that to Thomas Windham, who died in 1599—with the following quaint lines:

" Liv'st thou, Thomas? Yes—Where? with God on high.
  Art thou not dead? Yes, and here I lye:
  I that with men on earth did live to die,
  Dy'd for to live with Christ eternally."

Nollekyns did the bust which adorns the monument of the statesman Windham, and which is on the south side of the chancel.

Felbrigg Hall is a stately mansion in the style which prevailed at the time of Henry VIII. It was several times enlarged by the Windham family, for the most part in a style corresponding with the ancient south front. This is in three storeys, its chief characteristic being a stately solidity, from which its large mullioned and transomed windows do not at all detract. It shows three bays running up to the level of the parapet of the roof, the outer two being irregularly octagonal in plan, and the middle one, which contains the entrance, square. The doorway is circular, and above is an entablature, with a frieze enriched with carving, supported by handsome columns on moulded pedestals. Over the doorway are carved panels, above which are two three-light windows, separated by a string course. The large windows are a peculiar feature at Felbrigg, and might, with advantage, be studied by those whose idea of "domestic Gothic" is a multiplicity of corners and as little light as possible. The upper storey is in the roof, the three gablets rising in the plane of the main wall, and opening upon the roof of the bays. In lieu of a balustrade proper, the pious aspiration, "Gloria—Deo in—Excelsis," appears, each letter being pierced quite through—a somewhat novel arrangement. There are two gables, one with a continuous bay to the level of those in the front, at the end next the stables, &c.; but at the other end, adjacent to the more modern part of the building, only one, with bays as before, the window in the ground floor opening direct to the grounds, French casement fashion. Heraldic animals serve as finials to both the main buildings and the angles of the bays, while above the roof tall chimneys rise in triple clusters. The fine effect of the building is considerably enhanced by the eminence upon which it stands. The stable quadrangle, in a similar style to the main building, was erected in 1825 by Admiral Windham, and the entrance gates to the park—600 acres—were put up in 1841–2.

A quaint account of the interior, and the pictures with which it was adorned, was given in the *Norfolk Tour* (1829): "The house, built in the style of the period of Henry VIII., contains some excellent pictures by Rembrandt, Bergham, Vanderveldt, &c. The dining-room is decorated with good portraits of the Windham family. In the drawing-room is a Usurer, by Rembrandt; and the portrait of an old woman, by the same artist, supposed to be his mother, deserves particular attention. There are also some good paintings of sea engagements—one in particular, by Vanderveldt, jun., with the effect of smoke from the vessels in the foreground, which is made to receive the light, is very masterly: the subject is the engagement between the English and Van Tromp, in which Sir Edward Spragg was killed. Its companion, by the elder Vanderveldt, a sea-fight, is a confused and wholly uninteresting performance. Over each of these pieces is a Storm, by Vanderveldt, jun., in his usual style of excellence. At the other end of the room are two very fine views of the River Thames—one at Billingsgate Market, the other before the alteration at London Bridge. Over one of these pictures is a landscape, by Bergham ; and over the other a small but highly-coloured picture—the Finding of Achilles at the Court of Lycomedes—said to be by Rubens. From the drawing-room you proceed to the cabinet, where the small pictures are by much the best. Two or three Storms, by Vanderveldt, jun., in his best manner; Cows Stalled, by Sagtleven ; Scheveling Market, and a small landscape, by Paul Brill, are excellent : the trees of the latter are very finely touched. Some of the larger pictures are very good, particularly two views of the Cascade of Terni, by G. B. H. Busuri. The rest of the collection in this room is chiefly composed of Italian landscapes and small views of Italian ruins, in opaque colours. One of the best pictures in this house is an Italian seaport in a hazy morning, by Vernet, every part of which is truly and delicately expressed. A portrait of Rubens, and another of his wife, adorn one of the bed-chambers—whether by himself is doubtful. That of Rubens is, however, very like one of him in the British Museum.

" The library is fitted up with much elegance in the pointed style, and admirably corresponds with the building of the south front. Here is a collection of prints from the best masters. The gloom thrown into the apartment by the deep projecting munnions, the painted windows, and the sombre hue of the wainscot, renders it a retirement truly adapted to study."

In ancient times the Manor of Felbrigg was held by the Bigods, prior to its occupation by the Felbriggs. By order of Sir Simon Felbrigg it was sold after the death of his wife Catherine, the purchaser being Lord Scales, one of the knight's trustees. He sold it again to John Windham, who had had a lease of it from Felbrigg. John Windham, who had married the Lady Margery, relict of Sir Edward Hastings, of Elsing, and daughter of Sir Robert Clifford, of Buckenham Castle, made Felbrigg his seat; but was considerably troubled by the stand taken by Sir John Felbrigg, who claimed the manor by hereditary right. In Windham's absence Sir John made a forcible entry into the house, and when Mistress Windham locked herself up in a room to keep some sort of possession, he threatened to set the place on fire. Finally, the lady was dragged out, tradition says by the hair of her head, and the Felbrigg sat once more in his ancestral hall. Windham, however, obtained the King's order to the Sheriff, Thomas Montgomery, to be put into possession again, and the upshot of the business was the payment by Windham of two hundred marks to get rid of Felbrigg's claim. The latter, on receipt of this sum, released all his right and claim to the lordship, and conveyed it to John Windham by fine. This was in the 39th year of Henry VI., a time at which, *teste* the Paston letters, people who had power at their back did practically as they pleased. The Windhams came from Wymondham Town, where, in the reign of Henry I., Alward de Wymondham was a witness to William d'Albini's foundation charter of the Priory there. Edric de Wymondham, who died in 1277, was Treasurer of the King's Council and Baron of the Exchequer.

John Windham, son and heir to the first of the name, was an unfortunate man. By his wife Margaret, daughter of Sir John Felbrigg, he obtained the manors of Crownthorpe, Banningham, Colby, and Ingworth; and, assisting Henry VIII. at the battle of Stoke, in 1489, he was knighted for his valour. Four years later, on the 6th May, 1503, he was beheaded on Tower Hill, in company with Sir James Tyrrell, having been condemned as a traitor to his sovereign for joining a conspiracy in favour of Edmund de la Pole, Earl of Suffolk. He was buried in the Church of the Austen Friars in London, far away from his Norfolk home. His son and

heir, Sir Thomas, fell on better times. Knighted by Sir
Edward Howard, Admiral of the English Fleet, at Crowton
Bay, near Brest, he became Vice-Admiral, Knight of the
King's Body Guard, and a member of the Privy Council.
From his will, dated at Felbrigg, October 22nd, 1521, it
would appear that he then held the Manors of Crownthorpe,
Wicklewood, Hackford, Aylmerton, Runton, Barningham,
Ingworth, Tuttington, Colby, Briston, Wolterton, Melton,
Melton Cockfield, and Felbrigg. He was buried in Norwich
Cathedral. His brother, Sir Thomas, married Elizabeth,
daughter and co-heiress of Sir John Sydenham, of Orchard,
in Devonshire, and became the ancestor of the Earls of
Egremont. Sir Edmund Windham, by his wife Susan, a
daughter of Sir Roger Townshend, of Raynham, had three
sons and a daughter named Amy. Roger married one of
the Heydons of Baconsthorpe, and died without issue.
Francis, Judge of the Common Pleas, married Elizabeth,
daughter of Lord Keeper Sir Nicholas Bacon, died without
issue in 1592, and was honoured with a quaint monument
in the north chancel aisle of St. Peter Mancroft Church,
at Norwich. The tradition that he died of gaol fever has
no foundation in fact. The estates then went by entail to
Thomas Windham, the third son of Sir John Windham,
of Orchard. Thomas had two wives, and his son, John
Windham, four, and yet the line failed again for lack of
issue. William Windham, John's brother-in-law, took the
estate next, and died in 1689. His son, Ash Windham,
named after his grandfather, Sir Thomas Ash, of Twicken-
ham, was lord in 1740. William Windham, his son, was
a colonel in the Norfolk Militia, a great patron of manly
exercises, and an associate of the wits of his time. The
friend and admirer of Garrick, he left that distinguished actor
his executor when he died in 1761, his son William being a
minor.

William Windham, the statesman, was born in 1750 in
Golden Square, London, and educated at Eton, Glasgow,

and Oxford. He gave small promise then of his future greatness, and took so little interest in public affairs that it was a standing joke of one of his acquaintances that "Windham would never know who was Prime Minister"; while at the age of twenty he refused the post of secretary to his father's friend Townshend, who had just been appointed Lord Lieutenant of Ireland. In 1773 he joined Lord Mulgrave in his voyage of discovery in Polar regions, but he was attacked by an illness so severe that he was obliged to be put ashore in Norway. His first essay as a public speaker was at the Swan Inn, in Norwich, on the 28th January, 1778, and it was occasioned by a call for a subscription on behalf of the Government for the carrying on of the American War. Windham favoured conciliation, not from anything like cowardice, as he had amply vindicated his courage before by quelling a mutiny of the West Norfolk Militia, of which he was an officer, by seizing the leader, and felling some of his supporters amidst a shower of stones from the rabble. In 1780 he was a candidate for Norwich, but was unsuccessful; in 1783 he won the seat, to be defeated in 1802. He took part in the impeachment of Warren Hastings, held for seven years the office of Secretary for War under Pitt, and was one of the leaders of the Opposition during the Addington Administration. On his presenting himself for re-election at Norwich, after appointment as Secretary for War, he met with a rough reception, and at his "chairing" a stone was thrown at him. Windham, undaunted, jumped down from his elevation, collared his man, and handed him over to the officers. Windham's animosity to the Peace of Amiens lost him his seat in 1802; he tried for a Norfolk seat, failed, and finally met with luck at St. Mawes. He served another term from 1806 as Secretary for War, and also for the Colonies in the "Administration of all the Talents," which had only a twelvemonth's existence. In 1810 he died. Assisting to save the library of his friend North, when the latter's mansion in Berkeley Square was on fire, he sustained an injury to the hip, which subsequently necessitated an operation. With a feeling of tenderness for his wife, he sent her away, on a plea of business, and then prepared for the worst, receiving the sacrament at the hands of Dr. Fisher at the Charterhouse, and spending the rest of his time as if his hours were numbered. At first the symptoms were favourable, but a fever made its appearance, and on the 4th June this amiable and talented man breathed his last. On the evening of Sunday, the 10th, his remains reached Norwich on their way to their last resting-place at Felbrigg, and a large concourse attended them to the Maid's Head Hotel, where they lay in state for that night. On the following morning the journey was resumed, and at four o'clock, amid a great throng of county gentry and tenantry, the coffin was deposited in the family vault. Windham was generally regarded as a man of honour and liberal for his age; and he was not only temperate, but highly accomplished at a time of intemperance and much ignorance even in high places. He was opposed to Parliamentary reform, but he was in favour of Catholic emancipation. He would not support the war with America, but in readiness for the projected invasion of England he would dare everything, and raised a corps of Volunteers at Felbrigg on his own account. His wife, the daughter of Commodore Forrest, survived him, and erected to his memory the noble monument in Felbrigg Church.

Upon William Windham's death the Felbrigg estate went to his nephew, Vice-Admiral William Lukin, the son of Dr. Lukin, Dean of Wells, and formerly Rector of Metton, a living held conjointly with that of Felbrigg, his mother being a Doughty of Hanworth Hall, Norfolk. The Admiral took the name of Windham, in accordance with the provisions of his uncle's will, and under his *régime* Felbrigg was well cared for. He married Anne, a daughter of Peter Thelluson, and by her had thirteen children. And among his many grandchildren occur many well-known names of the present day — Lords Revelstoke, Cromer, Listowel, Lady Suffield, Colonel Hare, Lady Yarborough, Mr. Windham Holly, &c.

Admiral Windham's daughter, Maria, married her relative, George Wyndham (another branch of the family settled at Cromer Hall, Norfolk), and of her children, only one, the present Lady Alfred Paget, survives. Under his grandson, William Frederick Windham, the son of William Howe Windham, by Sophia, fourth daughter of the Marquis of Bristol, and the nephew of General Sir Charles Ash Windham, a gallant Crimean warrior, and the hero of the Redan, Felbrigg was sold to Mr. John Ketton, a Norwich merchant, who made his fortune out of cotton-seed during the time of the Russian War.

Over the career of the last of the Windhams, who fell so low as to drive the Cromer coach at a pound a week, we draw the veil Some day, perhaps in another generation, the story which was brought out at the famous trial (by which the unjustly-aspersed General Sir Charles Windham practically beggared himself in endeavouring to save the family property), and the recital of the prodigal's freaks, will make a curious chapter of local history. At the present there are those alive to whom it would mean nothing but pain, albeit it was so long ago as the 8th February, 1866, nearly four years after the sacrifice of Felbrigg, that he was laid to rest in the last home of his race in the church in the park attached to his ancestral home.

It may, however, be interesting to record the following incident, that when he was dying the only member of his family that he telegraphed for was his uncle, the General, who arrived in hot haste, and being met by his friend, Mr. P. E. Hansell, they proceeded to the hotel, to find that life was already extinct. The General clasped the still warm hand of the dead man, and, deeply affected, remarked, "Poor boy, I tried to save you, and I tried to save the property; now both are gone."

The present owner of Felbrigg, Mr. R. W. Ketton, is well known and respected in the Cromer district; and has, ever since his accession to the property, taken his due share in county business as a County Councillor and as a Justice of the Peace.

The above account of Felbrigg is taken from a series of papers on "The Ancestral Halls of Norfolk," published in the autumn of 1895 in the columns of the *Norfolk Weekly Standard.*

www.ingramcontent.com/pod-product-compliance
Lightning Source LLC
Chambersburg PA
CBHW031334070726
47496CB00018B/1855